Driven

Nicholas Kinsley

ForbiddenFiction
www.forbiddenfiction.com

an imprint of

Fantastic Fiction Publishing
www.fantasticfictionpub.com

DRIVEN
A Forbidden Fiction book

Fantastic Fiction Publishing
Hayward, California

© Nicholas Kinsley, 2015

CREDITS
Editor: T. J. Alden and Lon Sarver
Cover Design: Siolnatine
Cover Art: Cover creation by Jay Aheer. Adapted from photos © kevron2002, ArenaCreative, PicterArt, and scornejor at depositphotos.com.
Production Editor: Erika L Firanc
Proofreading: Jae Knight

SKU: NK1-000216-02 FFP
ISBN: 978-1-62234-268-6

Published in the United States of America

Without opening the door

to peer through the crack, Mitchell could see Trevor already. The slight tilt of his head as he spoke, clearly enunciating his words; the shadow of stubble across his jaw and upper lip, a shade darker than the chocolate brown of his hair; his broad shoulders, obviously muscular even hidden under his pea coat. He wondered if Trevor was wearing the maroon hat this time.

It was the memory of the pea coat that made Mitchell's heart sink. The man wore a fucking pea coat! It was judgemental, but in Mitchell's experience such judgements were usually correct. He was well aware of the divide between them, and people who dressed like Trevor were not the sort of people who had anything to do with people like Mitchell. So what if he could make Mitchell feel comfortable? What could they possibly have in common? Trevor was one of those upper-middle-class blokes—the friendly, well-dressed, sophisticated sort that still did it for Mitchell even more than ten years after Thomas—and Mitchell was a bloke with a criminal record.

Involvement with Kane aside, Trevor wasn't likely to be interested in Mitchell very long after getting to know him. It was probably best that there never be a chance to find out.

Also recommended...

You may also enjoy these other ForbiddenFiction works:

Don't... by Jack L. Pyke
"Don't... open me." Three simple words that tease Jack, taking him places from his dark past. For Jack, BDSM is a way to resist his worst impulses. Yet, the stranger calling himself The Unknown seeks to use that to seduce him. As Jack slips further down into the abyss, two men hold the power to save him. Will it be Gray, the Master who knows Jack's every secret? Or Jan, the first man to give Jack a reason to hope? With deadly ghosts coming out to play, Jack may lose everything, even his life. (M/M)
http://forbiddenfiction.com/library/story/JP2-1.000134

Love Is for the Living by Nicholas Kinsley
The zombies have arrived, and Blaine needs to escape. He'd always thought of his London neighborhood as a place of safety, but then his infected neighbors tried to eat him. Blaine packed a bag and fled through growing numbers of shambling, voracious monsters--*people, he had to remind himself, they're people*--toward his family in Bristol. He would surely have died without the turn of luck that brought him Commander Andrew Peterson. Together, they face the horrors and adversities of the apocalypse, trying to protect their loved ones, and — if they're lucky — find love for themselves. (M/M)
http://forbiddenfiction.com/story/NK1-1.000217

DISCLAIMER

Dedicated with love and appreciation to my dear friend
and brain twin, Vaughn.
No one could ask for a better cheerleader.

Contents

Chapter 1

Advanced Auto Repairs

It was a bitterly cold day in January when Trevor walked back to his blue Ford Fiesta after leaving the office and saw one of the rear lights broken. The plastic was almost completely shattered, jagged red pieces littering the concrete under the bumper. Reflexively, Trevor reached up to adjust his glasses, wondering if his vision was playing tricks on him, then remembered he was wearing his contacts.

For a few moments, he simply stared at the damage in the dreary yellow light of the parking garage, incapable of believing someone would actually do such a thing and have the nerve to drive away as though nothing had happened. That was, of course, what had to be the case, since he couldn't think of anyone who would do something like this maliciously. There was Rob, a web developer he frequently had to work with who was a bit of an arse and a homophobe, but Trevor didn't think the man would do *this*.

Staring blankly at his reflection in the rear window, Trevor sighed. It figured that, on a day he'd almost decided to take the tube to a meeting, some idiot had to back out of a space too quickly and ram into his rear lights.

He wasn't too averse to taking the tube, but it wasn't something he had a habit of doing. He had the money to afford a car, so if he didn't have to suffocate in a cramped carriage surrounded by smelly strangers, he wouldn't. He largely preferred enduring the slow, soul-crushing crawl of London traffic on the days he had to go into the office.

He was still standing listlessly beside his car when Stephen showed up. Stephen wasn't a bad guy, but he was also certainly no

1

friend, just someone Trevor endured sharing a lift with every morning. He didn't know much about Stephen, only that he was the type of person who enjoyed maths and was therefore more involved with the financial side of the company, working a few floors above him.

Now Stephen was coming up behind Trevor, tutting over the state of his Fiesta and frowning at the dented metal around the shattered plastic as though it were *his* car.

Trevor, friendly by nature, loathed Stephen. It wasn't even for a particularly good reason, in fact. It was simply Stephen's face, the way it was always pinched up and discerning, as if he were perpetually sucking a lemon or disapproving something. It may have also been the way Stephen's black hair was always perfectly coiffed, not a strand out of place.

"Well that's not good, is it?" Stephen said now. "Inconceivable to think someone here could've done that."

Trevor stifled a snort. That was another thing he hated about Stephen, the man's tendency to sprinkle his speech with unnecessary words like "inconceivable" when a perfectly good word like "hard" or "unfortunate" would work just as well. Trevor suspected the man had a small dick.

"Yeah. Don't suppose you know any good mechanics?" Trevor said.

Stephen beamed. It was obvious he was pleased Trevor had asked his advice, though honestly Trevor would've asked anyone who'd happened to pass by.

"In fact, I do," Stephen said, a happy lilt entering his voice. His face even pinched a bit less. "It's in the East End, not much too look at on the outside, but it's a hidden gem, I tell you." He stuck a hand into his pocket and pulled out his wallet. "I've got a business card in here somewhere, just give me a moment..."

Trevor kicked a shard of broken plastic across the garage. "Thanks," he mumbled.

Trevor hadn't expected much when he went the next day, and he was right not to. Advanced Auto Repairs was tucked under a railway, far off the main street, and though the woman Trevor had spoken to on the phone had been pleasant, the neighbourhood certainly wasn't. Trevor sighed, wondering why he'd thought it was a good idea to trust Stephen in the first place.

It was nearly impossible to get his car through the narrow alley. There was car after car lined up on either side of the road, and he worried he'd hit one just trying to get into the place. Finally, he found an empty spot nearly at the other end of the street and parked there before walking back to the main entrance, a hole in the wall that said "Advanced Auto Repairs" above it and a glass door through which Trevor had caught a flash of a receptionist counter.

Inside, it was a simple receiving area, white walls, white tile floor. To Trevor's right, six blue leather chairs were lined up against the wall with a short wooden table in front of them. The table looked newer than the chairs and had a box of Kleenex and a cup of black pens on it.

The receptionist counter was blue, too, as was the door behind it. A woman was sat there and Trevor quickly scanned the signs on the wall behind her head. First, the shop's hours, including what time they stopped taking cars. Then, stretched across nearly the entire width until it ended just before the doorframe, the name "Advanced Auto Repairs," stylised the same way as it appeared on the business card Stephen had.

"Hello," the woman at the counter sang cheerily. She was so short and her chair so low that her arms were above her chest where they rested folded in front of her. Trevor knew immediately she was the woman he'd spoken to, though she hardly looked like a woman. The soft curve of her jaw made the shape of her head almost a perfect circle, giving her a childlike appearance, and the oil-stained dark denim dungarees didn't help.

It was the straight brown hair that made her look womanly, the way she tossed it around gracefully. Her thin, pinkened lips curled up in smile that she probably didn't mean to come off as seductive. And upon closer inspection, her skin was rough and work-hardened, permanently sooty in some places under the otherwise creamy complexion.

Trevor felt an instant friendliness between them as he smiled back, looking straight into her large grey eyes. She had an evident strength of character and vibrancy, which Trevor always admired.

"I rang yesterday about a broken rear light," Trevor said.

3

The woman nodded and hopped down from her seat. "Oh yes, I remember. Trevor Lewis. We ordered the part after you called and it just came in today," she said as she walked around the counter. "Can I have a look? I'm Imogen, by the way."

"Sure. Nice to meet you, Imogen."

Trevor led her back out into the street and turned right. The wind had picked up as day began to shift into evening, and the already low January temperature had started to drop even lower. Trevor glanced over his shoulder at the petite woman following him and wondered how she didn't seem to feel the cold through the thin cotton of her jumper.

When he looked ahead again, his gaze slid right, to a single point, and got stuck.

The bloke he saw working in the garage was ordinary enough — straight, brown hair falling past his ears, sweat matting his fringe to his forehead; pointed jaw, but with a bit of squareness as it receded; lips plumped up as they pursed in concentration; dark, heavy eyebrows which lent him an air of intensity — definitely a man with a temper. His skin, nearly the same milky shade as the woman's, was smeared with grease and oil, and shining with perspiration.

Nothing particularly extraordinary, except the fact that the man was wearing only a vest in the dead of winter. Though Trevor worried instinctively for the man's health, his baser instincts had his eyes locking on where the vest was lifted, following the spattering of dark hair that lead from the man's navel and disappeared into low-hanging jeans.

The wind picked up again and blew the man's hair away from his grease-stained face. A moment later, the setting sun peered from behind the clouds and shone brilliantly through the dark brown strands, revealing them as a majestic amber. The man squinted and furrowed his brow as he focused on the car above him, methodically turning the spanner. The squint wasn't quite pronounced enough to hide the electric blueness of his eyes, even through his clear safety glasses.

Trevor's heart raced into panic when those blue eyes suddenly met his and caught him staring. A bold eyebrow lifted in silent question and Trevor's stomach dropped.

He was just about to turn away and try to play it off when the man's eyes slowly lowered, dragging his gaze down Trevor's body. Trevor looked straight at the man's crotch and felt his dick twitch.

"Sir?"

Trevor blinked and turned to Imogen waiting at his side. He nodded once and quickly continued down the alley.

He only made it so far. They'd reached his car and he was about to ask how long it would take when a voice called out above the general commotion.

"Imogen!"

She spun around and perched on the tips of her toes to see who'd yelled. Trevor followed her eyes, his stomach flipping a little because he had an idea of who needed her.

It hadn't been the dark-haired man, but he was looking right at them, standing a few metres down and poking his head out from behind a van. It was instead a youth with short red hair and an acne-ridden face, though it was obvious on whose account he'd done the yelling.

"Yeah?" Imogen replied in a near screech. Trevor winced. Her voice was normal enough at a conversational level, but at a higher volume, her pitch shot straight up.

"Mitchell wants ya."

Mitchell. The name seemed to slither into Trevor's brain through the holes in his ears and soak into his neurons, penetrate his nerve cells and radiate through his body along his spinal cord. It made his heart beat a little quicker, put him on the edge of his seat, as he knew anything that had to do with *Mitchell* would from then on send a spark through his system like a girl with a crush.

"Sorry, I'll just be a moment," Imogen said to him. Trevor nodded and leaned against his car, watching as Imogen walked briskly back the way they'd come. Mitchell stood waiting, silent and half hidden behind the white van.

Trevor forced himself to look away out of politeness, then after a moment ending up pulling his mobile out of his pocket. He nearly navigated to some mindless game to occupy the time, but kept his thumb hovering over the screen instead, right above the Grindr icon.

It certainly couldn't hurt to look, could it?

The app was loading before Trevor even remembered consciously deciding to lower his thumb. He closed the ad and started scrolling through the photos, looking for someone with straight hair and blue eyes, or at least a body that *might* pass for the one Trevor had only got a quick look at.

By the time he got to the end, he was torn between laughing at himself and just sighing.

"Sorry to keep you waiting."

Trevor jumped at the sound of Imogen's voice, putting a polite smile on his face as he slid his phone back into his pocket. "No problem. Must've been important, otherwise you wouldn't've been pulled away from a paying customer, right?"

Imogen grinned back, and once again Trevor was struck by how naturally likable she was. More eye-catching, however, was Mitchell over her shoulder, staring right at him as he used a tattered flannel to wipe oil from his bony hands. Trevor made himself shift his attention back to Imogen and Mitchell turned to go back to his work soon after.

"That's right," Imogen replied cheerily. "I'm afraid I'll have to keep you waiting a bit longer. It seems I'm needed after all."

"I see." Before, the news would've irritated Trevor, as he'd already had a time of it getting to the shop in the first place. Now, he found he didn't mind as much having to linger here a bit longer.

"Mitchell said he'll take care of you when he's done the car he's working on," Imogen continued. "He should just be a moment."

"Mitchell, huh?" Trevor's stomach was full-blown fluttering now. There had to be some reason for an already busy mechanic to willingly stop what he was doing to look at a broken rear light.

"Yeah. He's the owner, so he makes the rules." She rolled her eyes to show how much she thought of the fact. "Anyway, he's just over there by that white van if you get tired of waiting." She pivoted and raised an arm to point, not that Trevor needed her to. "Don't mind that glare of his. He doesn't bite. At least I haven't seen him bite anyone yet."

"Good to know, thanks."

"Why don't you bring your car up a bit closer in the meantime?"

"Alright."

It was almost five minutes after moving his car before he saw

Mitchell walking toward him, and by then he'd managed to mentally prepare himself for a conversation.

"Mr Lewis?" Mitchell asked as he reached out to shake Trevor's hand. His voice was soft and low, lower than the red-headed kid who'd called out for Imogen, but not too throaty. It had more of a huskiness, as ridiculous as the description sounded to Trevor. "You're the one with the broken rear light?"

Trevor nodded. Mitchell spoke so quietly it was hard to hear him over all the other sounds of the shop. "That's me. Some of the surrounding area is dented as well."

"Show me."

Trevor walked him around the Fiesta and extended his arm, revealing the damage. Mitchell bent over for a closer look, and immediately placed a slender hand on it. It was almost as though Mitchell was physically feeling the pain of the car, like a nature enthusiast who hugged trees and became one with the earth.

The longer Trevor watched, the more he got that impression. Mitchell's hand glided over the dented metal, fitting his fingers into each divot, as though he were feeling the problem through osmosis.

It got to the point where Trevor grew bored. His eyes drifted distractedly to the bare skin of Mitchell's lower back, uncovered by the vest. He followed the knobs of Mitchell's spine down to the band of his striped pants where they sat just above his waist and thought about how easy it would be to just pull them down.

Trevor cleared his throat, let his gaze linger a bit before bringing it back up. "You're not cold?" he asked.

Mitchell straightened his spine and rested his forearm against the glass window of the boot as he turned to Trevor. He looked him up and down again and this time Trevor became acutely aware of what he was wearing. He could be a little vain sometimes, and often took pride in his ability to dress well, even in winter, but standing next to Mitchell he felt almost *over*dressed. He wondered if he came off as too posh in his pea coat.

"I don't leave the garage much when I'm working, and I get hot in the shop shirt," Mitchell said and shrugged. "Guess it is a bit cold now I'm out here."

"I did notice you seemed perfectly comfortable earlier," Trevor

7

replied as he casually leaned his shoulder on the back of his car. He saw Mitchell's eyes note the movement and there was a moment when he was certain Mitchell was looking at his lips.

"And you seem perfectly comfortable now." He uncurled his loose fist and lightly tapped the glass with his oil-stained fingertips twice. "This'll cost you about three hundred."

Trevor glanced at his car, not in any real hurry to address it but letting the conversation flow. "Alright. How long will it take?"

Mitchell's lips pursed as he considered. He came off the Fiesta and crossed his arms, and Trevor could see the beginning of goosebumps on his biceps. He figured it served him right, but at the same time he wanted to give him his coat.

"Two days," Mitchell finally said. "If you come back around this time on Friday, we'll have it already parked near the front."

Trevor nodded, thinking that wasn't so bad. He was about to stick his hand into his pocket for the key, when Mitchell asked, "So this your car, or someone in your family, or what?"

"It's mine."

Mitchell's lips curled in a half smile as he jerked his head toward the Fiesta. "Coulda done a lot better. Titanium model's not bad, but... You know this is the kind of thing parents give to their kids who are just learning to drive, yeah?"

Trevor laughed. "I just liked the way it looked, and some of the features aren't so bad either, for the price. You saying I'm driving a teenage girl's car?"

"Ahh, I'm just sayin' you coulda done better, like," Mitchell said, his half smile stretching into an amused grin.

Trevor pulled his keyring from his pocket and started removing the Ford fob, glancing up at Mitchell as he worked at it. "What did you say your name was?"

Mitchell's smile slowly disappeared as he rubbed the back of his neck. He was shivering now, and underneath the grease smears his skin looked pale. "Mitchell. Mitchell Morgan. I'm the owner."

"Guess that makes you pretty important. Alright. Here's the key, Mr Morgan."

There was another nervous flutter in Trevor's stomach as their hands brushed. He hoped it wasn't just him.

"When you come back on Friday, Imogen should be able to handle everything for you. Have a nice day, Mr Lewis."

Mitchell started walking toward the front of the car. Trevor spoke before he could get too far.

"I'll probably at least see you then, yeah?"

Mitchell turned, hesitated, then nodded. "Yeah. Don't worry, I'll take care of your *Ford Fiesta* for you."

Trevor chuckled a little. "Why does it sound like you still think it's a teenage girl's car?"

"Have a nice day, Trevor," Mitchell said, waving as he laughed and opened the door.

Chapter 2
Define Crush

Mitchell had too much on his fucking plate to be thinking about some curly-haired, blue-eyed stud with a brilliant smile. His mind had needed the distraction at the time, so he'd let himself indulge in a little casual flirting. After catching Trevor checking him out, he'd been interested in seeing what the man was about, that was all. He'd fully planned on being too busy to be available when Trevor came back to pick up his car on Friday.

The job on the Fiesta hadn't taken long. It wasn't the light that had been hard to fix, but the reworking of the metal to get the light to fit. After that it was simple; he'd just smoothed out the dented metal himself, good as new, then added the plastic covering.

Perks of being able to psychically manipulate metal.

But when Friday came around, Mitchell ran into Trevor anyway. He'd just happened to be leaving the toilets and suddenly there he was, wide blue eyes staring right the fuck at him, brown curls sticking out from under a maroon beanie he hadn't been wearing the last time.

He'd smiled and asked Mitchell how he was doing, if he'd noticed anything else wrong with the car, and generally chatted with him a bit. Somehow Trevor had the power to make him feel comfortable in a way that most random strangers never really had before, even as Trevor continually checked him out, eyes lingering appreciatively over certain parts of his body.

Despite having a feeling that it would mean nothing but complications, Mitchell had done nothing to discourage it. He had ended up flirting back just as he had before, unable to help himself.

Trevor was so naturally warm and personable, and while usually Mitchell would find such a person annoying – always smiling too much, always cheerful – he found he liked it in Trevor. It wasn't over the top, but just the right amount of charm, confidence, and social grace.

And not done in an arrogant way either. Whenever Trevor spoke, his tone was easy-going and friendly, something that Mitchell sometimes wished he could pull off. His mother had always told him that friendliness was a trait he lacked and that he would have to practise at it. That he often came off as rude and apathetic.

Most of the time apathy *was* what he felt for things. He was also just quiet by nature and from too poor a background to be eloquent. Trevor, on the other hand, was good at this "life" thing.

Trevor and his Ford Fiesta had crossed Mitchell's mind a couple times since the last Friday in January, but for the most part he'd been focused on more important things, namely the car he was working on for his biggest client's next street race. Matters regarding Alfred Kane weren't exactly put after anything else.

Kane was one of the main reasons why Mitchell had been hesitant to get involved in anything more than a casual fuck for the past six years. A businessman and enterpriser above all, Kane was known by many, but his underground activity was known by far fewer. It wasn't, for example, exactly common knowledge that he had numerous police officers across the United Kingdom in his pocket, or that he had an equal number of media personnel at his command. When actions could be covered up or ignored by a convenient blind eye, operating within the usual bounds of morality wasn't really standard procedure.

Kane didn't know that it was his ability to manipulate metal, his ferrokinesis, that made him so talented with cars, but he did know that Mitchell could build one faster than anyone else and drive like no one else could. Early on, Mitchell had begun to see the effects of working for Kane all around him – the way stories were spun on the news, or the way some stories weren't talked about at all, the way even the internet didn't have much to say about him except for all the legitimate business he engaged in via his cyber security company, Kanine. Kane had enough money to do what wanted and take what

11

he wanted, and Mitchell was simply a very small part in a very large machine. Who knew how many average citizens working in the country led double lives the same way Mitchell did?

His part of the machine was to supply custom-made escape cars and street racing cars. Because Kane obviously didn't have his grubby hands in enough markets, he also liked to bet big money on street races. His escape drivers were used for all sorts of crimes, from small scale robberies to murders. Mitchell himself had at one time been more than just a supplier and occasional mission runner, had in fact been Kane's *first* escape driver and part-time legendary street racer, until he'd managed to work out a deal with him.

He'd enjoyed the thrill of that life for a while, but after raising enough money to buy his own garage and keep his business steadily afloat, there came a time when he just wanted to settle down and live life like anyone else. He'd endured working for Kane as long as he needed, and wanted out.

In hindsight, the way he'd gone about trying to get out wasn't the best. He was still under that git's employment, but there were worse deals he could've been forced to take.

Another thing Mitchell's mother had always told him was that he was a heartless little bastard, but that when he loved, he loved fiercely, and that was the other reason Mitchell was cautious when it came to romance. Mostly she'd started telling him that when he was fourteen and had been making heart eyes at one of her clients. Mitchell still cringed when he thought about the way that man had asked his mam if her boy sucked cock too, and how eagerly he had nodded to claim he did.

Mitchell would never forget Thomas, the first man he ever seriously fancied. The same man who'd led him down the path of becoming just as much of a whore as his mother.

Unlike the other blokes his mam fucked for money, Thomas wasn't creepy or malicious. While he never forgot that Melissa Morgan was a prostitute, he never treated her disrespectfully — which was more than could be said for some women who *weren't* in the business, but were treated like punching bags. Compared to the men Mitchell was used to seeing around their Liverpool neighbourhood, Thomas was the epitome of class, amiability, and sophistication — a bit like Trevor that way, actually. Mitchell didn't know why the hell a well-to-do gent like him would hang around the slums for a cheap cunt when he could probably get a fancy escort.

Even at fourteen he'd known Thomas never did and never would return the sentiment, that he probably only thought of Mitchell as that tart's bent son. Every time his mam explained to him that Thomas was married, that he seemed nice but was using Mitchell's feelings to take advantage and even getting off on it, Mitchell had said that even if that were true, he didn't care, that he wanted whatever he could get with him because he loved him. He'd said he was perfectly fine just getting paid to suck the man's dick and let him come on his face, and that love wasn't always easy.

That's when she cuffed him and called him an idiot, said he loved too fiercely and too foolishly, that it wouldn't be just his temper he'd inherit from her. Though Mitchell had noticed she'd never done anything to stop neither him nor Thomas. He'd wondered whether that was her trying to let him make his own mistakes or her simply not doing anything because it also just happened to help them survive.

At some point Thomas never came back, and Mitchell, in a bout of heartbroken depression, offered to keep doing things with other paying men. His teenage logic had been to fuck to forget, to fuck the memory of Thomas away... and he might as well keep helping bring in some money. He knew then that his mother's decision to let him make his own mistakes had taken just as much advantage of him as Thomas, considering she agreed.

Mitchell had moved up from occasionally sucking one man's cock to bending over for a different one three nights a week after he finished his coursework. His hair hadn't been as long then, but he hadn't gained the muscle he had now until later, so his naturally lean frame had been thin and a little effeminate. Mitchell had quickly learnt that the sort of men who liked shy, pretty, underage boys weren't usually as classy as Thomas.

He didn't *have* to keep doing it, but they'd been able to eat so much better after he started. So for nearly two years, he didn't stop.

He loved his mam, even after everything that she let happen to him, but as an adult he was able to realise how much her method of parenting had fucked him up. He didn't do relationships because of

13

her continuous warnings not to get attached to clients, and because the idea of giving that much of himself away, being so vulnerable, was terrifying. He didn't want to follow in her footsteps and fall fiercely in love with the wrong sort of person. At least he was lucky enough not to have the equipment necessary to get pregnant and be left behind as she was.

He didn't think Trevor was the wrong sort of person, not even a little, but from what he'd seen, he did think Trevor deserved more than the dishonest partner Mitchell would be. To lie to him, or to anyone Mitchell deemed fit to give a piece of his heart away to? Mitchell could admit his moral compass was a little different than others; if he had to, he could kill someone without feeling the slightest bit of remorse—and he often did have to on his assignments for Kane—but deceiving someone he cared about crossed the line. He was too loyal for that. Whoever he ended up loving, when the time finally came, he didn't want to drag them into this underworld hell he was trapped in.

He felt bad enough lying to Imogen, his closest friend, about what his "special projects" were. She probably had an idea, being the main one who handled the shop's financial records, but it was at least never brought up, and she certainly didn't know what the cars were used for beyond street racing. She, too, was ignorant of the darker side of his life.

So when Trevor came by the garage nearly two weeks after the Friday they'd spoken last, Mitchell was determined not to let Trevor see him. He would put an end to the flirting before he was in too deep and too attached.

But just because he wasn't going to go out and find Trevor to ask him on a date, that didn't mean he couldn't see Trevor when he came around. The second he caught sight of Trevor getting out of his Fiesta to walk into the entrance and talk to Imogen that Wednesday afternoon, he nearly dropped the socket spanner in his hand. He hurried past the other mechanics, into the back corridor of the shop, and pressed an ear close to the door once he got to the waiting room.

"...for a while," Trevor was saying. "I usually adjust the wheel and deal with it, but I figured I might as well bring my business here after last time. Do you do that here?"

Mitchell couldn't help the pleasant ball of warmth in his stomach at the sound of Trevor's voice, and his thoughts quickly leapt to last time. He'd known Trevor would be back soon. He'd noticed when he'd driven it—despite the car being new, the steering had a tendency to drift to the left. But it wasn't what Trevor had come in for, and it wasn't enough to make driving problematic, so Mitchell had left it and not brought it up, knowing—hoping—that he'd come back soon.

Fuckin' idiot, Mitchell chided himself. *Like you 'uv time fer these Bridget Jones flights o' romantic fuckin' fantasy.*

Of course, once Mitchell's mind thought the word "fantasy," it jumped to one of Trevor bending him over the bonnet of a Nissan GT-R and fucking him so hard he'd feel it for days.

"Sure thing," Imogen said. "We don't have any open bays right now, though, so it may take a few days before we get to it."

"Of course, that's fine."

Without opening the door to peer through the crack, Mitchell could see Trevor already. The slight tilt of his head as he spoke, clearly enunciating his words; the shadow of stubble across his jaw and upper lip, a shade darker than the chocolate brown of his hair; his broad shoulders, obviously muscular even hidden under his pea coat. He wondered if Trevor was wearing the maroon hat this time.

It was the memory of the pea coat that made Mitchell's heart sink. The man wore a fucking pea coat! It was judgemental, but in Mitchell's experience such judgements were usually correct. He was well aware of the divide between them, and people who dressed like Trevor were not the sort of people who had anything to do with people like Mitchell. So what if he could make Mitchell feel comfortable? What could they possibly have in common? Trevor was one of those upper-middle-class blokes—the friendly, well-dressed, sophisticated sort that still *did it* for Mitchell even more than ten years after Thomas—and Mitchell was a bloke with a criminal record.

Involvement with Kane aside, Trevor wasn't likely to be interested in Mitchell very long after getting to know him. It was probably best that there never be a chance to find out.

Mitchell jumped back a little as the handle turned and the door began to open toward him. He pressed himself against the wall behind it as Imogen walked in, out of her and Trevor's sight. After the door closed behind her, she arched a brow at him, wordlessly asking what the hell he was doing. He thought about making up some story, but knowing Imogen, she would've cottoned on soon enough anyway.

"Steering's off, right? Should just take a few hours, less if I work my metal magic. I'll take care of it," Mitchell said.

Imogen's brow raised a fraction higher. "Aren't you working on a car already?"

"I'm nearly done with it." A lie, but Kane would never know if Mitchell took a break to work on something else, and he was confident in his ability to get both done in time for when Kane needed it.

Her confused expression turned into a smirk. She simply looked up at Mitchell, crossed her arms, and said, "You know we have other punters that need repair work done before him. Really, Mitchell..."

Mitchell grunted. He knew she was right, and if it were anyone else he wouldn't have been adding to the workload he already had for Kane. But the thought of giving the job to someone else just didn't sit right with him, especially after he'd already handled the car once before.

"Listen, I don't blame you, Mitch," Imogen said. "He's cute. Friendly, well-spoken, never has dirt under his fingernails. You could use someone to help loosen you up. You're always so high-strung."

"Good to know I have your blessing and all, but I don't plan on going out with him. And before you ask, it's personal reasons, okay? I don't wanna talk about it."

"Didn't think you would," Imogen replied easily. "You're not really the talking type."

"But I'm still gonna fix his steering. Tell him it'll be done by tomorrow, but don't let him know I'm the one doing it. Just get the key from him and park his car around the back."

Imogen rolled her eyes but turned around to go back into the front room. "Yes, sir."

Alone again, Mitchell felt something he couldn't name rising in his chest. He wouldn't call it excitement, nor anxiety, and he didn't know if it was a good feeling or bad. He only knew that this thing with Trevor Lewis was starting to interfere with his other customers, his other *work*, and if he wasn't more careful, the lust-driven feelings he had for the man now might turn into something with much larger consequences further down the line.

Chapter 3
Adam

Mitchell hadn't been around when Trevor had picked up his Fiesta three weeks ago, steering newly aligned and working smoothly. Actually, he hadn't been around when he'd dropped it off either. But Trevor figured he'd give it one more try. The man was intriguing, they seemed to connect well the few times they'd spoken, and at the very least, there was definitely a reciprocated physical attraction.

He'd been wanting better tyres for a while anyway, wasn't feeling the ones the Fiesta had come with. As soon as he had the money, he once again made the trip to Hackney, planning to at least get Mitchell's number. If the plan ended up going to shit, well, he was going for drinks with his best mate, Kay, later, and could drown the loss of a good relationship opportunity then.

Before Trevor could even take off his hat and make it all the way up to the counter, Imogen smiled and said, "He's working in the back. Want me to let him know you're here?"

It was only his fifth time coming to the shop and already Imogen could see through him?

"Yes, thank you," he said and put crossed arms on the counter to wait. He was positive Imogen winked at him as she opened the door behind her.

Mitchell was wearing a red flannel shirt when he finally arrived, unbuttoned with the sleeves rolled up to his elbows. Trevor was gifted the glorious sight of Mitchell's chest, as well as the tendons in his forearms, and it nearly short-circuited his brain.

Mitchell's hair was a bit different today, as well. It was tied back in a ponytail, letting Trevor see the man's face without it being framed

17

by dark, lank locks. The style made him look remarkably younger. Trevor tried to subtly ruffle his own hair a bit, suddenly conscious of the way his hat might've left it.

"You're back," Mitchell said.

Trevor grinned, let his eyes overtly slide down Mitchell's chest and back up before responding. "Yep. I want new tyres."

Mitchell leaned his hands on the counter, his open shirt spreading further apart. Was he doing that on purpose? "Yeah? Anything wrong with them?"

"Nothing besides the fact that they're not the ones I want on my car," Trevor replied.

Mitchell snorted just softly enough for Trevor to hear it, then flicked his eyes over Trevor's shoulder to look past him. Trevor twisted his neck around to see what Mitchell was looking at but saw only the usual lot of cars parked in the narrow lane outside.

"What makes you think I'm not busy? That you're more important than other customers?" Mitchell said. Trevor turned back to him. "You could get your tyres changed anywhere. You could do 'em yourself."

Trevor tried not to deflate too much. He stood straight again to bring his eyes level with Mitchell's. "Last time I was here, Imogen said I'd have to wait a few days before someone even *looked* at the car for the steering, but then suddenly it was 'We'll have it ready for you tomorrow.' Sounds to me like something the owner could pull off."

Mitchell sighed, checked over Trevor's shoulder again before looking back. "Yeah."

"So *you've* done me the last two times. *You're* familiar with the car."

Mitchell's head dropped and hung between his shoulders as he went silent for a few moments, giving Trevor nothing but a view of the top of his dark, pony-tailed head. Trevor waited, stomach twisting with apprehension.

"Yeah, okay, alright," Mitchell finally said, looking up.

He didn't exactly seem enthused. "You're sure? I mean there's no... If you really don't want to, I can—"

"It's not that I don't want to, it's that I really fucking shouldn't. You've seen the place, you know space is cramped. And because we're good at what we do, we get a lot of business, like." Mitchell rubbed his forehead in frustration. "But I still wanna change yer fuckin' tyres. You see the problem?"

"If it's a bad time—"

"It'll always be a bad time." His eyes squeezed shut as he swore. "Fuck, that came out wrong, sorry. I'm a little... distracted."

"Look, Mitchell, I get it. Really." Mitchell looked at him a little helplessly, like he thought Trevor really didn't get it but that there was nothing he could say that would make him. "You seem like you're under a lot of stress, and dealing with some idiot who won't leave you alone is probably the last thing you need. But it also sounds like it's not necessarily the last thing you *want*. Right?"

"I..."

Mitchell's eyes went behind Trevor once again, but this time his expression changed completely. His lips thinned into a straight line and his eyes got a cold, measured look Trevor had never seen before, an icy glare that seemed a little dangerous. Whatever Mitchell saw, it wasn't something he wanted to be seeing.

Trevor turned around just as someone opened the door and walked in. It was an average-looking young bloke, with brown hair even longer than Mitchell's, falling past his shoulders where it extended from beneath a black beanie. As he walked up to stand beside Trevor at the counter, Trevor took in the sight of the man's shabby clothing, the tears in his coat. He looked like some druggie bohemian all of twenty years old. He stared resolutely back at Mitchell, cheeky and smirking.

Trevor put his key fob on the counter and slid it across to Mitchell's grey fingertips. "I don't mind if it takes a while. It's your garage, you'll do what you have to, and I don't need it in a hurry. But I wanna talk to you when I come back this time," he said, pointing a finger at Mitchell to let him know he was holding him to it even if Mitchell didn't make any promises.

Mitchell curled his fingers around the fob and nodded. He didn't smile, but Trevor wondered if he would have if the other man wasn't there.

He was pulling his hat over his ears on his way out when he heard Mitchell's quiet voice behind him.

"Come back tomorrow 'round three."

Trevor smiled and said, "Works for me. I'll see you then."

He walked out and headed to the left, hands deep in his pockets to fight the cold. He didn't even mind not getting Mitchell's number, not when things were looking up.

Mitchell had registered Adam's approach with an inward grimace and an outward scowl. He fucking hated dealing with that kid. Adam reminded him of both himself and the druggies he used to sell to back home.

He'd been expecting Adam to come today, and when Imogen told him a customer wanted to talk to him in the front, he'd actually thought it *was* Adam. He certainly hadn't expected Imogen to throw him to Trevor like that, though he supposed he deserved it after he'd snapped at her about him a few weeks back.

His heart had leapt ridiculously at the sight of Trevor's familiar features. He'd kept his calm on the outside, of course, but he'd felt it nonetheless, the quickening of his heartbeat that often started up when Trevor was around. He'd also made a bit of a fool of himself, but Trevor had been more than understanding.

He'd been both relieved and dismayed when Adam interrupted them. When Trevor had called him out on taking the job the last time, on being familiar with the car, he'd told himself that taking this one would mean he was giving in. He'd had to stop and consider everything seriously, make a final decision right then and there. And he had. He'd decided to just give in, let himself fall for the man.

Adam had come in like a slap to the face, an in-the-flesh reminder of why Mitchell had better not start caring about anybody else. His private working life could come crashing into his private personal life at any moment, horribly mixing the two even more than they already were. It was even worse when *he* was called in to Kane.

Getting involved with Trevor — with anyone — was beyond stupid. It was a fucking mess that Mitchell didn't need. As he walked Adam through the back corridor to his office, he decided to use the twenty-four hours until he saw Trevor next to make up his mind about what to do.

He closed and locked the door, then walked around Adam to sit behind his desk. Adam sat across from him, taking up the entire chair with his legs spread apart. Mitchell had never seen him without the black beanie on his head.

"So who's Mister Posh out there, eh?"

Mitchell sighed and leaned his forearms on the desk. "Just some punter. What the hell is it now? He can't want something else already, it's only been two weeks and the job isn't for at least another month."

Adam Serra was, in fact, a drug dealer, which was why Mitchell saw so much of himself in him. They'd both been in jail for it, only Adam more recently, because he was younger. Another major difference was the fact that Mitchell was never a user of the drugs he sold, whereas Adam definitely was, and even used his experiences to help promote sales. Also, unlike Mitchell, he was more than just a small-time dealer, and once Kane put him on the payroll, he'd suddenly had a much larger clientele.

As a footman for Kane, Adam ran a few errands — like relaying instructions to Mitchell in a passive-aggressively threatening way, and bringing Mitchell his payment in cash — and in return, Kane paid him a decent amount of money, as well as any cops in the areas where Adam did business, telling them to look the other way.

"Right, then." Adam pushed himself up by the elbows on the armrests into a slightly more vertical position. "Certain details of the operation have changed. Kane's words, not mine."

"Obviously."

"For this job — Tell me I explained it before, I don't feel like saying it again."

"You explained it."

"So they were gonna kill the guy, stuff him in the back, and bury him somewhere over yonder, yeah? Well, they wanna take the guy alive now and kill him later. And they wanna have fun with him a little on the drive."

Mitchell picked up the nearest pen and found the back of an envelope to write on. "How many will be in the car? I could raise the roof near the back a bit and get rid of the rear seats for more space."

"Yeah, that's what I was thinking, take the second row of seats

21

out," Adam said, nodding. "If you make the roof higher, won't that change the body too much? Won't be as aerodynamic and fast, or some shit like that?"

Mitchell shook his head as he wrote his notes. "Don't worry about things you don't understand. How many people?"

Adam rolled his eyes. "Four. Two guys up front and one in the back with the object."

"You'll be wanting something to keep him secure?" Mitchell asked.

"Yeah, handcuffs, one attached to each side."

"Length of the chain?"

"Can you make it adjustable?"

Mitchell visualised the interior in his head. He could install some sort of pulley system, somewhere out of reach of the prisoner. He wrote it down.

"Yeah. Anything to hold the feet?"

"Nah, rope should be fine. It usually is," Adam said. He'd sunk a little lower in his seat again.

"Places to hold the tools?" Mitchell asked. "Maybe magnetic strips along the sides or a compartment of some sort?"

"Maybe one of those little, you know, hidden spaces in the floors." He mimicked opening a floor hatch to demonstrate.

Mitchell wrote it down. "Floor compartment. Okay."

Adam leaned forward and rolled onto his feet. "That should be it."

"Great." Mitchell turned the envelope over and put it under his computer's keyboard, then got to his feet himself to show Adam out.

Imogen was back at the counter when Mitchell let Adam through to leave. She stared at Adam from the second he entered her vision to the second he walked out the door. Mitchell let out a long sigh and sank into one of the blue chairs against the wall once he was gone, tilting his head back to stare at the ceiling.

"Putting *that* to the side for the moment... How did your talk with Mr Lewis go?"

Mitchell snorted. "I can't believe you did that," he said without taking his eyes from the ceiling.

"If you don't give me a good reason why you shouldn't go out with this man, I refuse to actively work against what I think could make you happy," she declared. She crossed her arms and gave him her best disapproving scowl. "I think he's a good man, Mitchell, I've got a good feeling about him. And I've never seen you smile at *anyone* like that before. What the hell is it that's making you hesitate?"

"I've been busy with my private projects."

She knew this already; it was why he'd hired her not just as a receptionist, but a garage supervisor as well. He needed her to pick up his slack, take on some of the responsibilities that normally would've been his but that Kane had made it impossible for him to pay attention to. It helped that her passion for cars was right up there with his, and that he could count on her to be discreet with anything he asked of her. He just wished her moral beliefs weren't so upstanding so that he could tell her a little more of the truth about his "private projects." That it was sometimes a little more than just cars modded for street racing.

Imogen scoffed. "Like I haven't heard that excuse before. You don't have to stay here until arse o'clock in the morning working on your little side hobby. And Sean is more than capable of overseeing the mechanics when I'm playing receptionist. Nobody needs you to micromanage their work."

Mitchell let his head tilt forward again and gaped at her. "When the fuck do I micromanage people's work?"

Imogen ignored him, waved an arm around. "And if you're not here, you're visiting your mum. If you're not there, you're out driving and feeling sorry for yourself. It's like you *want* to have a miserable, sexless life."

"Trust me, if I want sex, I know how to get it," Mitchell replied dryly. He may have been shy but he remembered enough from his early teenage years to know how to find a quick shag.

He was only a few more remarks away from dismissing her or leaving the room himself. He wasn't in the mood to have his life choices criticised, especially when the critic didn't know the whole story.

"You're missing the point entirely," she said. "You don't see how much you need someone like that in your life, Mitchell. You don't have any friends—"

"Are you and your girlfriend not my friends?"

"That doesn't count! We never see each other outside of work. We never have, and I've known you since you worked for my father."

Mitchell sighed and looked away. She had a point. He had people he talked to on a regular basis, but he didn't really have friends.

Unless his mam counted.

"It's important to have people you can talk to, Mitchell," Imogen continued. "Someone you can tell everything. And you never know, Trevor might be supportive of, you know, your private projects."

Mitchell slid his eyes to her again. He was suddenly frustrated with the pretence when it was obvious she knew. "The race cars, Imogen, let's just fuckin' say it, alright?"

Imogen rolled her eyes. "Yes, Mitchell, the race cars. He might not take something like that badly. You never know."

Mitchell stifled his snort this time but turned to look out the window. It was raining now.

"He already makes you happy just by coming back for more and more ridiculous things to talk to you. Why don't you do yourself a favour and tell him you're interested?"

"Doesn't matter. I don't think he'd be interested in me for very long after he got to know me anyway," Mitchell said, voicing his inner worries in a rare moment of weakness. "We're too different. We'd have nothing in common. But even if he gets past me being Liverpool scum, you really think he's going to get past my freak psychic ability?"

"You want to keep making excuses, go ahead," Imogen said. "Do whatever the fuck you want. You always have. But I'm telling you, you could be missing out on something amazing. You'll never know *anything* if you don't at least try."

24

Chapter 4
Kay Then

Trevor had known Kay for years. They'd first met at university, where Trevor had studied to be a graphic designer and Kay had done film and animation. Trevor had been one of the few who'd hardly blinked at Kay being genderqueer, and Kay had been grateful for that ever since.

As if identifying outside the gender binary weren't enough, Kay was racially mixed as well, with a black mother and a white father. Their naturally curly hair fell to their shoulders and was dyed "ocean blue," which Trevor internally referred to as simply cyan. Their face was rounded and feminine, but a short stint with hormones had made their body hair longer and their voice deeper.

Trevor had been there for the hard times, in the beginning, when his usually outgoing and playful friend was depressed and angry enough to be dangerous. He'd been there when Kay was diagnosed with bipolar disorder. He'd been there to help Kay pull themselves together after they finished uni, helped Kay when two years ago they decided to become a barman in the meantime.

Kay was twenty-six but lived like they were twenty-one, staying out late at parties and without a permanent career figured out yet. They worked at a high-end club called Felicity, had strings pulled by their father to get the job even as a novice bartender.

It was partly because of Kay's usually exuberant, overzealous personality that Trevor almost always expected meeting up with them to end in a hangover the next morning. Kay did a lot of things that Trevor had tried once and never again, things like LSD and Ecstasy, but was a real mate and usually just stuck to alcohol when they were with

Trevor. They'd let Trevor know early on that there was no pressure to do anything he didn't want to, but that if he wanted to try some of the harder drugs, they'd be there to both hook them up and walk him through it. Trevor had taken them up on the offer a few times, but in the end, psychedelics and uppers just weren't his thing.

So when they got drunk together, it was usually falling-off-the-chair, quadruple-vision, plastered.

"*Pub número tres, abre la puerta!*" Kay exclaimed at the door to the third pub they'd visited, followed by a fit of giggles. They were a little too short to lean on Trevor's shoulder, but they did have a killer grip on it, dragging him down as they barely managed to walk upright.

"You might be done, mate," Trevor grunted. He had an arm around Kay's waist and was just about done himself. Horizontal looked like the best position to him at the moment, and the most horizontal thing in sight was the ground.

Kay held up an insistent, rigid finger. "One pint. And we'll drink it slow, won't chug it, alright?"

Trevor groaned. He was much more for passing out in a booth, but decided he'd try to power through it. He knew he'd regret it in the morning, but when *didn't* he regret things in the morning after hanging out with Kay?

"One pint," he acquiesced, and pushed his glasses up the bridge of his nose before dragging a cheering Kay inside. He would've worn his contacts like usual, only he hated falling asleep with them in, and he knew he'd be too pissed to take them out beforehand.

This pub wasn't too crowded. Kay and Trevor piled into a booth by a frosted window and shed their coats and hats for the third time that night. Then, since Trevor was the more sober of the two, he got up to get two pints of lager.

Kay was messing with their mobile when he got back, and slid it into their pocket as he set the glass down with a thud. They reached for it, but before they could touch, Trevor said, "Slow, remember?"

Kay rolled their eyes, brought the glass to their lips, and took a small sip before setting it back down. "Happy?"

"Just trying to make sure neither of us die of alcohol poisoning or some other such rot. Funny, how I actually care about you."

"Such a charmer, that Mr Lewis," Kay sang, batting their eyelashes. "Are you quite sure you've never thought about letting a magical queer unicorn fuck that bubble butt of yours?"

Trevor snorted, couldn't quite help picturing a rainbow strap-on shooting glitter, which just made him burst into guffaws. Unfortunately even if he was attracted to Kay, he preferred the real thing down below, though he'd never say something that insensitive aloud.

"Maybe some other time," he said between chuckles and sipped his own lager.

Then he remembered that another candidate had already occupied that vacancy, and that he'd been meaning to talk to Kay about it since the first time he'd exchanged smiles with said candidate.

He set his pint aside and, elbow on the table, rested his chin in his hand. "Actually, I did meet someone," he began, purposefully vague.

Kay's eyes lit up. "Yeah? What's he like? Is he boring? Tell me he's not boring so he can offset your utter *boring*ness."

Trevor gaped and feigned offence with a hand to his chest. "I am decidedly *not* boring!"

"Right. Let's think about this for a moment." Kay cleared their throat with a dramatic ahem. "Trevor Lewis. Hobbies include playing the drums, binge-watching television shows, Reddit, drawing those weird, fucked-up sketches—"

"Those are all perfectly valid hobbies that perfectly not-boring people have."

"Has a comfortable, mostly-remote job, yet doesn't take advantage of that fact to get completely and utterly fucked up every night—"

"Some of us prefer sobriety as our default state."

"Whatever. Go on and tell me about this bloke you've met." Kay put their drink aside to make room for their arms, crossing them over the table and plopping their chin down on top. "I'm all ears."

"His name's Mitchell."

"Last name?"

"Morgan."

Kay pursed their lips and repeated the name as if to discern the taste. "Mitchell Morgan. Hmm. Okay. Go on."

"He has long hair, not quite as long as yours, but he can put it in a ponytail. Past the ear, *just* above the shoulder range. Straight, brown. He talks incredibly quietly, and he doesn't adjust his voice much when it's loud around him, so then you have to strain to hear what he's saying. A bit shy, I think, but maybe he's just one of those soft-spoken types and doesn't like to raise his voice."

Kay quirked a brow. "Intriguing."

"Isn't it? The opposite of you, I know. Well, he owns a garage—"

"Like a mechanic? Or he just owns the mechanics?"

"What? Why would he just—Yes, like a mechanic. He's a mechanic, okay. So his skin looks like it can never quite be scrubbed clean and it's like his fingers have oil embedded into them."

"Dirty boy," Kay said, smirking.

Trevor laughed, unable to help it. "Anyway, I've been flirting with him for weeks—"

"Weeks?!" Kay sat upright, and immediately looked disoriented from the sudden change in position.

"No, no, no, not so much every day for weeks. More like I've taken my Fiesta in for repairs three times now and kind of let on that I liked what I saw each time I went."

Kay's shoulders dropped. "Oh. Alright then. And?"

Trevor grinned and stretched out his response by leisurely reaching for his pint and taking a drink. It lost some of its effect since Kay seemed too drunk to be bothered.

"Today was the third time I went to have work done. Told him I wanted new tyres. He almost declined, said he wanted to, but that he shouldn't."

"What, why?"

"Because he has a lot of other cars to work on, you know, other customers," Trevor said, waving a lazy hand in dismissal. "Some guy came in and interrupted us before I could finally ask for his number, but he ended up agreeing to do it and told me to come back tomorrow." Trevor put his glass down and looked across the table at his friend. "Kay, I'm totally in there."

"He sounds great, Trev. Just remember not to do that thing you have a tendency to do."

Trevor furrowed his brow. Maybe he was just too drunk to understand what Kay was getting at.

Kay sighed and rolled their eyes. "*You know.* That thing your last boyfriend Peter found weird and that one Grindr bloke went off about, called you fucking mental? The whole..." They raised their hand to their neck and feigned choking themselves. "You have to know when to stop, Trevor."

Trevor felt a sudden rock in his stomach and looked down at his drink. "I'll try to remember."

Kay picked up their drink and raised it. "Hey. I wish you the best with this Mitchell fellow. May he bring you at the very least a night of happiness, and make you less of a perfectly boring... bore."

Trevor shook off his worries and perked himself up. "Very well put," he said, nodding as he clinked Kay's glass.

"Thank you, I thought so myself."

Trevor drank. He locked eyes with Kay over the rim as he swallowed, saw that they weren't lowering their glass, and kept swallowing.

He upended the rest of the pint, chugging it down his throat. Kay groaned and had to stop.

When Trevor approached Advanced Auto Repairs the next day at three in the afternoon, Imogen was inside talking to a man Trevor had seen around but had never really took notice of. An ordinary black fellow with a shaved head and a wide smile. Trevor walked in and waited in one of the blue chairs as they finished up their conversation.

"Mr Lewis, hello," Imogen greeted him pleasantly when the man left through the door behind the counter.

Trevor stood and smiled as he walked up to her. "Good afternoon."

"Here to pick up your Fiesta? It's just outside, I have the keys here somewhere."

"Yes, I saw," Trevor said before she could find them. "I was wondering if Mitchell was around, actually. He told me to come back today. He must really love the work he does here if he works on Saturdays."

Imogen brightened. "Oh, yes, he is, and he does. Though he usually only pops in for a bit on Saturdays, doesn't stay the whole day. Neither do I, normally. Have weekend people for that. Anyway, yes, he's just in one of the bays, working. You go out and turn right—well, you know that, I suppose—and you should see him."

"Great, thank you." He started to turn and leave, but she stopped him.

"Oh, your key!" She placed the Ford fob on the counter, and as Trevor went to pick it up, she suddenly grabbed hold of his wrist. He blinked at the strength of the unexpected grip on his person then met her eyes. "Be careful," she warned. "Mitchell is..." She paused, frowning as she looked for the right word. "He's special, and a whole lot more sensitive than he lets on."

Her words made Trevor think there was more to her and Mitchell's relationship than owner-receptionist. He'd figured they'd be friendly, spending so many hours a day together for who knew how many months, but he wasn't certain of the details. If they were close friends, then Mitchell had most likely spoken to her about him. It also wouldn't have surprised Trevor if Imogen had simply been able to piece things together based on her own observations. He hadn't exactly been discreet.

Trevor nodded. "Special and sensitive. Okay."

"He's private, too," Imogen continued, loosening her hold on his wrist. "He keeps a lot to himself. So don't be surprised if it feels like he's keeping secrets at first."

"With all due respect, I haven't even asked him out yet," Trevor said, chuckling a little nervously.

Imogen let go of him. "I know. Sorry. I just thought I'd let you know that he can be hard to handle, especially since he doesn't communicate well. Hopefully he'll be different with you."

Trevor placed his key in his pocket and tried not to feel too unsettled. It wasn't a good sign if he was being warned about something before he even initiated a relationship with the man.

"Thank you," he said. "I appreciate the concern."

"Don't get me wrong, he's a good man to those he cares about," Imogen insisted. "He can just be a little... intense, I suppose is the right word."

Trevor leaned forward a bit, looking Imogen in the eye. "I know you mean well, but you're kind of making him sound like a psychopath."

Imogen laughed, and Trevor wondered if she was a little nervous herself. "Oh, no. No, no, no. He can be quick to anger sometimes, but I don't think... Well, never mind. He should be in the furthest bay down. Don't let him know we had this talk?"

"Of course. Thanks again."

He exited and turned right. He walked down the alley, past his waiting Fiesta, past the few other mechanics hard at work on this March Saturday. Finally, he got to the last bay and spotted the man he was looking for.

Mitchell was walking out of the bay and into the street, doing up the buttons on a grey shirt. The last two fingers of his right hand held what seemed to be a shirt he'd probably been wearing before. His movements were nimble and sure, covering up the sweaty, cream-coloured skin of his chest much too quickly for Trevor's tastes.

Trevor walked a bit closer and Mitchell caught his eye, stared at him and smiled a pleased little smirk when he realised Trevor had been watching him. There was a patch of grease on his forehead that moved when one of his heavy eyebrows raised the slightest bit.

"Something happen to your other shirt?" Trevor asked.

Mitchell flicked his wrist and let the ball of fabric in his hand unfurl. There were stains covering not only the sleeves but also the bottom half of the shirt, marring the abstract design.

"Transmission fluid spilled." Mitchell balled the shirt in his fist again. "You talk to Imogen?"

"Yeah, got my keys. She told me where to find you."

Mitchell nodded, tossed the soiled shirt on a wooden crate and slid his hands into his pockets. The way he stared into Trevor's eyes made Trevor want to look away, but he held his gaze. "So?"

Trevor took a deep breath. "So I was wondering if you wanted to maybe do something with me next weekend. Go for a drink, see a movie? We could even just hang out at my place and I could make dinner, if you like." His stomach was in knots as he waited for Mitchell's reply.

Mitchell grinned, nodded again. "A drink sounds great. Next weekend? Saturday?"

31

Trevor felt the tension leave his muscles as relief flooded his body. "Works for me. Let me get your number so I can text you the time and place?" Trevor pulled out his mobile.

As he punched in the digits and added Mitchell to his contacts, he wondered about Imogen's warning. So far, Mitchell seemed normal enough. He'd even made a joke about Trevor's car.

He was excited to see what the future with Mitchell held. Certainly it wouldn't be boring.

Chapter 5

Worker Bee on a Date

Mitchell wasn't used to feeling the good kind of nervous. Anxiety, sure. It put him on edge just *thinking* about the shaky ground he was on with Kane. The police? A strange man following him late at night? His heart wouldn't even start racing. He could remain calm in the face of things that would make most people quiver with fear. Danger that he knew he could deal with didn't much faze him.

But he'd never been on a date before. He hadn't seriously considered romance since he was in prison at eighteen years old and had nothing but time on his hands to ruminate about all the things he could've been out doing. Once he'd got out, at nineteen, he'd set his mind on making something of himself. He'd had plenty of casual sex, but had had no interest in anything more.

It was terrifying, hoping to make a good impression on Trevor and considering the possibility of revealing parts of himself that were usually hidden. He'd even thought about ringing his mother a couple times, but he refused to be *that* much of a mother's boy.

It was Saturday, the day of his date with Trevor, and Mitchell was sitting on the tube with his eyes closed. Teenagers at the other end of the car were being disruptive and annoying, but he was tuning them out. He was using a trick an old friend had once taught him. It helped calm his nerves.

He could sense metal all the time, and the sense was stronger the closer he was to the source. There was something about it that made the surrounding air charged and alive, signals that called out to him and that he felt more than saw. Like his other five senses, it was something that was always happening—always hearing, always smelling,

33

always touching, and for someone with his abilities, always being able to feel the metal around him.

It made places like cities look a whole lot different to him than what he imagined other people saw. People thought of metal objects as being made of the toughest, sturdiest, most reliable material, provided it was taken care of and didn't rust. Mitchell thought of it more like wood, not as effortlessly malleable as clay, but certainly not hard to manipulate either.

It wasn't a sense comparable to sight or sound; it was a unique sense all its own, and simply felt *different* in a way one couldn't explain to someone who didn't have it. It wasn't like sight, where the things one saw could be easily identified, and it wasn't like sound, where too much of it overwhelmed him. It was most like smelling, in the sense that it took concentration to filter the signals and pinpoint which was coming from what source.

It was a way to pass the time, was methodical and meditative. Mitchell mentally waded through the biggest things first—the carriage, the metal rail underneath it, the countless mobile phones in every passenger's pockets, the jewellery, the tiny screws in intricate things like eyeglasses. All of it sent signals to whatever in his brain gave him his gift, and he pushed away the ones he didn't want.

The point of the trick was to focus on something small, and the further away, the better, though of course his range was limited to whatever was immediately around him. He narrowed his focus down to an object his senses told him was mostly silver, with a bit a copper.

Sterling silver. Jewellery.

Mitchell held his focus until the object's owner got off at their stop. He repeated it twice more before he had to exit himself.

He tried to keep his mind blank as he walked to the pub where he was meeting Trevor. He tried not to check the time every hundred or so steps.

He failed at both. His mind kept showing him images of his hands fisted in a white sheet, his arms extended to hold himself up, and it was like he could already feel Trevor fucking him, making him clench and loosen his arse a little as he walked down the street. And even though he had slightly less than ten minutes left, he kept pulling out his mobile to check he wouldn't be late.

Finally, he arrived at the pub. Most of the tension in his muscles eased, but butterflies filled his stomach and his heart was pounding. What if Trevor couldn't handle him? His temper, his apathy, his ferrokinesis—it was a lot to ask of anyone. It was more than likely that this whole thing would end—

Mitchell took a deep, settling breath as he reached for the pub door, and told himself not to dwell on things that may or may not happen. He couldn't keep himself from taking chances simply because he didn't want to get hurt.

He opened the door and walked in, scanning the place for Trevor. When he didn't immediately see him, he checked the time again. He was six minutes early. It was possible Trevor wasn't here yet.

Mitchell ran a hand through his hair and put on the usual display of bravado and confidence as he walked leisurely through the pub, searching the sea of faces again. After a few minutes, he decided that Trevor definitely wasn't there, and found an empty table with two chairs in the back by the toilets. He texted Trevor to let him know he was there and where he was sitting.

Mitchell took off his coat and looked around the place again in the meantime. When he first started working for Alfred Kane, he used to worry that the man had eyes everywhere, had men following him. It'd taken a few months for him to realise that wasn't the case, that Kane didn't waste resources on surveying all his little worker bees twenty-four seven. As long as Mitchell supplied the cars on time, came running when called, and didn't do something stupid like try to snitch to the police that *weren't* on the payroll, Kane didn't give a damn what he did in his free time.

It was a normal Saturday night and everyone seemed to be having a good time. Though there was the usual exception, of course, like the lairy drunk brooding in the corner and the couple arguing in a booth across the way.

Then he spotted Trevor walking toward him, just in the middle of taking his hat off and half-heartedly fixing his hair. Mitchell let himself smile and shifted in his seat to put his arms up on the table.

"Hey," Trevor said, smiling back as he sat and took off his coat. "Alright?"

35

"Not bad. You?"

Trevor sighed, making Mitchell's stomach lurch. He couldn't have done something wrong already, surely?

Trevor leaned forward with an apologetic expression. "Look, I'm sorry, but you're gonna have to speak up. I can't hear a word you're saying, not in here."

Mitchell exhaled in relief. He could be louder. He could be much louder, though almost exclusively when he was angry. It felt odd and a little uncomfortable to raise his voice otherwise, but he didn't mind making the effort for Trevor.

"I said I'm not bad. How are you?" he repeated.

"Ah, I'm fine. You look good."

Trevor nodded at his clothes and Mitchell stopped himself from looking down. He knew what he was wearing — dark denim jeans and a black polo neck made of some material that stretched to fit him. He'd even brushed his hair before leaving, but nervously running fingers through it had probably undone that job.

"Thanks," Mitchell said, eyeing both Trevor's brown jumper and his usual just-above-the-ear curls. He leaned back but left one hand on table, letting an arm extend naturally. "You, too. But then, you always look good," he finished with a crooked grin. He even remembered to keep his voice louder than normal.

Trevor chuckled. "Thanks. I'd tell you the same but I think it's a bit obvious."

"You're absolutely shameless when it comes to flirting, aren't you? At my place of work and everything."

Trevor shrugged and beamed at him. "What can I say? I'm a guy that goes after what he wants."

Mitchell got up, laughing but inwardly delighted. "I'll get the first round. What're you having?"

Trevor sat back in his chair, extending his legs. "I'll start with a cider and see how I feel. Don't wanna get so pissed I make a fool of myself."

"Ah, but if I like you drunk then you know for sure I'll like you sober," Mitchell joked. He was pleased when Trevor laughed. "Cider it is. I'll be right back."

He went to order, getting a lager for himself. He wanted a little more of his confidence to be less feigned, wanted to loosen up a bit, and he wasn't a fast drinker anyway. He'd nurse his pint and maybe Trevor would down his cider, switch to a real drink afterwards.

"Cider for the teenage girl in the Fiesta," Mitchell said as he set Trevor's glass down.

"Stick to cars and leave the jokes for those who do comedy for a living," Trevor quipped, rolling his eyes but smiling. He picked up the cider and brought it to his lips as Mitchell took his seat. "Ta."

Mitchell took two large swallows of his lager and put it down, resolving to repeat the action once more before slowing. "Did you want a bit to eat?" he asked. "I ate earlier so I'm alright if you are."

Trevor shook his head. "Had something before I left. What I really want is to ask you some questions."

Mitchell's heart skipped. "Questions?"

Trevor nodded as he swallowed a mouthful of cider. "Sure. Get to know you a bit besides who you are at work."

"Okay."

Trevor pointed a finger at him. "And don't forget to speak up."

Mitchell shrugged, interested to know what kind of questions Trevor would ask and if he'd be able to give honest answers. "Go."

"Start with something simple. What would your perfect date be?"

Trevor looked especially pleased with himself, and Mitchell couldn't deny it wasn't a bad look on him. Trevor was naturally charming and stylish, the sort of man that radiated self-assurance, and it seemed even smugness he pulled off well, looking the slightest bit impish.

Mitchell took another two gulps of his lager as he considered the question. He'd never given it much thought, honestly.

"Haven't really thought about it, but I guess you can't go wrong with food," he said after a moment. "Good food, maybe a good film, topped off with good sex."

Trevor nodded with a grin. "A man who likes the simple pleasures in life. Can't argue with you there."

"How about you?"

"Me? Well, I like art, music. I'm generally pretty relaxed. I'd be fine having a drink at a place that plays local bands and things."

"Like an artsy type. Should've figured," Mitchell said, chuckling.

Trevor furrowed his brow. "Why?" He raised a hand and curled fingers in his hair. "Is it my hair? Because you're in no position to judge, yours is even longer than mine."

Mitchell shook his head to quickly dispel the notion. "Didn't mean no offence or anything, like. Just, I don't get on with most people right away. Not like I did with you. A lot of people think I'm..." He waved a hand, searching for the right word. "Too intense. Intimidating. Unapproachable."

"You're certainly that, but I've never been one to let something like that stop me. I know I come off as a posh pretty-boy — "

"I wasn't going to say anything."

"Pfft, fuck off." Mitchell chuckled into his lager as Trevor kicked him playfully under the table. "I know I don't look like it, but I *can* be intimidating. We all have dark thoughts, even the best of us."

Mitchell doubted Trevor's dark thoughts matched up with his, but the statement at least made him feel a little more hopeful.

"Anyway, second question," Trevor moved on. "Tell me about some of your friends. What are they like?"

Mitchell's stomach dropped. "My friends?"

"Sure. Good way to get to know a person is based on the sort of people they surround themselves with, right?"

"I guess so."

"So?"

Mitchell looked down into his lager. Two questions in and here was where he would have to start lying. At least it wouldn't be a complete lie. Imogen *was* his friend, just more of a work friend, as she'd said.

"Uh oh," Trevor said. "You're frowning."

Mitchell raised his eyes and relaxed the muscles in his face. Trevor was looking at him with a concerned expression. "Sorry, just thinking about something. I don't have many friends."

"Sorry?" Trevor leaned forward, cupping a hand behind his ear.

"I don't have many friends," Mitchell said again, louder. "Just Imogen and her girlfriend, Lydia. You know Imogen, my shop manager?"

"Ah, Imogen. Yeah, she's nice. I wasn't aware she was shop manager."

"We've been mates since I worked for her father. She grew up working on cars, started on them younger than even me."

Trevor nodded. "Very cool. Have you ever seen an anime called Full Metal Alchemist?"

"'Fraid not. I don't watch much TV, let alone anime."

"Ah, well. I don't watch it either, but some friends of mine do. There's a girl in it that Imogen kind of reminds me of."

"Speaking of your friends..." Mitchell nudged, eager to get the attention off of him.

Trevor took a drink from his cider. It was just under half gone. "Best friend's name is Kay. They're wild. Blue hair, lip piercing. You think I'm the artsy type, you haven't seen artsy 'til you've seen them. Though they like to call it 'the queer aesthetic.'"

"They?"

"Genderqueer. They/them pronouns."

"Got it."

"Then there's the people I have to deal with at work." Trevor sighed. "Stephen, God, I hate Stephen. Actually, he's the one who told me about Advanced Auto Repairs. Called your place a hidden gem."

"You may hate him, but I think I'm in love."

Trevor made a gagging noise. "You haven't met him. He's like... Damn, who is he like? Have you seen that movie with Steve Carell, he's a forty-year-old virgin? And that's actually the name of the movie."

Mitchell shook his head. "I told you, I don't watch much."

"Well, Stephen is the office loser. Annoying, and he doesn't even know it. I'm glad as hell I only have to go in for meetings and such."

"What do you do?"

"I'm a graphic designer at a company called Webprint, and basically they specialise in online advertising. There's loads of tech people—web developers, software engineers—that I have to work with too, and those are the people that usually get on my nerves. But anyway, other companies come to Webprint when they need advertising done; a social media plan, a logo, a whole website design, whatever."

"What do you do as a graphic designer?"

"Logos, icons, web page layouts, online adverts, those sorts of things. Some quick freelance work on the side for extra money if I have the time. I have to know some coding for the web pages bit, front-end stuff, which helps tremendously when I do freelance jobs. But I love drawing, and I love the internet, so I figured I'd combine them."

Mitchell took another drink of his lager, surprised to find that that was the last of it, though it did explain the buzz he was feeling. He hadn't realised he'd been sipping from it that frequently.

He set the glass down with a thud. "I have a random question for you, now."

Trevor folded his hands on the table. "Sure."

"What's your greatest fear?"

"Wow. Good question." Trevor pursed his lips at the table as he thought about it. "I suppose I have a rational and irrational fear. The irrational one is being eaten alive by wild animals. You know the Greek myth about the guy who gave fire to humans, and was chained to the rock? Had his insides pecked out by a hawk or something every day and it regenerated at night."

"Prometheus. It wasn't his insides, just his liver. And it was an eagle, not a hawk."

Trevor blinked.

"Sorry, I—"

"No, it's fine," Trevor reassured him. "Just a little surprised. You're a lot more knowledgeable than you look."

Mitchell shrugged. He was used to it. Mechanics, like athletes and actors and people in labour-intensive careers, weren't known for being intelligent, just for knowing a lot about cars. He also knew that the London accent he put on to cover his native Liverpool one slipped sometimes, making it *sound* like he was using an accent he didn't have. And of course people always thought someone who couldn't talk "properly" was stupid.

"I admit I didn't go to university, but I've done a lot of reading," Mitchell said. In the case of Greek mythology, it was because of his gift. As a kid it had been comics, cartoons, and films that he devoured when he could, eager to relate to *someone* who could do the sorts of things he could. Around the age of sixteen, seventeen, he'd turned to myths and legends and all sorts of tales.

It was around the same time that he'd started applying what he knew about electricity, metal, and chemistry to learn how to build cars, going to the library to help fill in the gaps. He'd stolen them, taken them for joyrides, then dismantled them to see how all their pieces fit together before selling the parts. He knew he couldn't teach himself to become a mechanic, that he'd have to somehow find someone to take him on as an apprentice, but he'd had to have some kind of goal. He hadn't wanted to spend the rest of his life selling drugs.

"Nothing wrong with that," Trevor said before moving on. "The story of Prometheus really fucked me up when I was young and impressionable. The thought of such pain and suffering, having something torn out of me, it's terrifying. I can deal with a lot of gory things, but not seeing someone be ripped apart."

"And your rational fear?"

"Not having a place to live, not having anything to eat. I don't know that I'd be able to make it on the street."

Mitchell looked at his empty glass and sighed, wishing he had more. "There are always ways to make money. You won't believe the things people will pay you to do."

Trevor nodded. "That's true. If it ever came to it, I'd just have to readjust my mindset, I suppose. Do whatever needed to be done." He threw back the rest of his cider and stood up. "I'll get the next round. Be right back."

When Trevor returned with another lager for Mitchell and a Snakebite for himself, talk turned to things like clubs, places they'd gone on holiday, and drugs they'd experimented with. Trevor had gone to more clubs, gone more places, and done more drugs than Mitchell. Mitchell left out that he used to sell, but did say that he used to smoke cigarettes.

"For how long?" Trevor asked.

"From the time I was seventeen to maybe seven months ago. I went through a phase where I decided to try to better myself. Eat healthy, take relaxing baths on Sundays, meditate, keep the flat tidy. Didn't last, but I quit smoking."

"That's good. I'll be honest, I wouldn't really date someone who smoked regularly."

"I can understand that. I still have a pack in my ice box, and I'll have one if I'm anxious or upset, but it's a rare thing."

"Brilliant." Trevor said, taking a long drink from his Snakebite.

"So. When you went out to clubs, ever hook up with anyone?"

Mitchell laughed. "That was the only reason I ever went in the first place. Do I look like the clubbing type?"

"There's dating apps for that sort of thing these days," Trevor said, hitching a brow.

Mitchell shook his head. "I've thought about it, but... I don't know. It's not like I wouldn't be able to take care of myself if it went bad, but there's something about people being able to know where I am that makes me feel uncomfortable, like. Even without a photo of my face up."

"Hey, it's alright. Not for everyone. I was just wondering, when you hooked up with them, if there was a way you preferred to do it."

Mitchell looked back at Trevor evenly, feeling a pleasant flutter in his stomach when Trevor held his gaze. Personally, he wasn't one for beating around the bush, would've came right out and asked top or bottom. Trevor had a bit more class, though, so Mitchell figured he'd follow suit.

"How do *you* prefer it?"

Trevor shrugged. "I enjoy both pretty equally. Wasn't sure if you were the same or if you're the sort that's into just one thing."

The truth was that Mitchell really was the sort to enjoy just one thing, but then, he'd never had the chance to get with someone he trusted enough to try it the other way. It was easier to just take it and not have to worry about making someone else feel good, and he was too self-conscious about performance to have his first time be with a random bloke he picked up. He'd *like* to try, at least once, but he was fairly certain he'd always like being fucked better.

He took another drink, and by this time the tipsy buzz was definitely taking hold. "I'm very much a bottom, but it's not set in stone or anything. Always open to new things."

Trevor grinned. "Great. How does one more drink sound before we head out?"

Chapter 6
Body Language

As soon as Trevor had seen Mitchell sitting there at the table, cleaned up and looking positively fucking delectable, he'd wanted to touch him all over and have Mitchell's hands just as all over him. The way the fabric of his polo neck clung to him, stretched across his chest and his lean muscles, came off more sexy than Mitchell had probably intended. Or maybe he knew exactly how he appeared in the otherwise simple garment. Either way, it was a step up from the equally attractive but grimy look he had going the times Trevor saw him at the garage. It made him want to have Mitchell pressed against him, sliding his hands up the tight shirt and feeling Mitchell's rough skin under his fingertips as they kissed.

Which was exactly what Trevor was doing now, as he devoured Mitchell against the wall next to his bedroom door.

They'd had to work to find a rhythm at first, especially since Mitchell threw himself into it like he was incapable of taking things slow. He'd been the one to push Trevor against the wall in the first place, hands already working at undoing the button of Trevor's jeans. It had driven Trevor nearly mad with desire to think Mitchell wanted to be fucked that badly. He'd had to grab Mitchell's wrists and move Mitchell's hands to his chest instead, before clutching his hips and pushing *him* against the wall.

Then he grabbed Mitchell's throat, holding the prominent Adam's apple in the curve of his thumb, and forced parted lips to his. Kissing was a whole other language, and Mitchell seemed to be able to understand Trevor perfectly. It got Trevor so hard that he pressed his cock right against the bulge in Mitchell's jeans and moaned.

43

Mitchell made a quiet "nnh" noise and dragged his hands down Trevor's back to the swell of his arse. He parted his lips just a fraction further and Trevor took it for what it was, venturing deeper into Mitchell's mouth with his tongue. Mitchell's lips shaped around it, sucking gently a couple times before sliding back a final time and joining his tongue with Trevor's.

God, he's so fucking *sexy*, Trevor thought. He only kissed Mitchell for a few more seconds, tightening his hand on Mitchell's throat as his desperation increased. Then he pulled away, putting enough space between their bodies to quickly undo his trousers. He wanted to feel Mitchell touching him so fucking badly.

He managed to get his dick out of the fly of his pants, and wrapped thumb and forefinger around the base. "Here," he said, pushing his hips forward again. He sighed gratefully when Mitchell's hand took it without the slightest bit of hesitation and started stroking it up and down as he mouthed at Trevor's neck.

It was only a few moments later when Mitchell gripped Trevor's hip and forced him back against the wall a second time. Trevor let out a surprised huff of air, and had just a second or two to get his bearings before Mitchell started sinking to his knees. His expression was completely blank, but his eyes never left Trevor's, some sort of murderous bedroom eyes that left Trevor's heartbeat stuttering.

"Fuck," he gasped when Mitchell took in his whole length. He put his hands on Mitchell's shoulders for balance, then let one slide through Mitchell's long hair to the back of his head. He didn't add any pressure; he didn't need to when Mitchell was doing such a perfect job of it by himself.

His muscles fell into a cycle of tensing and relaxing, and he could feel the way Mitchell was purposefully teasing him, getting him worked up and out of breath but not close enough to finishing. Mitchell was mesmerising to watch when he was deep-throating, eyes closed as he twisted his neck this way and that. His mouth stretched over Trevor's cock and he looked so fucking content, so fucking *dirty*.

"Like a slag," fell from his lips, barely said under his breath. He hadn't meant to say it aloud, and hadn't thought Mitchell could hear it, until Mitchell's eyes suddenly flew open, pinning Trevor to the spot.

Trevor's stomach twisted when Mitchell started pulling back, deliberately slow as he held Trevor's gaze. "I, I'm sorry, I didn't mean it like—"

Mitchell reached the head of Trevor's cock with puckered lips, coming off it with a smack while a string of saliva connected his lower lip with the tip of Trevor's dick. He didn't look offended. In fact he gave off the completely opposite impression as he extended his tongue and pressed it flat to the side of Trevor's cock, licking all the way down to his balls before sucking one in his mouth.

Trevor's jaw went slack as his lips parted. He didn't breathe, not until his body demanded it and he took in a large breath.

Mitchell rose to stand again a moment later. He kissed up Trevor's throat, a couple times on his jaw, as he ran his hands up Trevor's chest. When he pulled away just enough to be face to face, his lips twitched in a slight grin and he kept his eyes down.

"Fuck me like one if you want," he whispered.

All Trevor's senses screamed *yes, yes, yes.* He slowly trailed the pad of his thumb up the prominent vein in Mitchell's throat, made Mitchell tilt his head back when he reached the underside of his jaw.

"That how you like it? How all your club guys have done it?" he asked.

"Yeah, but you're different, like. Never wanted to go on a second date with any o' them, for one," Mitchell replied, looking down at Trevor from under his lashes.

Trevor smiled and pulled Mitchell's sleeve to finally take him into the bedroom.

He pushed Mitchell onto the bed and straddled his thighs, going straight to undoing Mitchell's jeans. Propped up on his elbows, Mitchell's hips raised from the bed as Trevor shuffled backward to pull the dark denim off, over strong legs and socked feet.

Trevor stood by the bed to finish undressing himself, while Mitchell sat up and pulled his polo neck over his head. His hair was sticking up from the static, strands of dark brown floating in the air.

Trevor bent to the trousers by his feet to get the condom from his wallet, then climbed back on the bed and reached out to smooth Mitchell's hair down. Mitchell blinked up at him then laughed.

"How do you want me?" he asked in a low voice.

Trevor grinned, crawled backward off the bed, and grabbed hold of Mitchell's ankles. With one strong pull, he slid Mitchell toward him until his arse nearly met the edge.

"Stand up and turn around first."

Trevor put the condom on while Mitchell got up and turned around to place his hands on the bed. The lube was on his chest of drawers behind him, stored in a square, silver holder like sugar packets on a cafe table. With his hands on Mitchell's hips, he urged Mitchell to walk back a bit and bend down more before he used it on him.

He heard the soft sound of Mitchell inhaling steadily as he eased his cock in. Then the sound of knuckles cracking as Mitchell's fingers curled in the covers. Trevor cast his eyes up the span of Mitchell's muscled back, from his spread arse all the way to his neck, and was so turned on by the fact that he finally had this man on his dick that he felt it throb, clenched by the hot walls of Mitchell's stretched hole.

He started pulling out and thrusting, easily setting up a rhythm that had Mitchell rocking back and forth. Each forceful shunt into him was punctuated with a sharp exhalation, until Trevor sped up and stilted breathing turned into desperate panting. Mitchell's spine seemed to extend as he pushed his arse back, inciting Trevor to go that much faster and harder. He held Mitchell's hips so tightly that he worried he'd leave bruises, but was too determined to fuck Mitchell as hard as he could to care. He saw Mitchell's hands out in front of him, clutching the covers and holding on as his entire body shook.

Trevor slowed when he got tired. He let his thrusts become lazy and less hurried, which Mitchell took advantage of by waiting until Trevor was lodged deep to swivel his hips in a circle and moan. He took over from there, Trevor more or less remaining firmly in place while Mitchell took the cock inside him at his own leisurely pace. Trevor was more than content to watch and enjoy while he caught his breath.

He placed a hand on either side of Mitchell's arse once he had, and stilled him. "Let's move."

For some reason he thought he'd have to specify that he wanted Mitchell lying on his back. He was surprised when Mitchell seemed to know and rolled over, spreading his legs. Mitchell held them up with hands on the back of his thighs as Trevor lined up and slid carefully back in.

Hands on either side of Mitchell's shoulders, he went straight to snapping his hips hard, pumping in and out of Mitchell's eager little arse. It was certainly more visually pleasing from this side, since Trevor could see every brilliant expression that passed Mitchell's face. Trevor sped up until he was practically pounding Mitchell, and Mitchell's eyes fluttered closed, his eyebrows drew together, and he let out a soft whine before choking it off and riding the wave Trevor rocked his body with.

It turned Trevor on so fucking much that Mitchell was trying to hold back a pitiful little whimper like that. He bent his arms at the elbows to lower his face to Mitchell's and kissed his panting mouth. He saw Mitchell's eyes blink open to register the change before settling softly closed again. He closed his eyes himself as he met Mitchell's tongue with his own and kept steadily fucking him into the mattress. Mitchell's hands glided up his sides and onto his back and he tensed with pleasure at the sensation.

Tired again, he pulled back for air and sat back on his heels, hooking his arms under Mitchell's knees to pull him up onto his lap. Mitchell propped himself up on his elbows and followed Trevor's lead, lifted his hips up and let them drop back down to bounce on Trevor's cock. He was apparently making himself feel just as good as Trevor did, because his head fell back and he let out a long, satisfied moan.

When Trevor felt the heat in his thighs building, he wrapped a hand around Mitchell's thick cock, making Mitchell's spine arch at the sudden touch. A moment later it sunk back down, deflating like a balloon as Mitchell's body visibly shuddered at Trevor stroking him while he fucked himself in Trevor's lap.

Trevor had expected to keep the rhythm and motion up for much longer than he did. When Mitchell extended an arm and pressed a palm flat to Trevor's chest before letting the fingers weakly curl, a shaky whine escaping his throat, Trevor realised quickly that Mitchell wouldn't take much longer to come. When he did, shooting over his stomach, his spine was taut and arched again, his head still thrown back.

The sight of Mitchell coming was hot enough by itself to get Trevor to finish. His dick pulsed at the way Mitchell took being fucked, and that one pulse led to the fire in his groin surging up. He eased his cock in and out a few more times until he felt the last of it.

Trevor pulled out and sighed as he collapsed next to Mitchell on the bed, one arm draped loosely across Mitchell's chest. He needed a moment to catch his breath again, and wasn't quite ready yet to stop touching Mitchell. Mitchell seemed content to lie peacefully for a couple minutes as well, lazily caressing Trevor's arm.

"Bathroom?" Mitchell said when each of their breathing evened out.

Trevor lifted his arm to release him and pointed a thumb at the door. "First door on your right."

Mitchell brought his legs together and rolled onto his side to slide off the bed. Trevor saw him pick up his pants on the way out.

Trevor had cleaned up as well when Mitchell came back, looking surprisingly feminine with one side of his hair tucked behind his ear. They dressed together, though Mitchell decided not to put his polo neck back on, which Trevor was perfectly fine with.

As a smooth transition, and because Trevor was a bit peckish, he asked, "Did you want a quick bite to eat?"

Chapter 7
Morning After

Mitchell's body registered a shift and he woke up. Someone was getting out of bed. He blinked his eyes open to soft morning light then closed them again to rub the crust away. Stretching his limbs, he rolled over just in time to see Trevor leaving the bedroom in only his red and white flannel pants.

Mitchell cracked his toes then folded his hands across his chest contentedly. After the first round of sex the previous night, Trevor had put a pot of pasta on to boil and showed Mitchell around the flat. He seemed to have a decent income, if the quality and taste of his furniture was anything to go by. It was simple, elegant, but with an obviously artistic element. Classy, always classy with Trevor.

Mitchell had seen Trevor's workroom, with his drafting table and a drum set Mitchell hadn't known Trevor knew how to play. Trevor had promised to play for him some other time, then led him back to the kitchen to finish preparing the pasta. After they ate, chatted a bit over a glass of water, they went back to the bedroom and Trevor fucked him again.

He heard Trevor in the adjacent room now, urinating, brushing his teeth. He thought about getting up and getting dressed, leaving before his presence made Trevor face the decision of whether or not to offer him breakfast, but felt too comfortable where he was. He let his eyes scan the bedroom as he lay peacefully in Trevor's bed on a fine Sunday morning.

He was glad for all the water Trevor had insisted he drink the night before; he was hardly hungover at all. Though he did need to use the toilet when Trevor was done.

49

Trevor smiled when he returned and noticed Mitchell was awake. "Morning. Ready for a little bit of a surprise?"

Mitchell furrowed his brow, feeling the slightest bit of caution creep in. He watched Trevor walk across the room to the nightstand and pick up a small black case he hadn't even noticed before. Trevor opened it and pulled out a pair of wire frame glasses, looking at Mitchell as he put them on.

"I usually wear contacts in public," Trevor explained.

Mitchell studied him a little, then decided he liked Trevor with his glasses on. As attractive as he was, people could mistake him for being all looks and no brains. The glasses made him appear more intelligent.

"I have a secret, too," Mitchell admitted, giving Trevor a mischievous smile. Trevor hitched a brow. Dropping the London accent he usually put on, he said, "Am really a Scouser."

Trevor's eyes widened. "Seriously?"

Mitchell chuckled and nodded. "Seriously."

"I knew you weren't from London because your voice gets a certain thickness sometimes, but I couldn't place it. Didn't know you consciously changed it to cover it up, though. I don't know that I'd be able to keep it up that long."

Mitchell sat up and folded his legs to sit cross-legged. "Ay moved ter London when ay was nineteen, so it's beun, like, nearly ten years. Am from Liverpool, originally. 'Ad lots o' practice, did a lotta self-trainin' in the beginnin'. Comes out as some sort o' weird 'ybrid now."

Trevor shook his head, laughing. "You're full of surprises, Mitchell. Never would've thought."

Mitchell shrugged. "Most days ay dun like it and wish it wasn't my native accent, but some days am or'rite wi' it and dun wanna lose that part o' me."

It wasn't too much of a sore subject, but Mitchell wasn't really in the mood for discussing why he felt ashamed of that part of his life, of himself. It wasn't the right sort of conversation to have on such an otherwise pleasant morning, and he berated himself for saying something stupid like that in the first place.

Trevor must have noticed the way Mitchell was hesitant to say more on the subject, because he tactfully nodded and dismissed it. "So, would you like tea or something?"

Trevor made them tea, which Mitchell liked black and bitter. Mitchell declined breakfast, more because he was starting to get uncomfortable being in someone else's space for so long and wanted to retreat back to his own than anything. He made the excuse of having to do laundry, and probably he'd go in to the shop to work on something for a bit, both of which were true. Trevor simply said "of course," and moved on to the next topic of conversation as they finished their tea.

Eventually, it was time for him to go, and he tied his shoes by the door. When he stood up, confronted with Trevor looking at him with his hands in his pockets, he walked over and placed his hands on Trevor's hips, smiling.

"I'll let you know when I'm free again, but text me whenever you like, in the meantime. Just don't come by the garage, my mechanics are starting to think you have a thing for the owner."

Trevor laughed, and Mitchell waited until he was finished to lean forward and kiss him. After a while, it was obvious that it was a lot more than just a kiss, especially when Mitchell's cock started to stiffen and he didn't bother to stop Trevor from pressing harder against it.

"You've gotta be fucking kidding me," Mitchell breathed when hands slid down the back of his jeans and squeezed fistfuls of his bare arse. "I just put all these clothes back on."

Trevor chuckled breathlessly against Mitchell's lips. "Come on," he said, pulling Mitchell toward the bedroom by his hold on Mitchell's buttocks. "It's not like it takes all day to do laundry. And I bet you're still all nice and loose from last night..."

Mitchell groaned and pushed Trevor to the bedroom faster.

Finally, Mitchell got home, where he immediately put his mobile on its charger and went to shower. He washed his hair, shaved, brushed his teeth, and felt much better.

After a quick breakfast—though it was almost noon and nearly lunch—he put a load of clothes in the wash and went through his email on his laptop at the living room table. Email turned into checking other things, browsing the internet, and time sped by on him until somehow it was nearly two in the afternoon. He sighed, not really wanting to go to the garage when he'd only just settled in at home after a night out.

He checked his calendar. It was the ninth of March, and Kane didn't need the car for the torture ride until the end of the month at the earliest. Mitchell had already been working on it a good few days when Adam had come by the shop on the twenty-eighth of February to let him know about the modifications to the order. There was still a good portion to be done, but not so much that Mitchell couldn't afford to relax a bit here and there while still being able to get his legal jobs done. Besides, there were still a few parts he was waiting for.

Hungry again after the small breakfast, Mitchell put the laptop down and went to the kitchen. He searched the fridge and cupboards for something to eat, then settled on ordering something that could feed him for dinner as well. He went to the bedroom and got his mobile to call a place he'd eaten from a thousand times before.

Once food was taken care of, he stared down at the phone he'd just hung up, pursing his lips. The excitement from the date with Trevor and the impromptu morning sex was still coursing through him despite the lull his day had dipped into. He wanted to talk to someone about it, someone that wasn't his mother, and thought about how Trevor had asked him about his friends, what Imogen had said.

He'd only ever had a few friends in his life, and only one from his time before London did he still keep in contact with – the woman who'd taught him how to tune his metal sensing, who had helped so many other people with psychic gifts. Naomi had been in her early thirties back then, so she was maybe in her late forties now. But the only time she and Mitchell interacted with each other was via holiday card, and it'd been that way since Mitchell had cut ties with her only six months after meeting her.

He sighed and dialled Imogen's number.

"Hello?" Imogen answered.

"Imogen?"

"Hey, Mitchell."

"Hey. You busy?"

"No," she said. "Just sitting here watching Lydia play video games. Did you need something?"

Mitchell sat down on his sofa. Of course she thought he needed something. He normally wouldn't call if it wasn't for a specific reason, and never was it anything personal.

He tried to come off as casual. "There was something I wanted to talk to you about, that's all."

"Sure," Imogen said. Mitchell heard Lydia swearing in the background, probably playing multiplayer.

Mitchell took a deep breath. "You remember I told you last Saturday — not yesterday, but the Saturday before — Trevor asked me out and I agreed?"

The change in her tone was instantaneous as she became excited. "Of course I do! Was that last night? Shit, how did it go?"

Mitchell smiled, relieved Imogen's enthusiasm made it so much easier. "So far, so good. So very, very good."

"Well, come on, you can't just say something like that and not give any details!"

Trevor settled into his usual Sunday routine and worked out for a bit after breakfast, did some yoga, and took a shower. He wanted to tell Kay all about his success with the dirty mechanic, but knew that Kay's sleeping schedule wouldn't have them wake up for at least another two hours. Then they'd shortly be off to work.

He decided to watch a horror film on Netflix in the meantime, in the mood to have himself thoroughly frightened in the middle of an ordinary Sunday afternoon. Something with lots of hacking and slashing, but not a boring and predictable serial killer movie. He turned the lights out, closed the curtains, and got comfortable in a blanket on the sofa before bringing up Netflix on his Xbox360 and browsing through the choices.

He ended up really liking what he chose, and wondered if Mitchell liked horror films. He hoped he did, and figured that that was probably the case since Mitchell seemed like the kind of person who would. Or at least not the kind of person who was too easily scared by them. Apparently Mitchell hadn't watched much of anything, too focused on work and whatever else he did with his free time.

It was just getting on evening when Trevor got up to sit in bed with his laptop. He signed in to Skype and messaged an online Kay to see if they were up for video chatting. They were.

"Hey, Trev, how's it going?" Their curly blue hair was tied up in a ponytail, the way they kept it when they slept so it wouldn't get out of control. They scritched the top of their head as they yawned, both sounds amplified by the headset they were wearing.

"Not too bad," Trevor said, raising his voice a little for the mic in his laptop. He himself only had in headphones in order to reduce the echo effect. "Had a date with that mechanic last night that ended up being fucking brilliant."

Kay grinned. "He's a good one, then? You give 'im the old Trevor Lewis lay?"

"I told you not to call it that every time I shag someone," Trevor said, laughing. "But yes, he's a good one. We get on great, similar sense of humour and everything. And when we kiss—"

"Aww!"

Trevor rolled his eyes. "Jesus, I didn't even finish yet."

"Sorry, sorry! Go on."

"When we kiss, it's like I can *feel* the connection, you know? It's like we get each other, with words and without them."

"You got all that from one date?"

"Why is that so hard to believe? It's not like it's unheard of for two people to just click. And I felt a hell of a lot more with him in one night than I felt with anyone else I've dated or slept with," Trevor pointed out.

"Fair enough. What's he like then, now that you've got to know him more?"

Trevor put his elbow on his knee and rested his chin in his hand as he cast his mind back to the previous night, to that morning. "We've talked about mainly surface stuff so far. Nothing too deep and personal, like politics or beliefs. But he seems quite laid back, very go with the flow. It's nothing he's *done*, really, more like the way he acts. Like if people were rioting out in the street, he'd probably pour himself a drink and shrug. Bit of a hedonistic quality to him that way."

"Right. Well, everyone's got a type," Kay said. Trevor could tell by their tone that they didn't much fancy the description.

"I know you don't care much for people who aren't as actively for things like human rights and the environment as you, but some people just don't care, Kay. Well, no, it's not that they don't *care*, it's more like they just don't feel strongly enough about causes like that to be all activisty for it."

Kay put up their hands. "Hey, I didn't say anything."

"No, but I know you were thinking it. Anyway, he's certainly keeping things interesting. Surprised me this morning with a Liverpool accent, said it's where he's originally from."

Kay laughed. "Surprise!"

"Yeah. I wanted to ask him loads of questions, 'cause I had sudden urge to know what he was like as a kid, but he looked uncomfortable enough admitting it to me. I kind of don't blame him. Even if he is well off enough to own a whole garage, he's still a labour worker, still considered pretty low by most, you know? And there he was surrounded by all the nice stuff in my flat. I wouldn't've wanted to emphasise the difference either if I were him. Not that I mind, but I mean, I can understand why he'd feel ashamed given the surroundings."

"That makes sense," Kay said. "As long as his past isn't full of like, criminal activity or something, he's probably an alright bloke. Just wasn't dealt the best hand in life and that's not his fault."

Trevor nodded. "My thoughts exactly. But honestly, even if he had been a criminal in the past, I think I'd be able to forgive it now. People change, and who he is now could be completely different from who he was then."

"Could be," Kay mused. "But I think of it like those people who go through a rough patch before supposedly 'finding Jesus.' You say you've changed, you might even *think* you've changed, but there'll always be that piece of you in the core of your being that's the same. You can't just pretend it never happened or that you weren't capable of doing something terrible at one point."

"Basically you're saying once a criminal, always a criminal."

"Yeah, I guess I am."

Trevor moved the conversation on to something a bit lighter before Kay eventually had to go get ready for work. The words stuck with him, though, try as he might to shake them off.

He kept remembering the dodgy-looking young man who'd come into the shop the day he'd dropped his car off for new tyres. The cold way Mitchell had glared at the man then had screamed danger, yet the man had simply smirked back. The whole exchange had left Trevor unnerved, an exchange that felt like it was between two individuals who couldn't possibly be up to anything good, but he'd mostly dismissed it at the time.

He dismissed it again now, positive that he was being paranoid. It was probably just as Imogen had said. Mitchell was quiet, and therefore naturally reserved and secretive.

Chapter 8
Let's Go for a Drive

It was nine days later when Trevor saw Mitchell in person again, but they'd kept in touch through texting every day in between. Trevor managed to keep himself from asking Mitchell out again despite wanting to, remembering that Mitchell had said he'd tell *him* when they could next meet.

Not wanting to waste time he could otherwise spend getting to know Mitchell better, he decided to ask Mitchell at least one random question a day. Five days in, he started to worry he was being annoying, even though Mitchell always responded, even sometimes asked Trevor a question of his own. He was thrilled when Mitchell assured him that he wasn't annoying him in the slightest, that it was in fact quite the opposite. It was apparently something he looked forward to throughout the work day, and even if he couldn't always reply right away, he enjoyed reading them.

By the time Mitchell said he was free to meet up for a second date, Trevor had learnt all sorts of little facts about him, all of them making Trevor more interested. He hoped he'd provided Mitchell with an equally clearer picture of who he was as a person as well, and that Mitchell liked what he saw.

Remembering the shop hours sign from before, Trevor knew that Advanced Auto Repairs was open later than most garages. Mitchell had said that around seven, an hour from closing, they started winding down. Most of the bay doors were shut, many of the lights were turned off, and only the most dedicated employees stuck around to finish up one last thing before heading home.

That was the time he'd told Trevor to come by, so he could leave with him for the restaurant right from work. He'd asked Trevor to bring his car, too, because he wasn't really in the mood for the Underground.

When Trevor approached the shop entrance, it was almost half seven, and he saw Mitchell talking to Imogen through the window. They seemed to be among the last few around.

Trevor slowed his gait, not wanting to interrupt something important. Mitchell must have seen him in his peripheral vision, because he suddenly waved him over, not bothering to look away from Imogen. Trevor quickened his pace and used the brief opportunity to look his fill of Mitchell after the week and a half apart.

Mitchell's usually soft-spoken voice trailed off by the time Trevor walked up. He was wearing oil-stained jeans and a dirty vest. One hand on the counter, he turned to Trevor, looking him in his eyes for a long moment, then let out a sigh. "Hi."

Trevor flashed him a smile. "Hey."

"Have to go to my office to change my clothes. I'll be right back, okay?"

"An office, huh? Guess that means I don't get to see it."

Mitchell chuckled, and finally his lips spread in a smile wide enough to stretch his face, showing his teeth. He looked down, appearing coy under the curtain of his hair.

"I'll be right back." He turned toward the door behind him, opened it, and took one step in. Then, seeming to have forgotten something, he turned back to Trevor, reached out, and slid his fingertips down the back of Trevor's hand where it rested on the counter. He returned to his usual course as though nothing had happened.

Trevor didn't know where the gesture had come from, but he had no trouble understanding it. Imogen, standing off to the side, had wide eyes and a palm over her mouth, her gaze locked on Trevor's hand.

"So," Trevor began, clearing his throat. "How have things been here, then?"

Imogen blinked and refocused on Trevor, dropping her hand to her side. She placed a nonchalant elbow on the counter and shrugged. "Oh, you know, same as ever. How have things been you with you and Mitchell?"

Trevor laughed and leaned onto his forearms. "You're shameless, you know that?"

Imogen grinned and came to lean on the counter in front of him conspiratorially. "Maybe a little."

"Things with me and Mitchell have been fine, thanks for asking."

"He's, you know, talking to you and everything?" Imogen asked.

"He seemed able to communicate just fine when we went for drinks, and we've been texting all the time. Not at all hard to handle."

Imogen exhaled in relief. "Good, that means he's comfortable around you."

"I take it that's a rarity?"

"You could say that."

"You know, I haven't really seen any of those other things you warned me about," he said. "I think you said something about him being quick to anger? Haven't seen the slightest trace of that in him. Intense? Maybe a *little*, but certainly nothing worth bringing up to someone. And everyone has some degree of privacy —"

"Has he told you about... No, never mind."

"Oh, come on! Told me about what?"

"Honestly, Trevor, if you have to ask, then it means he hasn't."

Trevor sighed in exasperation. "Imogen. Seriously?"

"Look, I'm sorry, but he's a friend, and I don't give away my friends' secrets. He'll tell you when he's ready. But don't worry, it's nothing I don't think you can't handle."

"Bloody..." Trevor huffed. Now it would bother him every second he was with Mitchell, and he definitely wasn't going to just *ask*, because that was sure to make Mitchell shut right up.

Behind Imogen, the door opened, and Mitchell stood in the doorway, cleaned up and changed into new clothes. His face and hands were free of grease, his dark brown fringe was swept out of his eyes, and the rest of his hair looked like it'd been combed.

The jeans he wore now were crisp and black, and fit the muscular curves of his legs in a way that made Trevor positively lust. His shirt was an ordinary black, cotton v-neck, and over it he'd thrown on a black leather jacket that would have looked new if not for the worn cuffs where his hands poked out.

"Hey," Mitchell said. "Fancy letting me drive?"

Trevor didn't understand why Mitchell would possibly want to drive, other than maybe wanting to surprise Trevor with where they were going out to eat. He decided the reason didn't matter either way, since he didn't mind letting Mitchell drive his car. Mitchell must've known Trevor wouldn't be too worried about something happening to it, since he was the same mechanic who'd taken care of it three times. If anyone could be trusted with a car, it was Mitchell.

Still, Trevor feigned offence. "You want to drive my Fiesta? After what you said about it?"

Imogen gasped and turned to look at Mitchell. "Mitchell, tell me you didn't make any rude remarks about Mr Lewis's *perfectly* appropriate car." Mitchell laughed as he walked around the counter, hands in the pockets of his jacket.

"Oh, fuck off about my car, both of you." Trevor took his key out to give to Mitchell nonetheless. "Here. Where are we going?"

Mitchell grinned a satisfied, knowing smile and walked ahead of Trevor with his chin up. "I wanna take you out for a drive before we go to dinner. Mind closing up for me, Imogen?"

"Yeah, yeah," she said. "Have fun, you two. And Mitchell, for fuck's sake, be safe."

Halfway out the door, Mitchell snorted.

Trevor followed him out. Mitchell unlocked the car, opened the passenger door for Trevor, then walked around to the driver's side. As Trevor slid into the seat, he thought it was weird being in his own car but not driving it.

He didn't mind it so much when Mitchell got in. Mitchell pulled an ancient-looking iPod out of his jacket, plugged it into the sound system, then dropped the key fob in Trevor's lap as he pressed the power button to start the engine. An electronic drumbeat came through the speakers, and the engine purred softly as Mitchell shifted gears and drove out of the narrow lane.

It was nearing eight o'clock by now, otherwise Trevor doubted Mitchell would've been able to go as fast as he was. More than once, Mitchell nearly ran over an unsuspecting tourist, and a few times he dodged around a bus, making Trevor worry his car would hit something head-on and be crushed, with them inside.

He couldn't figure out where Mitchell was heading or if they even had a destination at the moment, if Mitchell wasn't just driving aimlessly. He only knew that Mitchell seemed to have an uncanny knowledge of the roads, much more so than Trevor, as most of the streets they drove down had started clearing for the night. It was only when they got closer to the city centre that Mitchell finally had to reduce his speed.

Still, near Shoreditch, Mitchell managed to zoom down Old Street. Trevor had to ask. "Where are we going?"

Mitchell shrugged, which answered Trevor's earlier question about what they were currently doing. Mitchell turned smoothly down a side street that was less crowded as though he were headed somewhere, but then relaxed back into the seat like they'd be driving for a while.

Trevor tried not to trouble himself too much about it. Instead he openly stared at Mitchell, taking in his comfortable, open legs, and his fingers drumming the beat of each song on the top of the steering wheel. Even though a few turns were sharp and they'd nearly side-swiped a couple cars, Mitchell's breathing had remained calm, whereas Trevor had found himself gripping the side of his seat for dear life.

Trevor wasn't exactly comfortable with his car being driven so recklessly, and he wanted to say something, but didn't want to come off as being boring and unadventurous. That's what Kay definitely would've said. Some people would think a ride like this fun, which Mitchell certainly seemed to. In fact, Mitchell looked completely in his element and at ease behind the wheel, driving so skilfully and effortlessly that it kind of turned Trevor on. Despite all the quick gearshifting and brake-pumping, Mitchell was a brilliant driver, which made sense considering he'd told Trevor that cars were his thing. But Trevor also wanted to know if they were going to get to dinner *before* the restaurant closed.

He decided to just have faith that Mitchell knew what he was doing, because Mitchell didn't seem like the type of person to lose track of time or forget himself so carelessly. And watching him *was* mesmerising. Trevor sat back, hesitantly trusting Mitchell not to cause a wreck, and watched the early London evening begin out the window as he listened to Mitchell's music.

By the time they entered the City, Trevor had managed to keep his pulse from jumping every few seconds. They were on Queen Victoria Street, and traffic had thickened a little, but of course Mitchell was still managing to get too close to the car in front of him, or change lanes just in time to end up right in front of a looming bus. Trevor tried to calm himself by staring out the window and not paying attention to the way his car was being handled.

There went St. Paul's Cathedral on his right, and somewhere behind the buildings on his left was the sludge-brown of the Thames. Mitchell took them down Fleet Street, and there went St. Paul's again, closer this time. A little further down near Blackfriars Station, and there was the London Eye in the distance, though the last rotation had gone up long ago.

As Trevor opened his mouth to speak a second time, Mitchell's foot pressed harder on the pedal, and their speed increased, the engine purring. Mitchell's hand on the gearshift tightened and Trevor noticed his lips had pressed together as well, though they'd also turned up in a slight smile.

"I noticed you didn't go for many of the extras available for this model," Mitchell suddenly said, turning to look at Trevor. "No parking sensors or rear-view cameras, no spoiler on the back. Just the heated seats and satnav, even though you probably could've afforded more. The interior lighting is a nice touch, though."

Mitchell didn't return his eyes to the road ahead, and Trevor was definitely not okay with that, given both their speed and the flow of traffic. But Mitchell was staring at him as though waiting for an answer, not concerned with the other drivers. Mitchell was acting completely mad and it was slightly terrifying. Trevor couldn't be sure if he was the excited kind of nervous yet or not.

"So I'm cheap but I like the warmth in the winter." Trevor tried not to snap, but wasn't sure he quite pulled it off. He was too concerned with his safety to linger on it. "And they said this one came with the satnav and ambient lighting. Look where you're going, would you?"

Mitchell rolled his eyes and stared straight ahead again, but made it obvious it was only to appease Trevor.

From then on, the ride was decidedly dangerous. Mitchell drove like he was suicidal, swerving in and out of traffic, barely missing cars and doing turns that had the tyres skidding across the street. Trevor couldn't breathe from how hard his heart was pumping in fright. His knuckles had gone white where they clenched the door.

And yet Mitchell seemed to know exactly what he was doing. He only laughed when Trevor squeezed his eyes shut.

Slowly, one by one, Trevor reopened them. In the end, it was the way Mitchell pulled death-defying manoeuvres with a playful smile on his face that convinced Trevor of his mastery and let him relax.

After a while, he even started to have fun.

Chapter 9

The Diner

They were at a traffic light when Mitchell turned to Trevor and asked if he was ready to go to dinner. Trevor noted the time. They'd been joyriding for nearly an hour and now it was a quarter after eight.

"Yeah," he said. "Could've done earlier, you know."

Mitchell rubbed the back of his neck. "Sorry. I just wanted to show you how I like to have fun sometimes. If it makes you feel any better, the place I was thinking of going to doesn't close for a while yet."

"It's fine. It wasn't at first, I admit, but then it wasn't so bad. You're absolutely mad, I hope you know that."

Mitchell chuckled. "Trust me, I know."

The light turned green and Mitchell made a sharp U-turn, the tyres squealing loudly over the music. Trevor cringed and mourned for his poor Fiesta.

Mitchell stopped the car abruptly in Soho, near Carnaby Street. He pocketed the iPod, shut off the engine, and got out. Trevor felt like he'd been picked up in a tornado and deposited a thousand miles away from home.

Carnaby Street wasn't particularly busy, but it was as lively as expected for this hour on a Tuesday. Most of the shops were closing or about to close, and as they walked past, Trevor wondered when Mitchell would be alright with holding his hand in public. He'd already brushed it in front of Imogen.

"This place alright with you?" Mitchell asked, stopping in front of The Diner. Trevor had never been inside, but he thought he remembered hearing about it once or twice. In his experience it was hard *not* to hear about a place in Soho.

Trevor nodded once and followed Mitchell in. The restaurant was nice enough, and loud as hell due to the number of people packed inside. Trevor noticed it was American cuisine, which wasn't bad, he supposed. He followed Mitchell's leather jacket to a table and slid into the seat across from him.

Mitchell ran a hand through his hair, brushing his fringe from his eyes again, and sighed as he picked up his menu. Trevor looked down at his and started scanning it for something he liked.

Soon enough, a waitress came to ask what they wanted to drink. They both ordered water.

"And do you know what you'd like to eat?"

Mitchell raised a single heavy brow. Trevor shook his head.

"I'll be back in a few minutes then," she said. "Take your time."

Trevor looked over the menu a while longer before giving up and consulting Mitchell. "What are you getting?"

Mitchell pointed his finger at a spot on his menu. *Banana pancakes.*

Trevor blinked. "Seriously?"

"Yes." His voice was drowned out by the much louder ones nearby, but Trevor could read the simple word on his lips.

"You know it's nearly nine, right?"

Mitchell smiled and leaned in so he could be heard. "You've never had breakfast at night, have you?"

"Uh, no. I'm apparently rather boring."

"I dare you to try it." He flipped Trevor's menu over and stabbed a slender finger downward, pointing to an item nearly centre-page. "Get that."

It was like Mitchell had performed some sort of magic. As soon as he had suggested something for Trevor to order, their waitress reappeared, notepad in hand.

"All set?"

Mitchell nodded once and moved his finger to his own menu, pointing to the line marked "banana pancakes." Trevor sighed. It wasn't as though he liked anything else on the menu all that much.

"Lumberjack breakfast, please," he said. "Eggs fried hard."

The waitress scribbled their order then took their menus. "Great. Be ready soon." She disappeared and left Trevor to face an intolerably smug Mitchell.

"Well, there you are." Trevor said.

Mitchell chuckled. "Let me start the question game this time."

Trevor regarded Mitchell's face, the carefree, happy expression smiling back at him, and tried not to think the worst. But he couldn't help remembering that Mitchell was keeping something from him, and he was still dying to know what it was, how serious or inconsequential.

"Alright," Trevor said.

The smile suddenly disappeared as Mitchell became serious. "Do you believe in ghosts?"

Trevor burst into shocked laughter. "What?"

Mitchell did nothing but stare unblinkingly back.

"I don't—Sure? I don't know," Trevor said. "I mean, I watch a lot of horror movies, so I don't really have the excuse of saying I've never thought about it. But I guess I sort of think of it like, it's just stuff reserved for cinema, dramatic storytelling. So, no, not really. Do you believe in them?"

Mitchell shrugged. "Yeah."

"I see."

"Will that be a problem?"

"Not at all. As long as you don't start saying things are haunted or possessed, it should be fine."

Mitchell half smiled. "I used to know someone who could see and talk to dead people. She said they were usually one of two things, sarcastic as fuck or confused as fuck."

"Yeah, stuff like that."

Mitchell laughed. "I was just kidding. Thought you could tell."

Their waitress passed by the table quickly, setting their drinks down before hurrying off somewhere else. Trevor thought he heard her say she'd be right back with their food, but couldn't be sure.

They each took long sips from their glasses, then Mitchell said, "What about God?"

Trevor proceeded cautiously, but he agreed that it was probably a topic they should discuss sooner rather than later. "Raised to believe in it, but pretty much agnostic about the whole God thing these days."

Mitchell exhaled. "Okay."

Trevor laughed, feeling tension dissolving. "Worried for a second there?"

"I don't think a religious person would really be able to handle someone like me."

Trevor didn't know what the hell that was supposed to mean. What did someone even say to something like that? Luckily, their food arrived before the delay in Trevor's response could get awkward. The waitress placed their respective plates in front of them, the food steaming and filling Trevor's nose with the incongruous scent of breakfast at night. His mouth started watering, and he dug in as soon as he could.

"Sorry, that was a weird thing to say," Mitchell said after they'd been eating a little while. "I'm more spiritual than religious, in case you were wondering. Also pretty agnostic about God, though."

"Spiritual?" Somehow applying the word to Mitchell didn't seem to fit.

"In the sense that I think everything's connected. Everything in the universe is made up of the same stuff, and..." He trailed off, shaking his head, as if chiding himself and resolutely saving it for a better time. "I just see things in an... interesting way."

Seeing an opening, Trevor contemplated his next words. He swallowed a bite of food and wondered what Mitchell's reaction would be. "Imogen did tell me you were special."

Mitchell froze, his fork lodged in a fluffy piece of pancake. "Special how?"

"Oh, she didn't say how. Just told me things like you have a quick temper, you don't usually communicate well, and you're more sensitive than you let on. That you're special and really private." Trevor took a quick bite of egg. "But listen, don't be upset with her. She obviously cares about you and just wanted to sort of prep me, I guess, for being around you."

"All of those things are true," Mitchell said evenly, raising his eyes to stare into Trevor's. "Especially the part about me being private."

Trevor broke the eye contact first, looking down at his plate. "Noted."

"Everyone has a right to privacy, Trevor."

"Yes, well, there's privacy and there's lying, isn't there?"

Mitchell's hands curled pleadingly around Trevor's wrists, urging Trevor to look back up.

"Stop. I like you, Trevor, so fucking much. I have things I don't usually share right from the start, just like anyone, but I'll tell you everything eventually. Just, in pieces, in case you end up not sticking around. I have to be careful. Not just because of what it is, but because I'm scared of what you might think of me. Give me some time, alright?"

Trevor let a few seconds pass, and Mitchell took his hands back. "I have a question for you now," he said.

"Yeah?"

"Do *you* have a car?"

Mitchell visibly relaxed, chuckled a little. "I have many. A garage full."

"You know what I mean."

"No, I don't own any. Never have."

"Never will?"

"Maybe. Don't really see now why I'd need to, though." He shrugged and took another bite of his pancakes.

"Ever thought about being anything other than a mechanic? Or have you always wanted to work on cars?"

Mitchell circled his finger around the rim of his glass, the hint of a smile on his face. "Cars have been my hobby for ages," he said. "I have a knack for them."

Trevor remembered the garage's slogan, the same one that accompanied the shop's advert everywhere.

"The magic touch?" he teased.

Mitchell smiled, albeit a bit sadly. "Something like that."

Trevor took a bite, putting some distance between his last question and the next. "How did you get to own your shop at such a young age in the first place? You said you were twenty-eight, and you seem to have had the place for a couple years at least."

Mitchell's face clouded over and he leaned back, his food seemingly forgotten. He rested an arm on the back of the booth and let his eyes drift to look out the window. His voice, when he finally spoke, sounded like he was a thousand years away.

"I took out a loan," he said simply. "I always knew, even when I was a kid back in Liverpool, that I wanted to own my own garage, not have to take orders from anybody. Nothing was going to hold me back, certainly not money."

Trevor swallowed his food and licked his lips clean. There was something about the tone of Mitchell's voice that let on that he was lying about the loan, or at least not telling the full truth of how he'd acquired the shop. He thought back to his and Kay's conversation about criminals and tried not to let it colour his judgement. He just wished Mitchell trusted him enough to be honest with him, but at the same time, he couldn't blame the man for being cautious with what information he shared. It was still only the second date, and Mitchell had explained that he needed a bit more time.

"That's good that you were so persistent and determined," Trevor began. "My father was dead set on me going into business or law, so I had to go to uni using some of the money I inherited from my mother at first. Eventually he came round and helped out."

Mitchell remained silent, but his expression had softened throughout Trevor's speech. He was looking down, not quite smiling.

"What about your family?" Trevor asked.

The not-quite smile faltered. "It was always just me and my mother. Never had a dad."

"Ah, so reverse of my situation."

"Guess so. I don't think my dad is dead, though. Just never met him and never really cared enough to go looking."

"Do you and your mum get along? I don't always see eye to eye with my father."

Mitchell nodded. "Yeah. In a few ways she's my best friend, as pathetic as it sounds."

Trevor grinned. Before he could say anything, Mitchell shot him a warning look, which only made him start laughing. "What's she do?"

All trace of humour in Mitchell's face drained away. Trevor imagined a turtle slowly retreating back into its shell.

Instead of replying, Mitchell asked, "What's your dad do?"

"He's a solicitor."

"'Course he is."

"And your mum?"

Mitchell shook his head again, more insistently. "Nothing."

"Nothing?"

"She has a job, kind of, but mostly I just send her money. I don't wanna talk about it."

Now Trevor had to know. Another secret? How could he not be curious? "It can't be *that* bad."

"Well she's sure as fuck not a solicitor," Mitchell snapped.

Trevor was taken aback. Why was Mitchell getting so upset? "I'm lost, did I offend you or something?"

"Look, Trevor, you know I'm not like you. I'm not..." Mitchell sighed and stabbed his pancake with his fork.

"Mitchell—"

"You really wanna know?" Mitchell looked up.

Trevor swallowed and nodded. He wanted to know.

He waited while Mitchell shoved the bite of pancake in his mouth, chewed, put the fork down and rubbed his temples.

"She's a whore."

Trevor blinked. "You mean like—"

"Sleeps with men for money. Yeah, that's exactly what I mean." Mitchell let his hands drop back to the table, eyes lowered.

Trevor touched Mitchell's wrist, half mirroring Mitchell's earlier action. "What your mother does for a living has nothing to do with how I feel about you, Mitchell."

Mitchell pulled his wrist from under Trevor's hand and held it in his own, took a slow breath before speaking, but still kept his eyes down. "I... I used to help her. A few times a week. Before I found another job."

Trevor's mouth ran away with him before he could shut himself up. "Not together, surely?"

"Not technically..." Mitchell yanked his hand out of Trevor's and put his face in his hands. "Christ. I'm making it sound like we had threesomes or something. That's not how it was. I don't wanna talk about it."

"Mitchell." Trevor grabbed his wrist and pulled a hand away from his face so he could look him in the eye. Was this what Imogen had been talking about then? Was this what Mitchell had thought would make Trevor think differently of him? "I'm not the type of person to judge. I know it doesn't seem like it, but it takes a little more than incest to scare me away. You can talk to me. Seriously."

He saw Mitchell swallow hard, saw in his eyes the way he was considering the situation. Finally, Mitchell exhaled and said, "It was only a few nights a week, like I said, and we never touched the client at the same time. Sometimes the client was just mine, and my mam would go to the other room. But when they wanted both of us, it was more like taking turns. Some men liked to, to fuck the mother before having a go at her boy. Maybe switch back and forth before coming on both of us. They paid extra for it, sometimes a lot extra depending on what they wanted to do. It was usually in the same room, so, I mean, I guess, yeah, I've seen my mam fucked plenty of times, and she's seen me as well. But that's it. The two of us never... We were offered money to cross that line a few times and always turned it down. The only reason we did as much as we did was because we had to, like."

Jesus. Trevor tried not to appear outwardly shocked, keeping his face composed. It was appalling, but still not enough to lessen his feelings for Mitchell. He pitied Mitchell more than anything, was sorry he had to go through it.

"Don't think she whored me out or anything," Mitchell hurried to add, like he could hear Trevor's thoughts. "My mam's a good woman, really. I offered to do it, to help. It started with one client I kind of took a fancy to when I was fourteen and after him I figured I could, you know, keep doing it to bring in money, at least until I was older and could figure something else out. We needed it, so she didn't disagree," he finished with a shrug. "I sometimes hate her for letting me make a decision like that, but we're so close I could never really *hate* her."

"Why didn't you just find a job?" Why didn't Mitchell's mother find one for that matter?

Trevor regretted the words as soon as he said them. Mitchell sneered at him and said, "Of course, why didn't I think of that? A kid with no work experience who lives in a neighbourhood where people steal car parts and sell drugs for money, I'll just go out and 'find a job.' Easy."

"Sorry."

Mitchell sighed again, continued eating. "It's okay."

"Were you at least always safe? Were you ever mistreated or hurt or threatened?"

"It's not exactly a safe business, Trevor, but I was as safe as I could be. It got a bit rough at times, but Mam told me that was to be expected. And if I was ever threatened, I knew how to take care of myself. We were never unarmed."

Trevor took a deep breath and leaned forward. In the back of his mind, he hoped his food hadn't gone cold.

"Mitchell, seriously, I want you to know that this doesn't change anything for me. For us. The only thing that would really make me have to consider calling everything off is if you murdered someone or something."

Mitchell chuckled. "Right."

"You haven't, have you?" Trevor joked.

Mitchell rolled his eyes. "I have another question for you."

Trevor sat back, returned to his food. "Alright."

"Do you believe people can be psychic?"

"You mean like seeing the future?" Trevor asked, laughing.

"Yeah. Or like, telekinesis and mindreading."

"Ghosts, God, psychics. What next?"

"So you don't believe in it, then?" Mitchell said, an eyebrow raised.

"I'd have to see it to believe it. If I had solid evidence, sure."

Mitchell nodded. "Yeah. Yeah, most people are that way."

Chapter 10
Essex

Trevor didn't dare approach anything else that was too personal, lest it explode in his face again. They talked about their favourite things, their pet peeves, and the more recent past for the rest of the meal, until Mitchell pushed away his plate with a contented sigh.

"Wanna get out of here?" Mitchell asked, smiling and pressing his calf against Trevor's under the table. "Back to your place?"

Trevor didn't have much left on his plate, so he quickly shoved a few bites into his mouth before pushing away his own meal. He already started thinking of the fastest route back to his flat. "Definitely."

Mitchell caught the waitress's attention and waved her over. Trevor reached for his wallet, but Mitchell shook his head. When she arrived, Mitchell pushed a couple notes into her hands and told her something Trevor couldn't hear. She glanced down and blinked, eyes wide.

"Thank you," she whispered in awe. Trevor wondered how much Mitchell had given her. Mitchell shrugged and slid out of the seat, jerking his head and motioning for Trevor to follow.

As they walked back to the car, through hordes of laughing drunk people spilling across the street, Trevor wondered for the second time what Mitchell was like as child. He had a feeling Mitchell wasn't telling him everything about his past, and he couldn't even imagine the sorts of things that Mitchell deemed too horrible to reveal. The fact that Mitchell had had to always have a weapon at the ready, and that maybe he'd had to use it a few times, unsettled Trevor the most. He'd never realised how strong Mitchell was.

It made him wonder if Mitchell would be able to handle seeing his artwork well.

Trevor was already waiting patiently in the passenger seat when Mitchell slid into the driver side. Mitchell pushed the power button just as his mobile rang.

Mitchell punched the dashboard hard enough to make himself pull back and swear. Trevor flinched, jolted by the sudden aggression.

"Fuck," Mitchell hissed. He looked apologetically at Trevor. "I'm so sorry." He shoved his hand down the front pocket of his jeans and took out his phone, swearing again when he looked at who was calling. "I've got to take this."

"It's alright," Trevor said. But he was curious to know who could cause such a reaction. "Whatever."

Mitchell bit his lip and frowned until the persistent ringing spurred him into action. He hurried out and slammed the car door behind him, then leaned against the driver window. Trevor heard a muffled, "What?"

He didn't hear much more of the conversation because Mitchell kept his voice lower than usual. Most of Mitchell's side of the conversation seemed to be monosyllabic answers and angry hisses. He obviously didn't like whoever was on the other end, and Trevor wondered if it was something to do with that dodgy fellow from before.

Mitchell hung up the phone and put it slowly back in his pocket. At his sides, each hand curled into a tight fist, quivering with tension.

Mitchell spun around and walked around the car to open Trevor's door. Trevor furrowed his brow and stepped out, closing the door behind him. "We'll have to save it for another time," Mitchell said, sounding genuinely sorry. "I have to go to Essex tonight."

"Essex?! That's at least an hour's drive from here!" Trevor exclaimed. What the hell was in Essex that Mitchell had to go to so late, and in the middle of the week?

"I wouldn't go if it wasn't an emergency," he said. "I don't *wanna* fucking go, believe me."

Trevor put his hands on Mitchell's shoulders. "Calm down, yeah?" he said. "We can easily reschedule." He leaned in closer and parted his lips at the same time Mitchell did before fitting them together in a kiss. He pulled Mitchell in by his shirt until their bodies were pressed against each other and opened his mouth enough to let his tongue out. Mitchell groaned.

Finally, he slid a hand up the back of Mitchell's neck and pulled away. "Just come straight to my place next time. We'll stay in. You know where it is, so just text me when you're free and I'll tell you if it's an alright time to come by."

Mitchell smiled and tucked the right curtain of hair behind his ear. "Alright."

He stepped back and stood awkwardly, seemed reluctant to leave. Then he rummaged through his pocket and pulled out his wallet. Trevor furrowed his brow in confusion. Why was Mitchell taking out money?

"For petrol," Mitchell explained. "For the joyride before."

"Don't be ridiculous, Mitchell."

"Take it." Mitchell pressed the notes into Trevor's hand and squeezed his fingers over it so tightly Trevor couldn't refuse. He just nodded dumbly and felt a bit lost when Mitchell's touch left him.

"See you around, then," Mitchell said with a slight smile. "Sorry this is all we had time for." He pushed his hands into his pockets and spun on his heels, giving Trevor a view of the back of his leather jacket.

Trevor watched him leave, trying to savour the sensation of the kiss on his lips before he couldn't feel it anymore. "Bye."

There was a gorgeous black Mercedes parked right by Trevor's Fiesta that caught Mitchell's eye the second he saw it. The body wasn't the sort of thing Mitchell usually went for, but he could tell instantly it had brilliant acceleration and would drive smoothly. Mitchell pulled his leather gloves out of his pocket and slipped them on as he walked up to the car. He glanced around — left, right, left again — before placing his hand on the side of the door and sensing all the pieces of metal connected to the lock, willing it to give way.

The inside was fucking beautiful as well — leather interior and state-of-the-art sound system. Whoever owned this lovely piece of technology would be in a right strop when they saw it gone.

Making the car go required control over a little more than a few metal pieces. Mitchell had to make the wheels spin manually, had to move the whole steering assembly by controlling the sway bar, the tie rods. It'd taken a painful amount of concentration at one time, but was something he could do somewhat effortlessly now. He was attuned to the complex metal puzzle of the car, like he was any machine he'd long ago figured out, and drove it through traffic as if the engine were really on. The only trouble was that, because it *wasn't* really on, none of the lights were lit. It was illegal, but then, a lot of the things he did were illegal.

Besides, Mitchell had other things on his mind as he drove the stolen Mercedes-Benz. He couldn't believe he told Trevor about his mother being a ten-pound cunt, about *him* being one! He also couldn't believe Trevor had reacted so reasonably, so calm and collected. He was apparently a lot more strong and open-minded than Mitchell gave him credit for.

He had been all set to get out of there and have Trevor fuck him into incoherent bliss again when he'd gotten the call from Nathan, Kane's closest man and most senior bodyguard. Mitchell hadn't had his presence requested in so long that he'd taken it for granted. Now, after months of simply having them come to him, he had to come when called like a loyal pet.

Tonight he'd been told to come to Kane's private racing field in west Essex and do as Kane said, or else.

The only kinds of races held at the middle-of-nowhere, two-lane strip of winding road were the kinds of races Kane held to impress new business partners, make a lot of money in front of them, and show things off. There was nothing more impressive than Mitchell, the driver no one knew by name but who'd never lost a race. The last time he'd had to race for Kane was last June, nine months ago, but if he was calling Mitchell in to be his show pony and easy win, it meant he was expanding business again.

Mitchell made the wheels spin a little faster as he merged onto the motorway. He loved the feeling of the car running smoothly, each individual part listening to his every command.

What was Trevor doing now? Mitchell wondered. It wasn't that late. Maybe he would finish the evening watching a film or doing something even more boring and mundane like work on a design for a client. Or maybe he would mess around on his drum set, improvising for a while. Whatever it was, it was sure to be nothing like the eventful night Mitchell had ahead of him.

Mitchell shook the thoughts away. Once again, he found himself ruminating on their differences, which would just get him nowhere.

He'd lied to Trevor about more than one thing back in the restaurant, and where he got the money for his garage was one of them. He'd never taken out a loan—he'd gotten the money from street racing, first for himself, then for Kane.

It had begun as simply offering his services after hours, back when he worked for Imogen's father, John, and was still technically an apprentice, though vastly better than most. Someone had come in to the shop wanting work done that was too close to street racing mods for John's comfort, and he'd declined to do it. Twenty-year-old Mitchell, a year out of prison for drug dealing, was always on the lookout for a way to move up, and had seen the client as an opportunity. He'd caught up to the bloke before he could leave and said he'd do it.

He'd had to buy all the parts himself and work afterhours, but it'd been an investment he'd been willing to put down. He'd simply explained to the guy that it would cost extra because he had to go behind his boss's back, but that it would be worth it—he had the magic touch when it came to cars.

John, unlike most of the other mechanics in the shop, had loved Mitchell like the son he'd never had. He'd helped Mitchell tremendously by getting him started in his apprenticeship, helped him get a full driving licence, gave him all the opportunities he could ever hope for. Mitchell was the perfect employee; he never complained, he always did as he was told, and he worked efficiently. Though perhaps he could've worked better with others.

John had trusted Mitchell as much as he'd trusted Imogen, and Mitchell had lost no sleep over taking advantage of the fact. John saw Mitchell's willingness to stay late and work as nothing but passion for learning, and let Mitchell stay behind to close up if he was the only one left. He'd trusted him so much, that when Mitchell left a car covered by a grey sheet in one of the bays and lied about what it was, who it was for, John had believed him.

It had started that way, at any rate. Eventually Mitchell didn't just work on race cars in the spare time he had between automotive courses and the garage. He drove them.

And why the fuck not? He'd made contacts in the scene and had a way in. He'd proved his worth making the car, so it was easy to convince them to let him have a go at least once. He'd made a good deal of profit from the modding work, but no great sum that would get him out of the shit flat he'd been staying in at the time. As he worked his way up, raced for higher and higher stakes, all that had changed. And the people in the street racing world weren't the only ones who'd noticed his talent for driving.

Mitchell sighed and shifted in the seat, stretching his legs. If only people could know they were in the good old days while they were still in the good old days.

Mitchell reached Kane's private racing field in a little under an hour and a half after parting with Trevor. He drove up to the gate, showed his face to the man on guard, and continued in.

Eventually he drove by a row of cars that were a bit flashier than his Mercedes, decked out in garish colours and patterns. He parked at the end, in the midst of other cars not participating in the race. He got out and locked the doors with a flex of his brain, then began walking into the heart of the crowd gathered in the street up ahead.

He was met by one of Kane's large bodyguards, Harry, who Mitchell didn't actually believe could speak.

"He's expecting me," Mitchell said.

Harry jerked his head to the right a little and Mitchell saw Kane's familiar figure standing next to a car in the line over Harry's shoulder. He even saw part of Kane's face — the hook nose, the black beard, the bushy eyebrows. Mitchell brushed past Harry silently, heading straight for him.

Kane's wide face lit up the second he laid eyes on Mitchell, making Mitchell's stomach clench. "Ah, my favourite driver!" he exclaimed. "You're just in time."

Mitchell walked up as close to Kane as he felt comfortable, which wasn't very close. A gorgeous, slim, black woman in a fitted black dress was standing nearby with a glass of wine. She seemed to be measuring Mitchell up, which by now Mitchell was used to. Still, it never failed to make him feel like he'd just switched one form of whoring himself out for another.

He scanned the area for anything that stood out as odd as he went through the pleasantries and was introduced to Kane's guest. After his split second survey, and shaking the woman's hand, Mitchell looked back to Kane, who was staring at him with piercing black eyes set in a false-friendly face. The man's hair had grown out a bit since the last time Mitchell saw him, the black fuzz on his shaved head not cut quite as close, though it still came to a widow's peak above his harsh eyebrows. After all these years, Kane still looked like he was in his mid-forties, his appearance not having changed a bit, unlike Mitchell's hatred for him, which seemed to grow exponentially with each job.

The woman at his side tonight was Miss Sydney Arnold from New York. She was hoping to come to a sort of mutual trade agreement concerning certain product shipments and wanted to meet the man she'd be doing business with. She was apparently very impressed when Kane had told her he could get her an undefeated driver, make the race a little more interesting.

Mitchell didn't even think about refusing, but felt something sharp and pointy warningly pressed against his lower back nonetheless. Well, Kane *was* trying to show off what big balls he had in front of the elegant American lady, demonstrate his overarching control.

Mitchell turned his head and glared over his shoulder, right into the dark, sunken eyes of Nathan.

Nathan grinned back at him, wide, cracked lips revealing gleaming white teeth, contrasting his ebony skin. "Glad you could make it," he purred in Mitchell's ear.

The hidden blade pushed a little further, digging into Mitchell's spine. Mitchell kept his face passive and calm, hardening his stare right between Nathan's eyes.

"I've got a lot invested in this race, as I'm sure you can imagine," Kane said, interrupting Mitchell's focus. Mitchell's eyes flicked to Sydney, whose smile never faltered. "You'll get to keep half the winnings. That's certainly generous of me, isn't it?"

Mitchell allowed himself another quick glance around. It wouldn't be difficult to make the blade turn around in Nathan's hand. He could do it with a single thought, could plunge the point into Nathan's navel and mentally push until it had gutted him through. But then there'd be a scene, and more importantly, as guarded as the private racing area was, more men would just flock to Kane's side. It'd be a massacre that would end with Mitchell losing either way.

Mitchell grit his teeth and felt disgusted with himself. "Take me to the car."

Kane's racing events were invite-only, but everyone was allowed a plus-one. It ended up totalling upwards of five hundred people, and they mostly congregated near the entrance, at the starting line, and further out, where more depraved things were happening in the dark field at the finishing line.

Videos and photos were strictly prohibited. Kane liked to argue that street racing wasn't a thing to be recorded, but to simply be enjoyed in the moment, when the thrill and excitement was fresh. That it was like an art form and its pleasure should be fleeting to get the most out of it. Mitchell thought that was just a way to get people to keep coming back to his private events. It dressed the whole thing up in a much more glamorous light than it really was.

Live broadcasting to televisions onsite, however, was perfectly acceptable. Kane had a decent set-up out here, with perched cameras every so often along the road to show the race from above. Spectators could watch from wherever along the stretch they liked, or at either end under gazebos with wide-screen televisions and wine.

The last time having raced being a little under a year ago, Mitchell could admit he was a bit excited. The thrill and adrenaline rush, which he had always loved, was still there, even under all the pressure. The rush and excitement was partially why he'd kept up his habit of stealing cars, even though nowadays he had enough money to buy however many he wanted.

He knew he would win. There was never any doubt about that. Not only was Kane's long stretch of road just a simple sprint, driving from point A to point B, Mitchell had his special talent to fall back on.

He had briefly met the other drivers: a female brunette named Lindsay, dark blond Declan, Richard, fiery red-haired Isabelle, and shifty-eyed Cedric. Well, they'd been introduced to him — nobody outside of Kane, Adam, and Nathan actually knew his name — but he hadn't really said anything back, preferring instead to simply stare and size them up silently. They were all so pathetic, and frankly quite annoying once they'd found out he was *the* driver that Kane always bragged about.

Richard, who looked like the youngest, had practically jumped up and down when he realised it was Mitchell who had built the car he was going to race in. Declan displayed the standard level of bravado in a street racer and claimed he would be the one to destroy Mitchell's title. Lindsay had batted eyelashes at him, while Cedric and Isabelle appeared too stunned to speak. Mitchell had tried not to give them all too condescending a look, but they made it so *very* difficult.

While the other racers were busy revving their engines and intimidating each other at the starting line, Mitchell acquainted himself with the car he would be racing for Kane. It was a Mitsubishi Eclipse GT that had been painted with bright colours he could've done without, but the performance exhausts were fucking *boss,* and it had a nitrous oxide system worth killing for. Mitchell could win without the fancy additions, but it was nice knowing they were there.

Mitchell completed his interior examination just in time for the barely-clothed starter girl to slink her way past his window and to the front of the line. The six of them were lined up three by two, and Mitchell was in the second row. His pulse quickened at the familiarity of it all and it was like he was twenty-two again, young, impulsive, and eager to do anything for quick money. He felt the weight of all the bets on him and against him, the numerous eyes watching, waiting to see who would win. He thought of Kane's ever-appraising look and the intrigued expression on Sydney's face.

Glancing to the left and right of him, seeing his fellow racers tighten their hands around the wheel, he remembered he wasn't twenty-two, but twenty-eight, and leagues above the rest of them. He'd come a long way and done a lot of things since those days, whereas they had no idea what they were getting into.

That didn't mean he couldn't have a bit of fun.

Mitchell let his mouth curl into a smile and put all thoughts of Kane and obligation in the back of his mind. He focused on the vibrating metal body of the car, the humming of the engines around him, and the arc of the starter girl's arm as she raised it slowly above her head. His stomach was filled with butterflies, his nerves were at the top of a rollercoaster, and in the next second, her arm would slice through the air, crashing down.

"GO!"

Mitchell pressed the clutch pedal, slammed the gearstick into place, and floored the accelerator. He chose the driver up ahead and diagonal him, reaching out with his senses to compress the callipers, and forced the brakes to remain engaged. He sped forward while the car next to him was stuck behind, and already made second place right out of the starting line.

The trick was the turns. Since it was a sprint, there weren't many, and the few he had to negotiate weren't sharp. He was better at overtaking his opponents on turns, because he could drift like he was born to, whereas pushing past with speed alone required him to get a little underhanded. This particular driver ahead of him — Mitchell thought it was one of the girls, either Lindsay or Isabelle — would be easy to pass, but he made a point even in his earlier racing days never to take the lead too early on. He'd tail her as far as half a mile from the finish line, then snake by.

In the meantime, Mitchell worried about keeping those bright lights in his rear-view mirror behind him. The road being only two lanes wide, Mitchell was forced to get a bit creative. He mirrored the driver's actions, feinting left and swerving back to the right just as quickly. A couple times the front bumper hit the back of Mitchell's car and Mitchell ground his jaw in irritation.

It was Declan, no doubt about it. He was tempted to make the bonnet fly up and blind the arrogant bastard, but he wasn't nearly close enough to the finish line for him to be a problem for long. And if Mitchell had to pull any more tricks out of his ferrokinetic sleeve, he wanted it to be near the end.

The remaining length of road was shortening pretty quickly.

Mitchell stopped toying with Declan and turned his focus ahead. He did a quick calculation in his mind. He would need to either speed up quicker or slow her down. And all that was assuming she wasn't saving a nitro boost for the last leg.

Mitchell's power over metal was strong, thanks to years of practice and refinement. He could do something as inconsequential as bending a spoon to something as remarkable as keeping a helicopter in the air—for nearly half a minute anyway, until his nose started bleeding. So it was really quite effortless to apply a bit of drag to the driver's car, causing it to slow significantly and with no apparent cause while he zoomed past. He let go of his mental hold on it as soon as he was within a few metres of the finish line, then swerved to a stop in the circle of spectators.

Exhaling and relaxing his tensed muscles after the rush of the race, Mitchell allowed himself a victorious smile. He fucking loved winning.

Chapter 11
Mandatory Compliance

Mitchell hadn't even broken a sweat. If it weren't for the sight of Kane's face as he exited the car, he would've let himself enjoy the appreciation of the crowd a bit longer.

As it was, Mitchell ran a gloved hand through his hair and huffed out a breath. He walked straight up to where Kane stood, ignoring the numerous onlookers who wanted to talk to him. The bastard had his arms crossed, his feet wide apart, and a pleased grin on his usually sneering face. Sydney stood beside him.

The wave of hatred returned, and Mitchell had to force himself forward with every step, when really he wanted to get back in the car and go home. To make matters worse, the image of Trevor suddenly came to the forefront of Mitchell's mind, his warm smile and inviting personality, the way he'd calmed Mitchell with a kiss. Instead of walking toward him, Mitchell was walking toward Kane. It brought a maelstrom of emotions to his stomach—anger, hopelessness, frustration, desire, despair. Altogether it made him feel sick and heavy.

At within a metre or two of him, Kane turned and pushed through the bustling crowd toward the black limousine that held the winnings. Mitchell followed him wordlessly to where a man was waiting, and watched as the man opened the door for Mitchell to get in. Mitchell slid across the black leather seat.

Kane and Sydney slid casually in soon after, Sydney settling herself beside Mitchell while Kane sat across from them. He lowered the window and took a nondescript black case from Harry, who was standing outside. Even though the money wasn't entirely important to Mitchell, and even though he was only here because there was no turning down a request from Kane, he couldn't help feeling an excited little pull when Kane sat the case on his lap, popped the lid open, and put the stacks of notes on display.

Kane had said he'd get half the winnings. How much *was* there, exactly?

"You drive remarkably well," Sydney purred beside him.

Mitchell turned to look at her. She was sitting with her legs crossed and arms folded loosely over her thigh, a flawlessly manicured hand dangling leisurely next to where her black dress ended and the smooth brown skin of her knee and calf was exposed. This close up, Mitchell was able to see that diamond earrings adorned her ears, four in a row on each. Her smile was pleased and predatory, but simultaneously as relaxed as she was.

"Thank you," Mitchell said stiffly.

"And you've never lost a race? Never even been offered money to lose one?"

"I don't lose."

"Must be pretty dangerous, building up that much fame and glory. I'm sure more than a few people would like to see you fail."

Kane was splitting the money. He reached inside and split the stacks right down the middle with straightened fingers, taking out the left half and setting the stacks up in a neat pile on the empty seat beside him.

"But then, I suppose you have Alfred here to take care of you," Sydney said, nodding at Kane with a wicked grin.

"That is indeed how it works," Kane said, humming as he finished up. He closed the case and handed it to Mitchell, who was glad to take it. He wanted nothing more than to get out of there and go home already. "Ten thousand pounds."

Mitchell curled his fingers around the handle and made to pull away, but Kane kept hold. Mitchell narrowed his eyes. Now what?

"I've got a job for you."

Trevor had gone straight home, taken out his contacts in exchange for his glasses, and poured himself a glass of whiskey. Then he'd queued up an old episode of Doctor Who, needing to watch something light-hearted to take his mind off heavier things. Who could do that better than quirky and brilliant David Tennant?

He changed into more comfortable clothes and settled on the sofa, leaving the mostly full bottle of whiskey on the table as he drank from the glass in his hand. He would let himself think about Mitchell and the short date they'd had later; for now he needed to take a step back from the secretive man and his horrific past.

It definitely wasn't something he felt he could share with Kay or anyone else.

Kane put a hand out the window and snapped his fingers a few times. In a moment, Harry was there, leaning down to see how he could be of service.

"Bring us some wine. You'd like some more, wouldn't you, Sydney?" Sydney nodded once. "And why not some for our driver here as well. You could do for one, right?" he said, looking briefly back at Mitchell. "Yeah, why not, bring the lad a drink. Thank you, Harry."

Kane let go of the case, allowing Mitchell to pull it into his lap. Mitchell set it down upright between his thigh and the door.

"I want to tell you a little story about this man, Sydney," Kane said. He held up a finger. "No names. No, we couldn't make such a legend out of an ordinary man if just anyone knew his name. But ordinary man he is."

Mitchell's stomach churned and he fought to keep the bile from rising in his throat. He was sure Kane had told people about him this same way many times, but he'd never been around to ever hear it.

"Mr Ordinary Man used to be like any other kid with a custom-made car, racing on the street for prize money. He was the best then, too. Someone — not I, unfortunately — had the bright idea of using this resourceful, undefeated street racer to rob a bank. They came to the race, watched him win like he always did, then made him an offer. How much was it again?" he asked Mitchell.

Mitchell glared at him. "Fifty thousand pounds."

"Fifty thousand pounds," Kane repeated, looking right at Sydney with a gleeful expression. A movement to Mitchell's left made Kane look out the window, and he reached for the glasses Harry was carefully handing him through the window. He gave Sydney her glass of white wine first, then Mitchell, before taking the last for himself. Harry turned to face forward and stand by should he be needed again.

Mitchell looked down at his glass and sighed before taking a sip with the others.

"Yes, so, as I was saying," Kane continued. "Our wonderful young street racer agreed to be their getaway driver for fifty thousand pounds. And thus started a whole new line of work that he probably never thought he'd get into. He helped people escape from burglaries, murder scenes, and petty crimes that hardly required his services but that first-time criminals were paranoid about. Started doing quite well for himself. Certainly a step up from street racing."

"I'd heard that you were Kane's first escape driver," Sydney said, addressing Mitchell.

Mitchell didn't look at her, instead took another drink. Kane was either really trying to show off, and didn't care that he was being a dick to Mitchell, or was pushing Mitchell closer to his breaking point on purpose, just for fun. Mitchell wouldn't give him the satisfaction of getting angry.

"I picked him up when I took notice of how profitable his services were. He was still working on an apprenticeship to become a mechanic back then, which I took care of with a few calls. Got all his little documents in order so he could put those skills and services of his to good use right away. Though under my command he became a bit more like a glorified errand boy and taxi driver. Didn't you?"

Mitchell stared back at Kane, unblinking.

"I had Nathan bring him up to my office in the City," Kane went on, waving Mitchell's lack of a response away. "They gave him a warm welcome. Let him know who he worked for and what would happen if he tried to quit. I'm told he cried."

Mitchell hated it, but Kane was telling the truth, even about that. He *had* cried when Nathan and a couple of Kane's other men had abducted him and brought him in. He'd thought he'd taken bad beatings before when he was growing up, thought he'd had the worst he was ever going to get in prison, but never had he been beaten so badly

87

within an inch of his life. At the end of it, they'd dragged him to Kane and dropped him at his feet like he was some fucking present.

As a general rule, he never dared to use his powers to get out of something until he knew what was going on, and though it had hurt like hell, he'd stuck by his code even then. In the end it'd been a good decision, despite the fact that he often regretted not killing them in self-defence when he had the chance. Kane would've only become more interested in him, would've wanted to get his hands on him that much more. Anyone who could both offer services such as Mitchell's and do the things he could with metal, was more than just a treasure. Mitchell didn't need to add his ferrokinesis to the list of things Kane abused him for.

"Hmm," Sydney hummed disappointedly. "I'm sorry to hear that." Mitchell turned his glare on her and felt fiery rage boil inside him when all she did was smile back.

That fuckin' cunt, that fuckin' privileged Yank cunt, I'll smash every last one o' yer fuckin' teeth in yer fuckin' skull –

"Don't be so hard on him, Sydney," Kane said. "We all have a breaking point. He's come a long way since then."

"What's the job?" Mitchell bit out.

"Not so fast. I'm still giving Miss Arnold here a little background on how I run this part of my business. Relax, enjoy your drink."

Mitchell threw back the rest of his wine and swallowed it loudly. Kane sighed and shifted his attention back to Sydney, like Mitchell was a stain that was personally offending him.

"He was a model employee up until about two years ago. He'd drive for my clients anywhere, do anything. You won't believe what some people will pay to do."

"I have an idea," Sydney said, chuckling. "Don't forget I'm from New York."

"Of course. Yes, well, he was my on-hand escape driver for nearly five good years. Then... You know what I was just saying about breaking points?"

Mitchell tightened his hand into a fist. He wished he had more wine.

"Tell me, what did our young driver do?" Sydney said, delighted as if she already knew.

"One day, our young driver decides he's had enough. Doesn't want to be a glorified taxi anymore, because he's got himself a 'real job.' A job *I* got him certified for. So he requests a meeting with me, and comes up to my office. One of my men lets him in, and he stands in front of me with this blank face for a few seconds. I'm about to tell him to get the hell on with whatever he's got to say when he grabs the closest man and slices his throat with a blade he'd been hiding in his sleeve the whole time."

Sydney quirked a brow as she sipped from her glass. "Oh my."

"Blood *all* over my carpet. He's lucky I was understanding, as well as impressed," Kane explained. "See, I know people, and I know you can't handle them all the same way. Someone like our young driver, he'd got himself into a situation he didn't know how to get out of. He wanted things to change, but didn't have the first clue about how to change it. What he did have, however, was lots of anger and aggression. He didn't just slice my man's throat. He let him fall to the ground, then took the knife to him properly. Stabbed him again and again until he was all bloody and out of breath. Fascinating to watch, really."

Kane finished his own drink, looking down at it mournfully as though he wished there'd been more. He seemed to consider bothering Harry again, then thought better of it and sat it down next to the stacks of notes beside him.

"Once he'd got it out of his system, he said he didn't want to work for me anymore. That 'real job' business. Must've forgot I could take away what I'd given him just as easily. Naturally I laughed in his face. But then I told him I'd make him a deal. He'd build me cars at this garage of his—race cars, armoured cars, any kind of car I damn well wanted made—and I'd only call on him a few times a year. He'd have all the protection from the law I'd been providing him with, and would still make a good deal of money under my employment. But you see, his little breakdown had revealed something that I suspect he didn't think I'd consider."

"What was that?" Sydney asked, eyes flickering back and forth between Mitchell and a smirking Kane. Mitchell looked down at the floor of the limousine and kept his gaze locked there.

"Our young driver here is more than just capable of helping murderers escape. He can get his hands dirty himself," Kane said smugly. "And I have plenty of uses for versatile people like that."

He leaned forward, elbows on his knees and hands clasped together as he grinned at Mitchell. "I still need the car you're building for me by the end of month, but here's what I need you to do before then."

The episode of Doctor Who was wrapping up and Trevor was more than a little tipsy, the mostly full bottle of whiskey now half empty. The conflict was resolved and they'd moved on to another part of the plot to keep interest for the following episode. Being an old one, it didn't hold much enticement for Trevor, who started to let his thoughts drift.

He didn't just wonder what a younger Mitchell *was* like; he wondered what he looked like as well. Was his hair long then, too, did he look twinkish and feminine? How would he have appeared, splayed out on a bed and fucked in front of his own mother? Or standing naked by the bed while he watched her take it and waited for his turn? Did he ever cringe when he felt someone come on him, like a worthless human being that wasn't good for anything else?

Trevor was mortified to remember he'd called Mitchell a slag once before. Luckily, Mitchell had taken it well, even encouraged Trevor to fuck him like one. But that didn't mean Trevor wasn't just as revolted as he was relieved. Thinking of Mitchell selling his arse out for money, Trevor realised he'd probably fucked Mitchell the same way a lot of others had. Trevor had slept with all of ten or twelve people his entire life, but Mitchell? If he included the numerous club hook-ups Mitchell had mentioned, how many did that add up to?

Trevor tried to exhale slowly, let some of his revulsion go. All that was in the past. No reason to linger on something that didn't affect the relationship they were trying to build now.

He supposed in a way he should count himself lucky. There were lots of guys who'd love to have a lad with so much experience being treated like a whore. And Mitchell *had been* a whore. Thought of in the right light, it was practically like bedding a porn star.

Well, close enough.

Trevor shook his head to get back on track and instantly regretted it, as it made the room spin. He was inclined to think of Mitchell as a victim, as a scared little boy who threw punches to cover up the fact that he was frightened and alone, but that wasn't right. That may have been Mitchell at one time, but it was clear he'd grown into a man who could handle himself, into someone who worked hard until they were able to buy their own business.

No, the last thing Mitchell was was weak, though maybe he did still throw punches. There was no point in wasting time mourning the little boy Mitchell no longer was. The best thing to do with this new knowledge was to simply be sensitive about it if it ever came up later, but otherwise behave as if it changed nothing. Because really, it didn't.

At least now, after seeing Mitchell's temper in action following the call he'd gotten from whomever, Trevor had an idea of what he'd been like as a child.

Quiet and angry.

The limousine was driven back up the road to the starting line, where Mitchell left Kane and Sydney and stalked back to his stolen Merc, ignoring the stares of the attendants and the other bitter drivers. He got in, tossed the case of money in the passenger seat, and with a sigh, he took control of the wheels and steering, settling in for the long drive home.

Most days he could forget his past. It was almost like those five long years hadn't happened, or had only been a vivid dream. The man he'd been then was so different from who he was now. Now he wanted more.

But of course Kane would never let him forget. He could pretend to be a good guy all he liked but his inner demon wasn't gone completely — it was only locked away, held in check. And it was that beastly part of Mitchell that Kane wanted to put to use again.

Murder and torture were indeed things he was capable of, as Kane had told Sydney. That didn't mean he wanted to do them. It wasn't that he enjoyed killing people — he wasn't nearly that sick — it was just that something in his brain didn't work properly, and hurting others didn't faze him as much as it would someone normal.

It didn't help that he still walked around with all the simmering rage left over from the unfairness of his childhood, combined with the boiling hatred he felt for Kane. Whenever one of the dirtier jobs did start making him feel too much, he could imagine it was someone who'd wronged him to trick himself into getting through it. He could think about the nights he'd spent in prison, or the times when a client used him a little too roughly, and beat someone's face to a pulp without even realising he was doing it.

Most of the time he hated the fact that he had to work for Kane at all, thought it was bad enough he was using his shop to supply his cars. But he most hated the way Kane knew how to use his temper. While he struggled to practise patience and control in all other areas of his life, Kane encouraged him to unleash the full extent of his anger like a savage when it suited him. It was like Mitchell wasn't meant to have a normal life, no matter how hard he worked for it.

The trouble was, Trevor would never understand, and Mitchell didn't have much desire to tell him, especially after earlier tonight.

He leaned his head against the cool glass of the window and imagined he was somewhere else while still keeping one eye on the road, somewhere with Trevor. He ended up taking his imagination back to the morning he'd woken up in Trevor's bed, and held on to the feeling it had given him.

Soft morning light on his eyelids, the scent of Trevor on his pillow...

Mitchell ditched the car ten blocks from his flat and walked the rest of the way. It was nearly three in the morning on Wednesday, and he had to be at Advanced by noon. Imogen would be able to manage for the most part, and it wasn't like she didn't have the assistant shop supervisor for help. He'd get at least a good eight hours' sleep.

As Mitchell entered his flat and flicked on the light, he gave it a look around, a *good* look around. He'd furnished it with the bare minimum: a sofa, coffee table, telly, and bookshelf in the living room; a bed, chest of drawers, and nightstand in the bedroom; a simple square table with four chairs in the kitchen-dining area. He had a few trinkets, half-read books, a pack of cigarettes for when he needed to calm his nerves, and his laptop for everything else. The sad fact was, Trevor would not be impressed if Mitchell ever brought him over. His flat was nowhere near as put together, even though he had much more money. At least his bed was just as comfortable.

He went to the bedroom and undressed, letting his clothes fall to the floor without caring where they landed until he was in just pants and socks. He clicked open the case on the bed and put aside a thousand to send to his mam. Any more than two thousand at a time and God knows what she'd spend it on, or what dick would steal it from her. Then he carried the case over to his chest of drawers, unlocked the bottom, and poured the notes inside next to his book on ferrokinesis, a book Naomi had given him when he'd first met her.

Understanding Parapsychology: Metal Manipulation and Ferrokinesis, by Dr Vera Hunt. Mitchell hadn't read from it in years, but it had too much sentimental value to just throw away or sell.

He wasn't in a hurry to get to bed, to the intrusive thoughts waiting to keep him miserably awake, but it was inevitable. He climbed in under the covers, lay on his side, and closed his eyes.

His first date with Trevor had been brilliant, but now he felt like he'd fucked everything up. He'd never been as ashamed of his past as when he was around Trevor, and knew Trevor thought much more about what he had admitted to him than he was saying. The sad part was, being an underage piece of arse for sale wasn't the worst thing he'd done, and how could he tell Trevor anything more after the way Trevor had reacted just at that?

Trevor wanted something Mitchell couldn't give — a secure, trusting relationship where everything was all smiles and rainbows, where they wore matching pea coats in winter and went ice skating at Canary Wharf, or took romantic walks through Regent's Park in summer. It wasn't like Mitchell didn't want that, too. He wanted to do normal things like going to the cinema, or walking around holding hands with dopey grins on their faces, or waking up to the smell of breakfast after a long night of shagging.

He was at the age now where he wanted to settle down with someone, wanted it so badly it sometimes made him ache. But he had obligations and responsibilities to Kane. He was caught in a complex web of a world that Trevor would never accept and couldn't be a part of.

Mitchell groaned and buried his face in the pillow. It was stupid of him to have gotten involved with Trevor, with his easy-going charm and wide smiles and blue eyes and reasonableness and silky curls and, and just fucking *everything*, damn it. Yet it was also the single most thing that made him happy apart from working on cars. He couldn't remember ever looking forward to being in someone's presence so much, or wanting to spend so much time with someone.

He hoped watching all those horror movies meant Trevor had strong enough character to be with someone who was a bit frightening in real life.

Chapter 12
Parentals

Trevor woke up the next day feeling terrible, a pounding headache splitting his head in two. He didn't even remember getting drunk the night before, and struggled to think of why he had until the memories came rushing back.

He rolled over, burying his face in the pillow with a groan.

What he couldn't face sober last night, he would be forced to face today, Mitchell's big secret that Imogen had warned him about. Though he had come to some sort of tentative peace with the whole situation, hadn't he? So Mitchell had whored his body out at a young age, right next to his mother. It wasn't like worse things hadn't happened, like Mitchell was the bloody Antichrist. It was a shock, certainly, but nothing they couldn't get past.

Trevor sat up, holding his head. He needed water and something to ease the pain before he even thought about getting anything done today.

After chugging half a glass of water, relieving himself, and finishing the water with some paracetamol, Trevor thought maybe he was ready for some food. He made a light breakfast of toast and eggs, and smiled a little when he remembered that he'd had eggs just last night with Mitchell. He dropped the smile a second later.

He looked at the time and wondered if his father was too busy with work to be bothered. It was mid-morning on a Wednesday, and at the rate his day was progressing already, he'd be working on the concept art for a contract until late. He thought it over while he ate, and came to a decision between finishing his toast and sticking his fork into his eggs.

He just needed to talk to *someone* about it, and he was wary of how Kay would react. Their bipolar disorder sometimes made it difficult to talk to them about certain things. His father was logical and practical, level-headed. That, and they hadn't talked in a little while. He was just what Trevor needed.

It was nearly 11AM when Trevor picked up his mobile. His father, the respected solicitor David Lewis, probably wasn't busy at this time of day.

He answered on the fourth ring. "Hello?"

"Hey. Dad? Are you busy?"

"Just responding to emails, nothing I can't put on hold. How've you been?"

"Been alright."

"Still friends with that girl Kay?"

"Dad, come on. Every time? I wanted to ask your advice on something, don't be—"

"What is it, Trevor?"

Trevor sighed. "So I've met someone, yeah? He's absolutely brilliant, very laid back, laughs at the same stuff I do. But he's really secretive, said he'll tell me things about himself in pieces because he's worried what I'll think of him and that I won't stick around."

"That doesn't sound suspicious at all."

"No, no, I mean, I sort of get it. Everyone's like that, right? There are things I worry he'll be weird about as well."

"Like your disturbed little *drawings*."

Trevor tried not to groan into the phone. He did lean forward, elbows on his knees, and pull his hair. His father always referred to his personal artwork as something insignificant, even though Trevor thought some of them were actually pretty good.

"Yes, Dad, my drawings. Anyway, I don't find it too suspicious. Maybe a little, but you don't know him. I was told he's shy, which I've sort of seen, but he's less so around me. I wonder if because he's comfortable with me, his shyness, I dunno, manifests as nervousness or something. Being private combined with being shy..."

"What did you need my advice for, Trevor?"

Trevor rubbed his forehead. "Sorry, I was just, trying to give some background. He's a good guy, so try not to judge, okay? I mean, fuck,

I'm trying not to judge."

"Trevor."

Trevor sighed. "He told me one of his pieces, I guess, and... He was a prostitute, Dad. When he was fourteen. He and his mother were poor and men paid to take turns on them. If the person you were dating had had sex for money when they were a kid, how would that make you feel?"

His dad was silent for a few seconds, then said, "Well, worse things have happened to people, Trevor."

"I know."

"I suppose I'd feel sorry for them. It had to have been quite a sad life. Some sort of mental scarring, certainly. This man you're with, you say he's secretive? Are you sure it's not just that he's not alright in the head?"

Trevor scoffed automatically, feeling offended on Mitchell's behalf. But then he thought about it. He'd been temporarily terrified by Mitchell's actions with the car the previous night, his laughing during the joyride seeming absolutely mad. The jolt of fear he'd felt when Mitchell punched the dashboard out of nowhere was also rather memorable an occasion.

Not right in the head, though? Mitchell seemed to be alright enough. Just. Special.

So very apt, Trevor thought wryly, thinking of Imogen. *Special.*

"No, he's not like that," he said. "Quiet and a little unpredictable, but psychologically sound as far as I've been able to tell."

His dad sighed. "Be careful, son. You may like the person you think he is, but there are a lot of weirdos out there."

"I know that," Trevor snapped. "He hasn't been too weird, but he did have to randomly leave for Essex in the middle of our date last night. Besides that and a few other quirks, he's pretty... Well, I guess you can't be too normal if you grew up—"

"Hang on, he just up and went to Essex? Last night?"

"Yeah, what about it?"

"What did he have to go for?"

"He didn't say. He just said he had to go. Why?"

"What did you say his name was?"

"Dad, if you know him through some sort of case connection—"

"*What* did you say his name was?"

Trevor put his chin in his hand and pouted. "Mitchell Morgan."

His father repeated the name like he was learning a new foreign word. "Mitchell Morgan. What does he do?"

"He's a mechanic. He owns a garage, Advanced Auto Repairs in Hackney."

"I see..."

"Dad, do you know him or something?" That would be just Trevor's luck, for Mitchell to have gotten in trouble with the law and for his father to know him that way.

"No. I have a few friends who also went to something in west Essex late last night. I'd wondered if it was the same thing. The name doesn't sound familiar though. Tell me, how does he act when he's with you? Does he treat you—"

"He treats me just fine! We get on brilliantly, I told you." He was trying not to get angry, but something about his father's tone had him on edge. He wondered if this call was a good idea after all.

"What does he looks like?"

"Long brown hair, blue eyes, a bit broody-looking. A little pale, but not pasty white or anything, and usually has a dark spot of oil somewhere on him that's not been completely scrubbed out." There was silence on the other end for a while until Trevor broke it. "Hello?"

"Sorry, sorry. You did say shy and quiet, yeah?"

"Yes. Dad, come on, if you know him, just tell me."

"I, I think I might. I'm not sure. If he's with the same friends of mine who also attended the event last night, I might've seen him around. In passing, you know. Never spoken to him, but a man with a presence like his leaves a lasting impression."

Trevor's skin prickled. "What friends are these?"

"Business associates, clients, that sort of thing." He got serious before Trevor could say anything. "I mean it, Trevor. Be careful. I won't tell you to stop seeing him, because it seems like you really care about him. For your sake, I hope he cares about you."

"He does." Trevor said it with more conviction than he was sure of.

"I do have a bad feeling about him."

"You've never met him properly, you're only going based on assumptions. If things turn out well between us, I want you to meet him. The real him," Trevor insisted.

"I'd like to, but, we'll see. I have to think about it. Either way, don't let what he did as a young man affect your judgement of who he is now. People change, and none of us can help where we come from, what we've had to do to survive. It's where we aim to go and what we plan to do that's important. Make sure you know what his goals are and if they're goals you're ready to be a part of."

"We've been on one and a half dates, Dad. I think it's a bit early to talk about goals, but thanks. What you've said makes a lot of sense."

"I'm glad I could help, Trevor. If that's all?"

"Yeah, that's all. Bye."

"G'bye."

Trevor hung up feeling both better and more uncertain. Whatever weird, indirect connection his father had to Mitchell, it unsettled him, but he'd at least shaken off the remainder of his qualms about Mitchell's childhood. It was the present Mitchell he was interested in getting to know, not so much the Mitchell who had to endure older creeps fucking him. With each passing day, he was thinking he'd like to get to know the future Mitchell as well.

Mitchell's alarm woke him up at eleven. He dragged himself into the shower and bathed in the dark for a few extra minutes of fake sleep. He very purposefully did not let his thoughts drift to anything that had happened the night before; not through the shower, not through shaving and getting dressed, and not through breakfast.

He stopped to get a coffee on his way to the garage, at a shop not two blocks away from the tube station. He was nearly finished when he turned the final corner and saw his humble but well-known shop there to greet him.

Even after all this time, walking up to Advanced Auto Repairs filled Mitchell's chest with warm pride. He'd done a lot of things he wasn't proud of to get it, but the place was *his*, and nobody could say otherwise. Sure it wasn't in the best of neighbourhoods, but he was his own boss and got to work on cars all day. If he wasn't also involved in a night world of lies and crime, he would have claimed his life was perfect.

Mitchell drained the last of his coffee and tossed it just as he approached the open bay under the railway. Imogen was there with her sleeves rolled up and her hair in a ponytail, poking around under the bonnet of an old Chevy. Examining brake fluid or coolant levels or something, maybe.

Her blonde girlfriend, Lydia, was standing behind her. It'd been a while since she'd come by, bringing her vibrant smiles and playful personality with her. She had bright green eyes, was a lot more feminine than Imogen in flowery skirts and vanilla fragrance, and taught secondary school.

She had her hands low on Imogen's hips, was pressed up against her from behind and saying something in Imogen's ear that made Imogen burst into high-pitched laughter. Mitchell definitely did *not* think about what it would be like for Trevor to embrace him from behind like that while he worked.

Thinking about Trevor was too close to broaching the subject of last night, and he had other things to worry about before he could worry about that. Most of all, he needed to plan out the rest of his day. He wanted to get more work done on the car Kane needed by the end of the month.

"No snogging on the job, Imogen," Mitchell teased as he passed them, taking off his jacket.

When he glanced back, Lydia was shaking with silent laughter into Imogen's shoulder, green eyes sparkling with mirth. Imogen stuck her tongue out at him.

"We'll see how long that policy lasts," Lydia called after him as he entered the corridor leading to his office. Mitchell ignored her. He wasn't surprised that Imogen had apparently filled her in about Trevor. It had probably been the night Mitchell had phoned to talk about their first date.

He threw his jacket over the back of his chair and plopped down in front of the computer. He brought up the revenue log, still holding at bay the thoughts about last night that wanted to force their way in. Using money won at a street race for things at his business had to be done wisely, and with careful consideration.

He had four different bank accounts into which he regularly deposited money, and never in excessive amounts. It was why he always had cash on hand, because even though he was always pouring in his earnings, he was also continuously getting them, and needed to get rid of it somehow. Besides giving huge tips to servers, he invested in a handful of companies, anonymously donated to charities, and helped fund studies researching paranormal phenomena. He always sent at least a thousand pounds to his mam.

Looking through the budget helped Mitchell decide how he wanted to spend the ten thousand. He'd split it down the middle, put a thousand into each of his four bank accounts, leaving the last thousand for his mother, which he'd already put away. With the remaining five thousand, he'd pay the lease, replace lost and broken tools, restock things like loo roll for the toilets.

Technically, he'd been able to afford hiring a new receptionist for a while. Imogen would be able to focus more on her shop manager duties and less on the boring tasks of a desk-sitter. But he was also wary of bringing in someone new, inviting someone into his safe environment where he could peacefully involve himself in illegal activities. Besides, he liked the way things were now. Imogen was a friend and could be trusted with certain secretive matters. Having her up front, where she could report any suspicious characters, was a little bit of a strategic move as well.

Years of practice allowed Mitchell to finish going over the budget quickly. He sighed and slouched back in his chair, staring blankly at the numbers on the screen. Finally, he let some of his other thoughts trickle in.

The job Kane wanted him to do was on the twenty-eighth, and it was now the nineteenth. Mitchell wanted to fit another date with Trevor somewhere in there, sometime soon. They could pick up from where they left off like Trevor had suggested. Mitchell could go straight to his flat, they could relax, really get to know each other in private. He'd make up for last time by showing Trevor the better side of him, and hopefully he would be able to tell by then how serious he was about him, if he was worth the effort of trying to make things work. Part of Mitchell hoped he was, the other part thought life might be easier if he wasn't.

One more date then, and Mitchell would see where he wanted to take things from there. He pulled out his mobile and brought up the calendar. When Trevor sent his daily text message, Mitchell would ask if he was busy Friday night.

In the meantime, he closed the calendar and navigated to the keypad. He hadn't talked to his mother in far too long, and after what he'd come clean about to Trevor, it reminded him it was time to.

She didn't answer the first time, but that was normal. He dialled again, and this time she answered on the third ring.

"Mitchell!"

Mitchell smiled at the pleasure in her Scouse voice, and already felt himself calming a bit. "Hey, Ma."

"Fer Chriiist's sake, it's been ages since ay heard from yer."

"Ay know, la, am sorry, la, I've beun busy," he said.

"Well, tell uz 'ow y'are. Wus 'appenin' at yer place?"

Mitchell sighed, rubbing his forehead. He knew what the question really meant. "Ay 'uv an order ter fill by the end o' the munth, and a more delicate job on the twenty-eighth."

"Delicate job?"

"Someone's beun usin' 'is, 'is resources ter make their own product and do business on the side. Er so 'e said, y'know. Needs ter be dealt with."

"Fun," she remarked dryly.

"Yeah. Ma?"

"Son?"

Mitchell put his elbow on the armrest of his chair and swivelled around to face the opposite direction. He looked at his feet. "Ay met someone."

"Like a romantic someone?"

Mitchell's breath came out unsteady. "Yeah. 'is name's Trevor."

"Trevor, 'uh?"

"Eez, er, eez a bit posh. A graphic designer, well-spoken, wears expensive shoes, and all that."

"Good. You deserve someone smart. You was allus brighter than the twits around e'yer. 'Ave yer gorra photo of 'im?"

"Er..."

"*Mitch.*"

"Sorry."

"Or'rite then, describe 'im. Don't leave nothin' out, la."

Mitchell stood up, walked around his desk to lean against the other side. "Brown herr. Short. Currleh."

"A Jewfro, like?"

"Fuck's sake, Ma, no. They're no small curls, they're like... fuckin'... loose." Mitchell laughed at the absurdity of the conversation. Trying to describe a man's hair. Fuck. "It's smewth. Sort o' spirally. Wavy, like. Dead fuckin' soft, now that ay think about it. No like mine, y'know 'ow me 'air's all lank and jost sort o' 'angs thuz."

"Ay know you need a fuckin' herrcut, that's wa' ay know."

"Yeah, yeah, maybe when it's down to me arse I'll think about it."

"Or'rite, brown currleh herr, wa' else? Wa' colour's 'is eyes?"

"Blue."

"Wus 'is sign?"

Mitchell laughed. "Not now, Ma."

"You'd do bes' with an air sign who kin 'elp yer express yer feelins, like. Does 'e know about wa' you kin do?"

"Nah. We've only beun on two dates. Ay 'aven't evun thought about tellin' 'im that." Another thing he had to worry about Trevor freaking out over. He was starting to wonder again if he should just quit while he was ahead. "Am worried about the uvver things I've done, Mam. 'E might be frightened o' me like everyone else."

She sighed in exasperation. "You dun 'ave ter tell everyone everythin', la. Tell me you 'aven't fallun fe this bloke afti only two dates."

"Ay 'aven't! But ay 'uv ter 'uv someone ay kin be completely 'onest with, yeah?"

"Ay see, ay dun evun exist."

"No you!" Mitchell exclaimed.

"Or'rite, listun, when kin yer come and see uz?"

Mitchell groaned. "Mam, you're no 'elp."

"Speakin' o' help, am proper skint. Ay need something so ay dun get evicted."

"Wa'... *How?*"

"'ad ter pay a fella."

"Ay dun evun wanna know. Too busy ter deal with it right now.

103

I'll transfer yer two grand, or'rite?"

"Tar. Come home and see me!"

Mitchell ended the call a minute later, and even though he hadn't got to talk about things that he felt he probably needed to, he felt better. He did miss his mam, her equally tough love and affectionate embraces. He missed the days when he lived with her, when they had a flat with just one bedroom, had to share a bed.

Talking to her required more than just rolling over and opening his mouth these days. There was no way he'd have time to visit her this month, which he knew she wouldn't like. He had far too much going on, and would have to put it off.

He walked back around the desk and pulled open the drawer just beneath the table top. He rummaged around until he found an elastic band, then shook his hair before pulling it away from his face and up into a ponytail. He changed his clothes and, finished in the office, he returned to the garage.

The assistant shop supervisor, Sean, was bringing in a heap of metal that looked like it'd collided with a train, but Advanced was known for being able to repair cars that other places would look at and declare impossible. It was an especially valuable reputation when it came to people who preferred fixing up their long-time friend over buying a new one, something Mitchell could understand. Sean would definitely need Mitchell's talented hands to help with that particular project, and it wouldn't be a quick job, that was certain.

Mitchell sighed as he walked past the mechanics on task, out the bay doors and down the alley toward his own work. There was too much to be done, yet all he could think about was how much longer he'd have to wait for Trevor's daily text.

Chapter 13

Night In

Who was your best friend when you were a kid?

Trevor sent the message shortly after one in the afternoon. He was in his study, half lost in layer upon layer in Photoshop. He was pretty sure he was okay with the concept art he'd settled on for his current contract, and just had to send it to his employer before he began taking it from sketch to final product. Music was keeping him sane and productive, the sounds of Bloc Party acting as his current soundtrack. A normal working day, but with Mitchell now in his life things had become a bit more exciting.

He had to admit Kay's hope for him had been achieved, especially evident after the joyride last night. Mitchell was indeed thrilling, a pleasant change of pace. Trevor didn't know what to expect when it came to him, and though that feeling in itself was exhilarating, he also looked forward to learning all of Mitchell's mannerisms and habits and *knowing* what to expect. He wanted to get to know Mitchell inside and out, the good and the bad.

Which was why he'd gone right into the heart of it, asking about a childhood he'd taken the morning to wrap his head around. He was curious. Before Mitchell had been forced to help his mother bring in some income, what types of friends had he had, what did they do together for fun?

It wasn't the only thing he was curious about, but he could put off asking Mitchell what his connections to his father were for some other time.

It was a little over five minutes before Mitchell replied, one of his faster response times. Setting down his Wacom tablet pen, Trevor pushed his slipping glasses up the bridge of his nose and unlocked his mobile screen to read it.

Never really had one. Even at school. I'm still a bit shy now but it was even worse back then. Couldn't relate to anyone. Got much better with age.

Trevor stared at the words and wished he could offer some form of comfort through the screen. The intimidating way Mitchell came off as an adult seemed to be isolating enough; it must've been even harder to deal with as a child, especially surrounded by students he probably saw as far less intelligent than him. He wondered if Mitchell ever got into fights. It wouldn't exactly surprise him.

Two more text messages came in before Trevor could say anything back.

When I was 12 there was a woman who offered to be a sort of mentor. Introduced me to other people and taught me a lot more than just better social skills. A support group kind of. Made a few friends there but only went a few months. Still felt out of place.

Are you free this Friday? Want to make last night up to you.

Trevor smiled as he typed his response. *Come over after you leave work?*

I'll leave early.

Mitchell looked as attractive as ever when Trevor opened the door for him on Friday, albeit a little nervous. The smile he gave Trevor was shaky and wary, followed by a little wave that brought out his shyness.

"Hey," Mitchell said.

Trevor stepped to the side to let him in. He grabbed hold of his sleeve before he could get too far.

"Hi," he said, pulling Mitchell closer. He kept his eyes on Mitchell's lips, let his intentions of kissing him be clear. The moment he was close enough, he did. Mitchell slumped as some of the obvious tension left his body.

Having only had two dates, Trevor had been a little unsure whether or not they were at the stage where he could greet him like this, but the eager opening and closing of Mitchell's mouth against his was definitely appreciative. He pushed the door closed, not parting from Mitchell for a second.

It sent a jolt of pleasure down Trevor's spine when Mitchell slid firm hands over his hips to settle on his lower back. He felt Mitchell's fingers lace together as he brought their bodies closer, and was glad he'd put his contacts in before Mitchell arrived. The kiss would've been a whole lot more difficult with glasses on, even though he usually preferred to wear them at home.

He parted his lips more when Mitchell's tongue began to slide its way into his mouth, and let his own tongue move forward to join it. He raised his arms to drape them around Mitchell's neck, pushed fingertips into the thick roots at the nape. Mitchell started panting, but didn't break the kiss. If anything he held on tighter.

Mitchell's breathiness urged Trevor's hand to slide down; not far, just low enough to curl his fingers around the back of Mitchell's neck and hook his thumb around the front. He didn't mean to get so worked up so early, but before he knew what he was doing he was applying more pressure with his thumb, tightening his hold and cutting off more and more of Mitchell's air. Mitchell jerked back a little, a soft choking noise escaping from between his lips that made Trevor hot all over, but then he surged forward, twisting fingers in Trevor's shirt.

Trevor inhaled sharply when they finally pulled apart. He put his hands on Mitchell's shoulders and Mitchell gasped for breath in front of his mouth.

Trevor tilted his head and nibbled at the corner of Mitchell's bottom lip. "I was going to offer you something to eat," he muttered.

Mitchell chuckled and pulled away, let his hands drop and stepped back. This time his grin was wide and brilliant, cheeky and playful, even while he absently massaged the front of his neck.

"Haha, yeah, I could eat. Would actually be a treat since I don't usually get home until later to eat something. What is there?"

"I was thinking we could order takeaway."

Mitchell nodded, grinning. "Nice. Takeaway and sex, very classy."

Trevor grinned back and held up a finger. "No..." He grabbed Mitchell's hand and led him to the living room where he'd dimmed the lights and pulled up the first episode of *Hemlock Grove* on Netflix.

"Takeaway, sex, *and* Hemlock Grove."

Mitchell laughed. "Even classier. What's Hemlock Grove about?"

Trevor waved his hand about, gesturing abstractly at the screen. "Dark, supernatural... *stuff.*" Mitchell hitched a brow and pulled off his jacket to drop it on the sofa. "Anyway, there's a vampire and a werewolf who are totally gay for each other, and if that's not a good enough reason to watch it, I don't know what is."

Mitchell burst into soft, breathy laughter. "You are absolutely ridiculous."

"You'll see, you'll like it. I know you will."

"I'm sure."

"What did you want to order, then?"

Trevor walked to the bedroom to grab his laptop, expecting Mitchell to simply shout his response while he looked up something on the internet. He forgot that Mitchell wasn't loud like he and his friends, so he was surprised when he heard Mitchell's voice so close.

"You decide. I'll get something from wherever you want."

"Alright."

He pulled up a web browser as Mitchell fell onto the bed, landing with his arm out to lay propped up on his elbow. Mitchell kept the position for a few seconds as Trevor navigated search results, then gave a dramatic sigh as he rolled onto his back. Trevor couldn't see his face, so he darted a quick glance at him before returning his eyes to the screen.

A few more seconds passed before Mitchell lifted his head up to look at Trevor. With a grunt, he pulled his weight forward to sit up, hands folded in his lap.

"Let's have sex while we wait and watch Hemlock Grove when it gets here," he said with a wide smile.

God, Mitchell loved Trevor's dick. He had his knees spread apart on the bed, bent over with his spine curved in and his elbows holding up the rest of his weight. Trevor's knees were outside of his, and he was pumping his cock into Mitchell with quick, sharp thrusts that left Mitchell gasping. When Mitchell lengthened his spine, eased his hips back to take Trevor nice and deep, he moaned at how fast Trevor fucked him. The way he was hitting Mitchell's prostate felt so *fucking* good, and Mitchell eased back even more, his mouth open in a quivering O as he stretched his arms out in front of him like a cat.

"God, I love how you react to taking a cock up your arse," Trevor said, panting.

Mitchell's laugh came out breathy. He reached back to curl fingers in his own hair, eyes closed in bliss. "I love how you put yours up one."

Trevor slowed the speed of thrusts to long, easy motions, languidly pushing in deep enough for Mitchell's arse to meet skin. He shunted Mitchell forward at the end of each thrust and rolled his hips, the result feeling so spine-numbingly good that Mitchell whined and started frantically stroking his cock.

He came hard, eyelashes fluttering as his eyes rolled back in his head, his open mouth full of Trevor's duvet. Trevor kept slowly fucking him, rocking Mitchell back and forth on his cock as he ran a hand up the knobs of his spine. Mitchell swivelled his hips in a circle and exhaled each time Trevor pushed in to the base.

"Here, give me your arms," Trevor said, taking the one with the hand still on Mitchell's dick.

Mitchell gave him his other arm and let himself be pulled into an upright position. He tossed his head to the side to get his hair out of his face and wanted to brush a few lingering strands away but couldn't. It only bothered him as long as it took for Trevor to start fucking him again, gripping the insides of his elbows for leverage.

He was no longer slow. Mitchell's softening cock bounced between his legs as he rode the pounding wave of Trevor's, the sound of slapping flesh piercing the air. He tilted his hips forward and panted when he felt the angle that let Trevor fuck right into his prostate again. He felt drunk with pleasure.

One last deep thrust forward, then Trevor stopped, letting go of Mitchell's arms to hold his hips. Mitchell let out a long breath and placed his hands on the bed, careful of his come. He rocked easily on Trevor's cock a few more times, hesitant to let its fullness leave.

Finally, Trevor put a hand on top of Mitchell's arse and slipped out.

Empty but sated, Mitchell smiled and moved to sit cross-legged on the bed with his hands in his lap. He watched Trevor walk out of the room with the condom, waited for him to come back with a flannel. He thought about the food on the way, about the quiet night at home ahead. Like he always did around Trevor, he felt comfortable, relaxed. He felt he could be himself.

That was what made Trevor so dangerous. He gave off the impression of being open, like one could go to him with anything. Mitchell knew, however, that that sort of thing usually wasn't true. People had their own moral boundaries, lines they didn't cross. Trevor had made his clear when he put murder on the table, and any normal person would agree. As much as Mitchell wanted to be completely honest, he knew it was best he follow his mam's advice and just keep some things to himself if he wanted this to work.

Though how the hell he was going to do that when his business with Kane was such a huge part of his life, he hadn't the slightest idea.

Mitchell looked around the bedroom, at the expensive furniture and modern designs. He liked being with Trevor, liked being at his place, among his things. Just his *things* made Mitchell feel happy. He rubbed his hand across the thick duvet and smiled.

His mam would say he was infatuated again, but when Trevor was so perfect, how couldn't Mitchell think so much of him? It wasn't like it was another Thomas, someone taking advantage of him. Certainly not a loser who couldn't get it anywhere else than with a fourteen-year-old boy.

Honestly, Trevor was *too* good for him! They were compatible in every way so far, but Trevor was a much better man.

Trevor returned with a lime green flannel in his hand, and Mitchell decided he'd try to find out if Trevor had any secrets of his own. What darkness lurked in the corners of Trevor's mind?

"Here," Trevor said, tossing the flannel to Mitchell. Mitchell quickly cleaned himself up. "I checked the time. It's only been fourteen minutes since we ordered. We could—"

"Kiss on the bed," Mitchell finished, setting the flannel aside. He might've used the fact that his legs were wide open to his advantage, casually leaning back on his hands to be the perfect picture of invitation. His fucked hole was *still* throbbing, and he didn't have to touch it to know it looked pink and raw.

Trevor sighed and climbed back into bed, crawling up Mitchell's body before stopping just in front of his face. Mitchell saw the subtle twitch in Trevor's lips that was almost a smile. His heart pounded as he felt a hand slide up his chest and loosely wrap around his throat. He was beginning to see that his neck was something Trevor had a bit of a fascination with.

"Only for a few minutes. One of us should be dressed enough to answer the door," Trevor said.

He kissed Mitchell without another word.

"I do like this show," Mitchell said later, his feet up on the table. He was eating food from his lap, eyes glancing down every so often for another bite while they remained glued to the screen the remainder of the time. Trevor counted his programme suggestion a success.

"As I'd thought," he said.

"Attractive cast, suspenseful plot, lots of blood. What's not to like, yeah?"

Trevor smiled. "My thoughts exactly. I'm so glad you agree. Some people see this level of violence and kind of shudder away or think it's sick."

"If we're being honest, I think it's ace. I'd love to be able to turn into a wolf and rip people guts out with my teeth." He cringed. "Sorry, I know you said that's your worst irrational fear."

Trevor shrugged. "I've been trying to get better about it. And being a wolf is alright and all, but the shift looks rather painful. At least as an upir you get to look sexy while you're being a monster."

"No surprise, your main focus is appearances. Bet you'd gel your hair back like Roman, too, huh?"

Trevor sputtered, playing along when he knew Mitchell was only teasing. "I, I am an artist, therefore I think of things from a more aesthetic point of view!"

Mitchell laughed, reining it in to swallow the food in his mouth.

"Shut up and let me watch the damn show."

They were halfway into the second episode when they finished their food. They didn't speak again until the end, when Trevor stopped it from autoplaying the next one and moved to clear away the rubbish.

"Can I see some of your artwork?" Mitchell asked.

The question instantly made Trevor tense up. *Your disturbed little drawings,* he heard his father's voice say in his head. He finished gathering the empty containers and stuffed them into one bag.

"Sure." He set the bag down by the door and nodded his head in the direction of his workroom. "It's just in here."

He led Mitchell down the corridor and into his study. The electronic drum set sat across the room in the corner diagonal the door. On the other side, straight ahead, was his L-shaped desk in the other corner, his laptop plugged in and closed on top of it, the Wacom tablet sitting close by. He walked over and opened the bottom drawer in the desk, the drawer bigger than the top two.

Inside were his sketchbooks, loads of them. He tried to remember which held the better work but ended up pulling one out at random to save time. It was a large, black spiral notebook that had come with blank pages until Trevor had filled them up.

His heart was in his throat when Mitchell opened it. He watched Mitchell turn page after page, lingering on some, passing quickly by others. Trevor's heart pounded thunderously when Mitchell took particularly long on a few.

"You draw a lot of mutations and... deformities," Mitchell stated, staring at one sketch Trevor actually really liked. Most of his work he'd done in black pen, and had done this one in it as well. It was a skeletal human frame with two bald, veiny heads, the right head attached where the left one should've had an ear. The left head had a wide, toothy grin that extended across the face of the right one.

Trevor shifted his weight from one foot to the other. "I think they're cool. I know how that sounds."

Mitchell turned the page to a realistic portrait of a girl with long gashes on either side of her mouth, curved into a permanent smile. There was another long dark line down the centre of her face, carved from the middle of her forehead, over her nose, down to her chin.

Mitchell lingered a little on that one, then kept flipping.

"You ever look at medical reference photos?" Mitchell asked, holding up a sketch of a girl with an extra arm and leg coming out of her side. Trevor had a tendency to draw people as more angular and elongated than they anatomically were unless he was going for realism, and that was how this girl appeared. There was a spidery quality about her, emphasised by the quick strokes of the pen Trevor had used to give her a less rigid outline.

"Sometimes," he admitted. "There's this website, Reddit, and they have, well, everything. Deformities being one of them."

Mitchell lowered it, hummed thoughtfully, and turned the page. "Some people might say this is a bit morbid, like."

Trevor took the sketchbook back, slamming it closed. "It's not like that's all I draw. I do nature scenes, too."

"I think your art is really amazing, Trevor," Mitchell said, smiling easily, as though Trevor hadn't just ripped something from his hands. "It's so detailed, it looks great, and it's so cool you were able to do it with just an ordinary biro. I love your imagination."

Trevor exhaled in relief. "Thanks. I, uh, haven't really showed many people besides the friends I'm sure can handle it."

"I'm glad you thought I was."

"I mean, I'd've shown you at some point regardless, I guess," Trevor said as he put the sketchbook back in the desk. "I wouldn't date someone if I thought they wouldn't be okay with the things I draw. *That* would be a bit problematic down the line. But it's also not something you start a conversation with, you know?"

"Trevor, seriously, I get it," Mitchell said, chuckling. He stepped closer, put a hand on Trevor's arm and kept his eyes lowered. "I feel the same way. Trust me, you and your depraved little mind are safe with me. I *dare* you to show me your worst. Bet I won't even flinch."

Trevor couldn't help but rise to such a challenge. Part of him worried he would push Mitchell away, but mostly he believed him. He was looking forward to the thrill of sharing it with someone.

The second drawer in the dresser held his current sketchbook. He turned away from Mitchell to pull it out, and flipped to the most violent thing he'd ever drawn. He'd done it two days ago.

Seeing someone have their insides ripped out had always been one thing he could never bring himself to stomach well, as he'd told Mitchell on their date. He was, however, a man who liked to conquer his fears, so he'd finally sat down and forced himself to draw it, looking at medical photos online for reference.

On the last filled page in his sketchbook there was a drawing of a man strapped on his back to a surgical table, mechanical arms on either side keeping his chest pulled apart. The man's intestines were spilling out, his lungs fully expanded underneath his ribcage. There was a look of intense pain and agony on his face.

"Wow." Mitchell took the sketchbook from him. "The lines of these are so realistic, so intricate," he said, placing his finger on the large intestines and tracing the swirling path. "With the folds and everything. And you managed to show so many different shades with just the one colour."

"Medium," Trevor supplied. "One medium. When you use something enough, you kind of learn how to manipulate it."

"Yeah. Trevor, this is brilliant. I love it."

He handed the book back to Trevor and Trevor took it, smiling. "I can't believe how lucky I am," he said. "I usually go to the internet to show people stuff like this, but you're like, a real person I can talk to it about."

"And you show me new things I've not watched yet. Works out perfectly. Which, speaking of, we *could* watch one more episode and then you can fuck me on the sofa. Just a suggestion."

Trevor put the sketchbook on the desk and took Mitchell's hand, leading him back to the living room. He was grinning, excited. "After Hemlock Grove, I have the Game of Thrones DVDs. You'll like that too."

Chapter 14
Indulging

Mitchell had told Trevor that he didn't plan to stay the night, but they stayed up so late and exhausted so much energy having sex that it ended up happening. Trevor woke up the next morning to the feeling of his back pressed against Mitchell's, noticing right away that he had an erection and that Mitchell was as naked as he was.

He twisted his neck to see if Mitchell was awake. He wasn't. Moving carefully, Trevor leaned out of bed to find his mobile. He saw the third condom he'd used last night on the floor next to their mixed clothes.

He didn't have his glasses on *or* his contacts in, but after squinting and bringing the screen to his face, he was able to make out that it was almost 9AM. Trevor rubbed his eyes and put his mobile down before just as carefully sliding back toward the centre of the bed. He turned to lay on his other side, facing Mitchell.

Mitchell's lungs were expanding and contracting, his chest rising and falling. Trevor watched the steady rhythm of his sleeping body and wanted to run his hand up the spine.

He settled for making his way closer, close enough that he could align his body with Mitchell's and lie comfortably next to him. He hesitantly reached out to touch, then committed himself to the movement and caressed up Mitchell's arm, from elbow to shoulder.

Mitchell didn't wake until Trevor moved his hips the slightest bit forward, trying to make his legs comfortable. He ended up nudging the head of his cock against the crevice of Mitchell's thighs, which was apparently enough to also nudge Mitchell into consciousness.

"Mrnin," Mitchell mumbled. Trevor figured it was meant to be "morning," but didn't linger too much on it when Mitchell hitched his right leg up and rolled more onto his stomach.

Too groggy with sleep to think better of it, Trevor chased the feeling of Mitchell's skin, taking more without asking if that was what Mitchell was offering. It seemed to be okay when Mitchell sighed and tilted his arse up though, which had Trevor's cock throbbing, stiffening even more. He shifted his own leg higher up to lean forward and slide into the cleft of Mitchell's arse.

He grunted at the instant pleasure. Mitchell was still all loose and slick with lube, both from the liberal amount they'd used last night and the little natural bit that the inside lining of his arse had made. Probably some sweat from sleep, too. Trevor reached between them to hold his dick steady and rubbed the head over the fleshy rim of Mitchell's hole again and again. His thighs, holding him up, almost buckled when Mitchell pushed back against it.

"There's no condom," Trevor managed.

Mitchell sighed again, bringing his legs together to curl up, his back still arched enough to let his arse curve out. "Ay 'aven't got nothin'. And you won't hurt me if you're worried."

Trevor hesitated, trying to force his sleep-addled mind to think and not just shove inside while he rubbed spit-slicked fingers over Mitchell in the meantime. Mitchell had been with quite a few people in his time, but Trevor trusted him to be telling the truth.

It was apparently good enough for *some* part of him, because before he realised he was doing it, he was pushing the head of his cock into Mitchell's loose hole, his jaw dropping as Mitchell's heat engulfed him.

He put a hand on Mitchell's arse to spread it apart a little before sliding deeper in. Mitchell groaned and Trevor froze.

"Is it too—"

"Dun stop," Mitchell gasped, a hand darting back to grab hold of Trevor's hip. Before Trevor got a chance to keep going, Mitchell started rocking back to take it. Trevor let out a shaky breath and tightened his hold on Mitchell's arse, squeezing the cheek in his hand as he shoved his cock into Mitchell harder. He fucked Mitchell on his side, desperate and determined.

"Lift your leg and get up," Trevor grunted after a minute.

He managed to kick the covers off and roll onto his back without slipping out of Mitchell. Mitchell followed, careful not to let too much of his weight fall on Trevor by quickly putting his arms out on either side, propping himself up. From there, he launched into riding Trevor's dick on his own, lazily moving his hips back and forth while his hair fell into Trevor's face.

"Up or down, but you have to move," Trevor said.

Mitchell picked down. He raised an arm over Trevor's head, twisting his torso enough to let Trevor see his face for the first time that morning. Trevor's vision was still rather blurry, but that didn't mean he couldn't see Mitchell smile as he lowered himself and more of their skin met. Trevor started jerking his hips up to thrust into him.

"Very good morning," Mitchell said, breathless and laughing a little.

Trevor laughed breathlessly back. "Indeed."

"Ah-h-h." Mitchell's brows pushed together in a desperate slant and as his lips parted, his eyes stared into Trevor's. Trevor slowed the motions of his hips and planted his feet in the mattress to push upward, holding before sliding out and doing it again. Mitchell's eyes squeezed shut as he whined.

Trevor did it a few more times, then let Mitchell drop and started snapping up hard and fast enough to make Mitchell's entire body shake. Mitchell's arms stretched out above both of their heads as he panted and submitted to Trevor fucking him.

Eventually Trevor grew tired and had to stop. He huffed out a breath and lowered his legs.

Mitchell pushed himself up and Trevor remained lying back, too tired to move. As Mitchell manoeuvred himself to face Trevor, keeping Trevor deep inside, Trevor wondered how Mitchell had the energy. Mitchell had said he wasn't a morning person.

When Mitchell finished his revolution, was sitting astride Trevor the same way he had on the sofa last night, Trevor saw the lethargy in Mitchell's movements. As soon as Mitchell was satisfied with the position, he leaned forward until he was draped over Trevor, resting his head on the pillow beside his.

He rode Trevor slowly, taking his time and enjoying Trevor's cock at his own pace. Trevor slid his hands up Mitchell's thighs and over the skin of his back, clawing at it when Mitchell started picking up speed. He felt the press of their stomachs sliding together, Mitchell's cock between them, and turned his head to find Mitchell's mouth.

It was as they kissed, sloppy and uncoordinated, that Trevor slid his hands to Mitchell's arse, possessively squeezing and spreading him wide again. Tongue deep in Trevor's mouth, Mitchell moaned, and his hips rolled forward to take in more of Trevor's length. It wasn't long after that that he apparently got a boost of energy and started slamming down on it, determinedly riding Trevor to orgasm.

Trevor felt him quivering as his hot come shot into the tight space between them. Mitchell didn't let the space be too confined for long. He sat up with a contented sigh, placing his hands on Trevor's chest as he looked down at him with what looked like a soft, dopey smile even when everything Trevor saw was all blurry.

"Come inside me," he said, lifting up just so he could ease back down. He was still so fucking wet and loose from arousal, so fucking *pliant*, that it was driving Trevor mad. "If you want."

Trevor was suddenly up. He wrapped an arm around Mitchell's torso and held him as he tilted him back, laying him down. Mitchell brushed hair out of his face and raised his legs higher. A second after that, his eyes widened and his throat clicked in a surprised croaking noise, his neck in a tight hold under Trevor's hand.

It didn't take long for Trevor to come. One hand anchored around Mitchell's throat and the other gripping his thigh, he fucked Mitchell with quick, frantic movements of his hips. It was when Mitchell tried to tilt his head back and take in air that Trevor finished, his dick throbbing at the desperate little sound Mitchell made. He shot his load balls deep in Mitchell's arse, a full body shiver running through him when Mitchell's hand came up and half-heartedly tried to loosen his too-firm grasp.

He didn't move right away when he was done. He exhaled and relaxed all the muscles in his body, finally releasing his hold on Mitchell to let him breathe. He was trying not to feel dirty, but he did.

Eventually he slid out, leaning back on his knees and slipping free. He couldn't help looking down to see his come leaking out of Mitchell's puffy arsehole. Mitchell shuddered a little, a pearly white drop dribbling out as Trevor watched.

Trevor thumbed at it absently, pushed it back in while the rest of his hand kept Mitchell's balls out of the way. He tilted his head and rubbed circles into the abused rim as Mitchell's eyes slid closed and he sighed again, one hand massaging his throat. Trevor wondered if he knew how fucking content and satisfied he sounded.

"Can't stop thinking about who else has come inside you," he admitted quietly. His cock was still close enough to be convenient and he moved his hand to hold it, gently rubbed the head over Mitchell's wet hole the same way he had when he'd started the whole thing. "Can't get the image of other people fucking you out of my head sometimes. It's not that I'm jealous, I just—"

"Don't feel clean." Mitchell threw an arm across his face and his chest heaved with a deep breath. His voice was a little hoarse, strained for some reason. He gave a weak cough and it was much better when he spoke next. "Yeah. There are days when I feel like I'll never be able to get clean either. I wish I had a psychic power to make you stop thinking about it."

It startled a laugh out of Trevor, because it was such a weird and random thing to say. He shuffled back and stopped ruining the moment. "Forget it. It'll just take some time, that's all. Come on, let's take a shower."

Mitchell had never had such a good time with anyone else before. Even showering was made more enjoyable than normal by Trevor telling jokes while caressing his back with soapy hands. His neck was a little sore, as Trevor had surprised him by being even more forceful than usual, but most of the initial pain had gone. The steam from the shower helped.

Leaning back into Trevor's touch and moaning appreciatively when Trevor began massaging his shoulders, he wondered if he should bring it up. So far he'd treated it as something that Trevor simply did when he got excited, something that came with the whole sex package. There'd been another instance of Trevor half choking him last night, but after this morning, it seemed to be getting worse. Mitchell's throat had ached acutely, hurting when he swallowed and hardly allowing him to talk. It was almost like Trevor didn't even know he was doing it.

He understood that there was something about it that got Trevor off, because Trevor always reacted positively when he struggled. He personally loved rough sex when it was done right, loved being held down, but what Trevor was doing was different, and didn't really do anything for him. He could, however, let it do something for Trevor. He didn't mind that Trevor liked choking him, even found it to be incredibly hot when Trevor stepped out of his usually genial shoes and became a bit aggressive. But there were limits.

He decided not to bring it up now, but at some point in the future. It wasn't the right time now.

He turned around to face Trevor and slid his arms around his waist to hold him close. He didn't give an explanation for the impromptu embrace, but Trevor hugged him back without question, so he figured he didn't need to. Standing under the spray, Trevor let Mitchell hold him for several long minutes.

"So," Trevor said after a while, "a bit out of nowhere, but it kept slipping my mind to ask last night. What with Hemlock Grove, and fucking, and showing you my art."

Mitchell didn't let go, even though he felt like he should by now. It was too nice a feeling to give up easily, having a warm, solid body to hold close. "Yeah?"

"You said something about having a mentor when you were younger. A... support group? I was wondering why you stopped going."

Mitchell had forgot he'd even told Trevor that.

"Maybe things would've turned out better for you and your mother if you'd let them help you?" Trevor ventured.

Now Mitchell didn't pull away because he didn't want to look Trevor in the face. As skilled as he was at lying, he still preferred not to look someone in the eyes when he did it. He wouldn't be lying exactly, but he certainly wouldn't be telling the full truth.

"They wouldn't have been able to help with that, Trevor. They helped me with a lot, made me feel like less of a freak. I kept going as long as I felt they had something to offer me, but most of the time I spent away from the group with... my mentor."

Naomi had been able to teach him so much, expanded his mind and let in a world of possibilities. He'd learnt some helpful techniques from the others as well, particularly from one girl with pyrokinesis named Alisha. She'd had problems accidentally lighting things on fire, and Mitchell had had problems warping metal whenever he got upset. Naomi had been able to lay the foundation for that too, but it'd been a girl five years older than him who'd told him what worked best for her and made everything click.

It was during his time with Naomi that he'd met the woman who could see and speak to the dead. Still, as much as Mitchell tried talking to the other psychics living with her, he'd never felt like he belonged. Naomi, who could see the future, had known both where to find him and that he'd only be with them for a short time.

"At first I felt like I'd found a place where I could be myself," Mitchell said. "There were mostly older people there, though. The one closest to my age was two years older than me."

Wilson, a boy who could control plants. Mitchell had thought he was incredibly cool and had wanted to be friends, but Wilson, like Trevor, had always worn the most stylish clothing, had far better personal hygiene, and had a much larger vocabulary. Twelve-year-old Mitchell had looked at Wilson, compared them, and wasn't surprised when Wilson overtly put a bit of distance between them. Looking back on it now, Mitchell was certain his insecurities about his accent stemmed from the way Wilson had laughed the first time he heard him speak, and every time after.

"The point is, I was still awkward. I'd never fit in, even with them. So I didn't bother trying. I got what I needed from them and left."

Done explaining, Mitchell let himself look up to see Trevor's face. It was blank, like he was still listening. Then his eyes slid to meet Mitchell's. Mitchell stepped back, finally ending the embrace.

"Do you think things would've turned out different if you'd stayed with them? Even if they wouldn't have been able to help you and your mother's situation?" Trevor asked.

Mitchell laughed louder than he expected himself to. "Definitely."

121

All things considered, Trevor was thrilled with how the date had gone. He hadn't got any closer to finding out what Mitchell had had to go to in Essex, but they'd been having such a good time that the opportunity to bring it up had never arisen. He didn't want to spoil the date by asking about something that had made Mitchell freak out and snap. Mitchell was so much more relaxed in the privacy of Trevor's flat, and it was nice to see.

He wouldn't trouble himself with it for now. If he *really* felt he needed to know what sort of event it was, he'd probably have better luck getting it out of his dad.

"Well," Mitchell said at the door, after a large breakfast. "I've decided I want to see you again."

Trevor smiled and leaned against the wall. He'd put on his glasses and could make out things clearly now. "Oh? Good."

"It's just, it'll be a few days. I have a lot of work I need to get done at Advanced and this was sort of, y'know, like, indulging before I have to set my mind to the task. You can still keep texting me, though."

"A few days?"

"As in not until next month. Maybe two weeks."

Trevor tried not to deflate, but felt his heart sink nonetheless. "Oh."

Mitchell frowned apologetically. "I'm sorry."

"It's okay, I understand."

Mitchell leaned forward to kiss him and Trevor met him halfway. "Try not to think of me as being anything but yours in the meantime," he said with a smile when they parted.

Chapter 15
Guilty

Mitchell rarely felt guilty about doing a job anymore. The first few times Kane had sent him out on something more than an escape mission—after his stunt at the Kanine office when he'd proved he was capable—he'd felt terribly disgusted with himself, especially when the job involved prolonged torture. How had he been able to do such things and not feel remorse? What would Imogen think, or his mam? He'd looked at his accomplices and saw he really was just another cog in Kane's depraved wheel, was nothing more than an attack dog just like them.

Because he'd known he'd have to do it again, he'd steeled himself against the guilt at not feeling guilt, ignoring the inner voice that told him he really should at least *try* to feel something about these people who had hopes and dreams just like him, families. Instead of trying to subdue his anger and make himself personable like he did every day, he gave in to the apathy and let it numb him in order to get the job done. He used the broken switch in his brain along with built up rage to become something terrible and detached until it was time to resurface.

Eventually he didn't have to steel himself, and he started not caring about his not caring. None of the other attack dogs flinched, so why should he?

It got better once Kane agreed to only call on him a few times a year, easier to convince himself that he wasn't such a bad bloke in the time in between. But he still hated the whole fucking thing, being blackmailed and threatened into working for one man. A man who had a legion of just as capable bodyguards at his command but who apparently got a kick out of seeing how he could bend others to his will.

After submitting and giving up his body to so many men as a teenager, Mitchell had developed a bit of a thing with having to follow orders that were barked at him like he was a damned slave. It was why he always wanted to own his own business in the first place. The way Kane played with people, using them like toys in his own international game, was one of the things Mitchell most loathed in a person.

With Trevor now in the picture, he felt guilty again, only for a different reason. He still felt Trevor wasn't the kind of guy who deserved to be lied to. How much Mitchell enjoyed their last date only enforced the point.

That was why, waiting in the passenger seat of a black 2010 Subaru Impreza, he was chewing his fingernails and wishing he had a ciggy. He couldn't remember the last time he'd had one since he started restricting himself to "once in a while" occasions. A month ago, at least.

He pressed a hand to the window on his left, peering out into the night. They were stopped on the side of some dark road with no lights near Reading, and it was fucking raining. Fields were just past the sparse line of trees, a path leading through a thicket of wild grass and shrubs. Ezra, one of the other men Mitchell had come with, and the driver of the Impreza, was out there already, one of two shadowy figures in the darkness.

Mitchell lowered his hand and turned to face the second man Kane had assigned to the mission in the back seat.

"Got a smoke?"

Walter was fat, with a thick, porous face, and small, beady black eyes. His blond hair was thin and light, and fell to his ears all the way around. He grunted and leaned to the left to reach into his coat pocket and pull out a pack of Camels.

Mitchell exhaled in relief and took the offered cigarette between his fingers gratefully. "Light?"

Walter sighed and pulled out a lighter.

Mitchell put the hood of his coat up and stepped out of the car. He cupped a hand around the cigarette and lit it, inhaling the moment the tip flared red.

Opening the door only enough to toss the lighter back to Walter, he said, "Thanks." He shut it again and started down the path leading out into the field.

It felt weird out here, away from the city. Mitchell was used to the constant stimulation of his metal senses, to the large metal structures all around. Out here the biggest metal thing for as far as he could see was the car.

He crossed the dark, wet field until he reached Ezra, who was still trying to get their assignment, John Gilman to talk. He was keeping him at gunpoint, Gilman's mobile in his other hand.

Gilman was on his knees, sitting on his heels with his hands secured behind his back, his head down. Water streamed down his gaunt, white face from the black strands of his fringe, and his shoulders were hunched. He was shaking, though that could've been from the cold and rain, because he was otherwise firm, resolute in his decision to stay strong and not speak.

Mitchell thought the decision spectacularly stupid, because they'd get it out of him eventually and all of them knew it. But then, he wouldn't give in easily and without at least a little resistance himself. He could understand the man had to keep his dignity.

For years, Gilman had been in charge of Kane's marijuana greenhouse, and recently had been experimenting with strains, growing his own unique products using Kane's resources and selling them on the side. Since he was the type of man to give half his client list and keep the rest to himself if he thought he could get away with it, they were making damn sure that he didn't think he could get away with it. Then they'd kill him.

Mitchell took a long drag on his cigarette as he listened to Ezra.

"We're just getting fucking started, mate," Ezra said, pressing the barrel of the pistol firmly to Gilman's skull. Gilman's head was pushed aside a little, but he otherwise didn't move or react. "You tell me the fucking passcode and this'll go a whole lot smoother. Otherwise, my friend here will start having fun. You know what he likes to do for fun?"

Mitchell transferred his cigarette to his left hand and took out his switchblade, flicked it open. It was too dark and rainy for the steel to gleam in the moonlight, but the sound was triggering enough. Gilman's head snapped up and wide eyes locked on Mitchell's hand as his body tensed.

Already Mitchell's blood was pumping faster.

Trevor was at a party for a friend's birthday, a bloke named Shoubhik he'd gone to university with and still talked to every couple months or so. Shoubhik had a house in southeast London that had been a real piece of work when he'd bought it and he was still doing his best to fix it up. There were obvious places that needed more attention – the bathroom, for example – but it'd come a long way since Trevor had seen it last. He didn't feel uncomfortable leaning against the wall anymore.

Kay was beside him, or had been. They were slowly drifting away now, further into the crowd. After asking about how Mitchell was doing, nodding and giving the appropriate excited replies, they'd turned around to talk to someone else. Trevor didn't mind. Kay and he saw each other much more frequently, while large gatherings were the only times they'd ever see some of the people here.

Trevor wasn't really in the mood for getting drunk, or doing any of the other things a few of his friends were doing upstairs, but he didn't know how he'd have fun otherwise. He resorted to checking his mobile for messages, then pulling up a game when he saw he had none.

It struck him then that he didn't have any photos of Mitchell, none whatsoever. He'd have to rectify that soon.

"Hey, Trevor!"

Trevor looked up at the feminine voice greeting him and made himself put on a smile. It was Anya, a girl he'd been closer to in university before they went their separate ways. She had straight, red hair halfway down her back and features so soft that Trevor had often thought all she needed was wings to be a fairy; she was already pretty and majestic enough.

She came up to stand beside him with a drink in her hand. Trevor took in her slim build, her clear skin, and white teeth, and thought she'd certainly done a better job ageing than a lot of the other people here. Many of them had started to let themselves go, either to a stagnant lifestyle or one filled with drugs.

"Anya, hi. How's it going?"

"Not bad. I'd ask you the same, but it's clear you're enjoying this party as much as I am."

Trevor chuckled. "I didn't really want to come, but I needed to get out of my flat. Kay says I spend too much time watching TV and not enough out socialising."

"That's because Kay works at a nightclub and is ridiculously extroverted."

"Don't remind me. They keep pestering me to come by more often. Have you been to Felicity? That place is absolutely wild, especially considering how high-end it is." Anya nodded. "I like clubbing but I'm not a clubber, you know?"

"I know. You were always very..."

Trevor nudged her when she trailed off and didn't continue. "Very what?"

"Selective, I guess," she said with evident reluctance. "Don't worry about it. Let's not ruin the party."

What the hell is that supposed to mean?

"Selective how?" he asked.

"Don't take it the wrong way," she said, sighing.

Trevor rolled his eyes. "Anya, come on."

She shrugged. "You asked for it. I'm not the only one who's said this, okay?"

"Okay." Trevor was even more curious.

"You go out to things with us, but not regularly. You hang out with people, but just enough that you don't lose them as a friend, then go back to doing whatever you do by yourself. Honestly, most of the time you only reach out when *you* feel like doing something, and make up some excuse to miss it if you don't. You do it with Kay, too, because a few times they've come to me after you've turned them down."

Trevor felt struck. He'd never noticed the pattern before, but it was true, he couldn't deny it even from himself. He liked his friends, liked having numerous people to choose from if he was ever in the

127

mood for a night out, but that was just it. He kept them around for when *he* was ready. He rarely went out if someone was trying to force him to, because... He didn't know.

Was it that he didn't care about them, only about what they had to offer him? He'd hadn't thought so, but then he'd never taken the time to analyse his actions with regards to the people he called his mates. He did care about how their life was going, if they were doing well at their jobs, if their kids were growing up. Sort of. To an extent. He'd be sad if they died, anyway.

No, he didn't care. He could see that now. He cared about Kay, because Kay had come to be close to his heart, having been through mood swings and numerous psychedelic trips with him. Besides them, he couldn't say he would be sad to see anyone else go. The others were placeholders in his life, things he turned to when he was bored of the usual. And he would most likely continue to use them like that.

He hadn't realised he was so selfish.

"I see," he said. He scanned the faces of the other people at the party, wondering which had spoken about him behind his back. Surprisingly, he found he didn't care that they had, that it was mostly curiosity that made him want to know.

Anya put a hand on his arm. "I'm sorry."

"Don't be, it's fine. I'm glad you told me. I hadn't even noticed."

"How are things with you, really? You wouldn't normally be sulking in a corner by yourself, even if you didn't want to come. Did you lose your job or something?"

Trevor shook his head. "No, I'm still at Webprint. Sorry, I just have other things on my mind. It's not as easy for me to put on a smile and pretend to enjoy myself as it once was, I guess."

"Anything you're interested in talking about?" She was nearly done with her drink, took a large sip.

"No. Just wishing I was out with my boyfriend instead of stuck here." He put a hand on her arm this time. "Listen, don't let me ruin the party for you with my moping."

Anya looked him firmly in the eyes. "You're not ruining anything for me. If anything, I'm glad I'm talking to you. Look, my drink is almost gone, so I'll go get some more for the both of us. Make the best of this party, yeah?"

"Alright, sure." Trevor wasn't particularly interested, but she was right. Why mope when he could do something about it and perk himself up?

"I'll be right back."

She disappeared into the kitchen. Trevor looked at his phone again, checking the time. It was nearly half ten, and he'd been there since nine. Still far too early to leave.

He'd set his mind up to get drunk when Anya returned. She handed him a cup of something without telling him what it was, and a small sip revealed it to be something mixed with Dr Pepper. Some kind of rum.

"This is amazing, what is it?" he asked.

"Captain Morgan and Dr Pepper. One of my favourites, something Kay taught me. I thought you'd like it."

Trevor took a much larger drink, and felt it. "Mmm. 'S good."

"Thank you." She sipped her own, licking her lips when she lowered the cup. "So, boyfriend now, huh? He any interesting?"

Trevor chuckled. "You have no idea."

"Ooh. Do tell."

"He's a mechanic. Owns a place in Hackney."

"Clean cut Trevor Lewis with a mechanic! Well, that's something. What was your last boyfriend again?"

Trevor rolled his eyes. "God, that was ages ago, I hardly even think about him. Peter. He was a songwriter and guitarist."

"Oh, that's right. The sensitive one."

"Too fucking sensitive for my tastes," Trevor muttered into his drink.

His last boyfriend had not only thought Trevor psychologically unwell because of his art, they'd had a huge argument because Trevor had made an offhand remark about not caring about recycling. Peter had said it was people like Trevor who were killing the environment, said he couldn't be with someone who didn't care about the planet. Trevor had said that something so insignificant was hardly anything to end a relationship over, was in shock that Peter was making such a big deal over it.

Peter had cried angry tears when they decided to separate, yelled for Trevor to take his fucked up drawings and weird choking fetish and drown in the polluted Thames. In the end, Trevor had been glad to break things off, felt free.

"Anyway, what's this one like?" Anya asked. "What's his name?"

"Mitchell. He's rather quiet, hasn't been to uni but is very well-read. Not so much the artsy type like this lot, but able to appreciate it," he added as an afterthought, recalling Mitchell's remarks on his own art.

"I'd love to meet him. You should bring him round some time."

Trevor looked down into his drink. "Yeah, I want to. Maybe. He's a bit... shy."

"Come on, Gilman," Ezra said. "Make things easy on yourself."

Gilman's wide eyes went back to normal size as he blinked and flicked his gaze back to Ezra. "Eight, seven, four, two."

Ezra brought Gilman's mobile screen up and punched in the digits, unlocking it. "Good man. Now, we're gonna go through every one of your contacts and you're gonna shake your head 'no' if they haven't bought from you, nod your head 'yes' if they have. Understand?"

Gilman slumped and lowered his head with a sigh. He looked burdened under the weight of his wet clothes, hopeless.

"Oi! I asked you a fucking question!" Ezra shouted, prodding Gilman's head with the gun again.

"Please," he whimpered, not looking up. "I'm sorry. I won't do it again."

Ezra stepped back, disgusted. He turned and waved the gun in Gilman's direction, gesturing for Mitchell to go on. "He doesn't understand. Help him out."

Mitchell tossed his cigarette away and walked forward, heart racing. There was just the sound of the rain pounding on the ground now, but soon the air would be pierced by Gilman's screams. He wondered how loud it would be.

Gilman, panicking, tried to get up to run. Hands still tied behind his back, he shifted his weight to lift his knee, planting a foot on the ground to stand.

He didn't make it even halfway up. Mitchell brought his knife down in a sure, swift arc, driving it into his thigh.

"AHH!"

Gilman's cry turned into sobs as he took deep breaths against the pain. In the little light there was to see by, Mitchell saw the bloodstain spread through his trousers, mingling with water and dripping onto the ground.

"Do you understand now?" Ezra asked.

Mitchell yanked the blade free and Gilman cried out again, curling in on himself as much as his position allowed.

"P-Please," Gilman gasped.

"Give him another."

Mitchell slammed the knife into Gilman's shoulder, right above his armpit, and Gilman screamed.

"Alright, get behind him," Ezra said. "Lemme try this again."

Mitchell pulled the blade out and stood behind him. He grabbed him by the roots of his hair, yanking his head to the side to press the edge of the blade firmly against his neck. Raindrops fell from the top of Mitchell's hood onto Gilman's shaking shoulders.

"Gilman," Ezra began, thin lips spreading in a sinister smile. "John, buddy. There are no more chances for you, not after what you've done. Let's make that perfectly clear. You are not getting out of this alive."

Gilman's sobs increased. Mitchell shook him by the hold on his hair. "Quiet," he snapped.

"You do have some control over how you go, though," Ezra continued, nodding his thanks at Mitchell. "Quick and easy, hardly feeling a thing." He raised the gun, waving it around. "Or slow and painful, bleeding out on the ground while we dig your grave beside you. It's your choice, John."

Gilman simply cried, a sniffling mess for nearly half a minute. As they waited, Mitchell sighed, bored and wanting to get out of the rain to go home.

"Think my friend's getting impatient, John. I don't have to tell you which option he'd prefer, do I?"

"Okay," Gilman croaked. "Okay. I'll tell you."

"Excellent." Ezra brought up the phone again and frowned. "Shit, it's locked itself again. What was that code?"

"Eight, seven, four, two," Mitchell said.

"Cheers." Ezra put it in. "Alright, let's do this. You've got quite a few contacts, so — "

"I'll show you," Gilman said, voice still unsteady. "Untie my hands and I'll put them in a separate group."

Ezra beamed. "Cooperation, I like it!"

"I just want this to be over."

Ezra nodded. "Cut the rope. He knows I'll shoot him if he tries anything."

Mitchell stepped back, letting go of Gilman, and bent down to undo the rope binding his wrists together. He kept a hand on his shoulder when he was done, preventing Gilman from standing.

Ezra handed Gilman the phone. "Alright, try to be quick about it. None of us want to be out here in the rain for much longer." He looked up at Mitchell as Gilman began filtering the contacts. "Smoke?"

Mitchell shook his head. "Got mine from Walter."

"Ah, well."

It was done within five minutes. Gilman gave Ezra the phone back and it was another minute or so as he scrolled through, looking at the names. When he was done, he looked up, nodding at Mitchell. Mitchell gripped Gilman's head again.

He pressed a knee between Gilman's shoulders as he pulled his head back, exposed his throat. Gilman's freed hands came up, but were too slow. Mitchell had already taken the sharp edge of his blade and dragged it from one side of his neck to the other, slicing open wet skin. Thick blood poured from the cut, down the front of Gilman's shirt.

Mitchell kept his hold on him a moment, still gripping the knife from the follow through. He watched droplets of blood falling to the muddy earth at his feet, the moment seeming suspended in time.

For the first time in a while, his stomach twisted at what he'd just done, at how even this man's screams hadn't unsettled him when he'd had to act the executioner. He couldn't help imagining how Trevor would react to seeing him this way, what he'd think.

After a few heavy seconds spent pushing away the emotions he felt trying to creep back in, he let Gilman fall. The man was still weakly gasping for air, trembling and twitching like a landed fish as blood continued to pour from his throat and pool underneath him. Mitchell stepped back, checking himself for bloodstains. He held his switchblade out under the rain and carefully rubbed it with a finger to wash it clean, manipulating the metal to sharpen as he did.

"Come on, let's get outta the fucking rain and back to the car," Ezra said, bending down to pick up the discarded rope. "The faster Walter gets this grave dug, the sooner we'll all be home."

Chapter 16
Pickup

Mitchell was sitting in his office having lunch, halfway done with a chicken curry when two knocks on the door made him look up. He was hunched over the desk, face close to his food in order to easily shove bites into his mouth, but at the interruption he swallowed, licked his lips, and sat back. Imogen was standing in the doorway grinning at him.

"You're back," he said.

She'd asked to take a long lunch to go somewhere with Lydia. It being the first of April, Mitchell was expecting Adam to ring or come by at any minute to pick up the car for Kane. Imogen's request for a longer break couldn't have come at a better time.

Unfortunately, Adam still hadn't contacted him. So much for having Imogen out of his hair while he conducted business.

Imogen stepped in, closed the door, and stood with her arms crossed. She'd changed before leaving for her lunch date, into dark jeans, a black t-shirt, and a black blazer with the sleeves rolled up. Her straight, brown hair, which was almost always in a high ponytail or a single braid, was let out, falling nearly halfway down her back. Mitchell always forgot how long it really was.

She was still beaming at him, an air of excitement radiating from her. "Guess what," she said, eyes sparkling.

Mitchell looked her up and down again. He was so often caught up in his own world, but he did try to make an effort to stay involved with Imogen.

It wasn't just the obvious happiness he noticed, letting him know that something had happened between before she left for her date and now. It was what his senses were telling him, something different about her. Even amongst all the metal in the shop, Mitchell could tell Imogen had more than usual on her.

It wasn't change. Not the right metallic signature for coins.

"You're wearing more metal."

Imogen nodded, her smile broadening. "Uh huh."

Mitchell closed his eyes, cutting off one sense to focus more on the other. After years of practice, it was only a moment before he was able to pinpoint it.

He opened his eyes and looked at where one hand was hidden in the bend of her elbow, where her arms were crossed under her breasts. He couldn't see it, but he knew it was there.

"You're wearing a ring," he said.

"Yes." The choked-up quality of Imogen's voice made Mitchell's eyes dart up to her face. Tears had formed but hadn't fallen. She was still smiling. "Lydia asked me to marry her."

"How?"

"She asked if I'd been to my father's grave recently, after we finished eating at this ridiculously posh French restaurant neither of us were properly dressed for. I said no, I hadn't. She asked if I'd be okay with going there, said it was a nice day, maybe some flowers would be nice. She likes cemeteries anyway, you know, thinks they're relaxing. I said yes."

Imogen walked forward, finally coming to sit in the chair on the other side of Mitchell's desk as she continued. "We got flowers on the way there, went and sat down. It was still rather cold, but sunny. After a few minutes she pulled the box with the ring out of her pocket, opened it and handed it to me."

She was getting teary-eyed again, and wiped her eyes with the back of her hand. "She said she was sorry she never got to meet my dad, but she hoped he would've approved of her. I told her he definitely would have. And she, she said she's glad because she wants to be part of my family and wants me to be part of hers. Because she wants to spend the rest of her life with me."

Her tears were falling now, and she was laughing a little hysterically with joy. Mitchell got up and walked around the desk, pulled her up by the hand. She was so small and short that when Mitchell put his arms around her, he practically engulfed her.

She didn't react right away, instead stood tense and frozen for few seconds. The level of affection was a bit uncharacteristic for Mitchell, so he tried not to take it too personally, assumed she was simply shocked. Eventually she put her arms around his waist and pressed a cheek to his chest, hugging him tightly.

"That's wonderful, Imogen," Mitchell said, genuinely happy for her.

"It's in a few months. Lydia wants our anniversary to be in summer so that every year we celebrate, we'll have fairer weather," Imogen said, finishing with a chuckle.

"Very wise."

He let go and pulled away. Imogen looked up at him, eyes full of warmth. "You're invited, of course, you and your mother. And Trevor, if he's still around, which I have a feeling he will be. It'll be relatively small. Low key."

Mitchell wasn't sure he wanted to bring his mother to such an event, and it required more consideration than he had time to give it now, so he put it off to think about later. He did hope Trevor was still in the picture when summer came around, but didn't want to get those hopes up too much.

"I can't wait," he said, a little surprised to find he meant it. "But when I asked how, I meant it more as, how are two women getting married? It's not legal, is it?"

Imogen furrowed her brow. "Have you not been paying attention to the news? Mitchell, the legislation passed last year. It became legal in March and the first weddings happened a few days ago."

Mitchell blinked and felt a little out of breath. "I had no idea."

"Honestly, Mitch, you've got too much on your mind all the time. It's like your head is in the clouds. Though I admit being with Trevor has helped, as I knew it would."

The buzzing sound of Mitchell's mobile vibrating on the desk interrupted them. Mitchell spun around and grabbed it, looked at the screen.

"I need to answer this," he said, turning back to Imogen. "We'll talk later?"

Imogen nodded. "I just wanted to let you know the good news

before I got back to work. Don't forget to finish your lunch, by the way."

Mitchell answered the phone just as Imogen was closing the door behind her. "Hello?"

"I'm on my way," Adam said. Mitchell could hear the commotion of a busy street in the background, traffic and people around him. "I'll be there in maybe ten minutes. Is it ready?"

"Waiting at the furthest end of the street, near the last bay. Meet me there, don't go inside."

"See you then."

Mitchell hung up and sat back down to hurry through the rest of his lunch. When he was done, he cleared up the rubbish and opened a drawer in his desk to grab the key to the custom car. After freeing his ponytail and ruffling his hair, he chucked the red elastic band in the same drawer before pushing it closed. Finally, he picked up his jacket from the back of his chair and left, heading for the other side of the shop with the key in his pocket.

With Adam not there yet, Mitchell unlocked the car and sat in the passenger seat. The windows were heavily tinted. He'd installed handcuffs, attached to each side by a chain, adjustable thanks to the pulley system he'd integrated. Behind both the driver and passenger seat was a floor compartment. Mitchell figured one for clean tools and one for dirty, though he doubted they'd be used that way.

He twisted his neck to look into the back of the car. With no seats in the back, the space was open, the floor made of clean steel that made the interior more similar to a prison transport than the Cadillac ATS Sedan it was built around. The modified roof of the car further changed its shape, raised more in the back. The whole back half of the car had had to be redesigned to fit, but manipulating metal to bend to his will was what Mitchell did best.

The sound of the door opening made him turn around. Adam slid into the driver seat, passing a raggedy black rucksack to Mitchell.

"Payment for both jobs, the Gilman one and the car," he said, slamming the door shut. He laughed and flicked the red tree hanging from the mirror above the dashboard. "I like that you always think about the little things."

"Yeah, Kane does too," Mitchell muttered as he unzipped the

bag full of notes. He looked through it mostly for show, not wanting Adam to think he made a habit of not checking. He trusted Kane to give him the right amount, but didn't trust Adam nearly as much to not keep a bit for himself.

Adam turned to look into the back just as Mitchell had, whistling. "Very nice. Elegant, even. Doubt this one'll be destroyed. Too good not to use again, 'specially if more rich cunts after this wanna pay to torture someone who fucked their wife."

A vibration in his pocket made Mitchell pause his survey of the money. He was pulling out his mobile before he could think better of it.

It was a text from Trevor.

Ever had any pets? If not, ever wanted any?

Mitchell glanced at Adam, who had turned to face him and was waiting. He killed the screen and put his phone away, zipped up the rucksack.

"Great," Mitchell said. "Key's in the cup holder and the tank is full. Phone when you're coming by for the next job."

He got out and shut the door, carrying the rucksack on a shoulder. As he walked past the bays back to his office, Adam drove out of the lane to the main street. Mitchell watched yet another of his creations disappear, never to be seen by him again.

Back in his office, before putting the money in his safe and after closing the door, he replied to Trevor.

Never had any. I wanted a snake when I was younger, but other than that, no. I'm not a pet person. You?

By the time he'd stashed one hundred thousand pounds in his safe, Trevor had sent a text back. His reply was so long it took up two messages.

My dad got me a dog as a kid. I guess he figured that's what you do when you have a nice house and steady job, like the next step. I was excited at first but lost interest, like with a toy. Neither of us took care of it so one day I came home from school and it was gone.

He said he gave it away to someone who would actually love it. I cried but didn't really care after about a week. I'd never wanted a dog or asked for it in the first place anyway. Basically I'm not a pet person either.

Mitchell imagined a young Trevor as he put his hair back into its ponytail and replaced his leather jacket on the back of his chair. Round-cheeked, curly-haired, as friendly as he was now. He imagined Trevor drawing in his bedroom, exasperated with a dog that wouldn't stop barking, a dog he hadn't even asked for.

What else had young Trevor done, been like? Why had they talked so much about Mitchell's past but so rarely about his?

Mitchell would have to get back to work shortly, but he allowed himself a few more minutes to talk to Trevor. Finally done with both jobs, his criminal schedule cleared, he felt free, a load off his shoulders. He wanted to take advantage of the reprieve until the next task came along. Sometimes it was days, sometimes months.

Any good horror films out? You should take me to the cinema this weekend. Can't stay the night, promised mam I would visit Saturday.

Trevor's reply was fast, as usual.

No, nothing good out now unfortunately. What I really want to see comes out next Friday actually. We could stay in at yours and you can kick me out whenever?

Mitchell's stomach lurched when he read "stay in at yours," but he supposed it was time, and only fair. Truthfully, he did want another night in after nothing but work. The time alone was nice, much more intimate and romantic. It would work out if they went to his; Trevor could go home that night, or as Mitchell was leaving the next day to catch the train at noon.

Sounds good. Come by the shop around 7.

Chapter 17
Worker Bee at Home

Trevor didn't know what to expect when it came to Mitchell's flat. A man as quiet and mysterious as Mitchell, Trevor drew a complete blank when trying to imagine the place he called home.

As Mitchell drove Trevor's Fiesta from Advanced out of Hackney, Trevor realised he'd thought that's where Mitchell lived—Hackney. He looked out the window as they passed through neighbourhood after neighbourhood, curious to know how far they were going.

It was when they crossed the River Roding on the A13 that Mitchell said, "Nearly there."

Trevor kept his face composed all the way through Mitchell parking on the pavement outside a modern tower block. Following Mitchell into the lift and taking it to the top floor, he adjusted his expectations and reminded himself that Mitchell was, after all, a business owner almost a year older than him. By the time they were outside Mitchell's door, Trevor had prepared himself to be surprised, had been expecting the unexpected.

Mitchell opened the door and stepped inside. Trevor went in, not sure what to make of what he saw.

It wasn't that the furniture wasn't expensive, or the layout of the place in poor taste. It wasn't even that it was particularly messy. In fact Mitchell was incredibly tidy, though whether that was in preparation for Trevor's visit or not, he didn't know.

It was that there wasn't much furniture at all. It was so basic, so... minimalistic. Like his own flat, much was the same colour, but unlike his silver and brown, Mitchell's things were mostly silver and black.

He nearly laughed, but caught himself for fear of Mitchell taking his laughter the wrong way. Really, he realised, he should've expected that Mitchell be a man of simplicity.

Mitchell walked further in, dropping his jacket onto the sofa. There wasn't much else to drop it on, as the only other things in the room were the coffee table, the television, and a bookshelf.

"I'm a bit dirty from work so I'm gonna shower really quick," Mitchell said. "D'you mind?"

"Not at all."

"Great. Make yourself comfortable, alright? I'll just be fifteen minutes, twenty at the most."

Trevor nodded, taking a few steps forward. "No problem. I'll just check out your bookshelf while I wait, eh?" he finished with a playful smile.

Mitchell eyes slid to the bookshelf. He wasn't exactly smiling back. "Uh... Yeah. Sure. Be right back." He spun on his heel and disappeared around the corner.

Trevor toed off his shoes and put his jacket next to Mitchell's on the sofa. The bookcase was dusty, and only the top two shelves held books. The far left of the third shelf held a half full glass jar of coins, with the rest of the space dedicated to intricately shaped trinkets of some sort, in the fashion of wooden carvings only made of different types of metal. The bottom shelf was empty.

Trevor knelt down and took a closer look at the titles on the upright spines. Thick books on mechanics, electricity, engineering. Thinner books on physics, mythology, astronomy. A self-help paperback on social confidence and making friends. Psychology, anthropology, trigonometry...poetry?

Curious to see what poetry Mitchell read, Trevor pulled the book from the shelf. It was a thin hardcover, with no title on the front, uneven pages, and obviously old. He opened it to the title page, saw "Poems of Inspiration." There were two handwritten messages underneath. Trevor read the first.

To whom it may concern:

It is no secret that Mitchell hides much of himself. An unfortunate combination of personality and upbringing. There are equal parts good

141

and evil in him, and it's difficult to say for certain down which path his future will take him. You are his crossroads, his chance at happiness.

I want you to read something on page 203. Remember it when you think of Mitchell. Remember that even during his darkest times, there is still a boy who longs to be loved.

Trevor read the message again, wondering who it was to, who else had picked up the book and read it. Surely Mitchell must have, but it was clearly not addressed to him, though the book seemed to be a gift he received.

It was almost like it was written exclusively for Trevor.

He would go to page 203 later; first, he read the second message.

Mitchell,

I know you have trouble believing in God. So do I. So do many people like us. Many of these poems mention a powerful Creator, but don't disregard their message too hastily. There's one I want you to read in particular, on page 92.

Remember that while money certainly solves much of life's problems, having it does not ensure happiness. Be careful.

Love,

Naomi

Trevor was more interested in reading Mitchell's chosen poem than his own, and was glad the page numbers worked out in his favour. He flipped to page 92, wondering if Naomi was Mitchell's mentor. It seemed likely considering the phrase "people like us." The others in Mitchell's support group, perhaps? Less privileged people with some form of social anxiety?

Mitchell's poem was called "The Future." Trevor read the short explanatory passage above it, then moved on to the poem itself.

'Tis well that the future is hid from our sight,
That we walk in the sunshine, nor dream of the cloud,
We cherish a flower, think not of the blight,
And dream of the loom that may weave us a shroud.

It was good, it was kind in the Wise One above
To fling Destiny's veil o'er the face of our years,
So we see not the blow that shall strike at our love,
And expect not the beam that shall dry up our tears.

Though the cloud may be dark, there is sunshine beyond it,
Though the night may be long, yet the morning is near;
Though the vale may be deep, there is music around it,
And hope 'mid our sorrow, bright hope is still near.

Trevor didn't much understand why a poem about not knowing the future would apply the most to Mitchell out of hundreds of poems in the entire book, but he could guess. Hope must've been in short supply given his childhood, and Trevor could imagine that at times Mitchell longed to know things would get better. Maybe he'd even tried to visit a psychic once; it would explain why he'd asked on their second date if Trevor believed in them.

He turned to page 203 next, finding his poem. Reading this one, he could again see some element referring to Mitchell's past.

There is no hope, and yet I keep on fighting.
There is no chance, and yet I fight the more.
Fate's holocaust is loosed against me, blighting
My dream of triumph that I held of yore;
Sick am I, sick unto the very core
Of heavy wrongs there is no way of righting,
Yea, I am weary of the battle roar
Beneath black skies no sun is ever lighting.

I see no gleam of victory alluring,
No chance of splendid booty or of gain,
If I endure I must go on enduring

143

And my reward for bearing pain – is pain;
Yet, though the hope, the thrill, the zest are gone,
Something within me keeps me fighting on!

Trevor reread it once more, then slowly closed the book and put it back. He was done with the bookshelf, he thought. It was getting him a bit down, making him think about things he'd rather not ruin the start of a date with.

He picked up one of the metal trinkets instead, turning it in his hand and admiring the smallest details. Then he put it down and got up to look in the kitchen. He could still hear the sound of the shower, and figured he had a few more minutes to check out the sort of things Mitchell ate.

It wasn't the most stocked of kitchens, but like the rest of the place, it had the basics – milk, water, butter, wine, bread. In the icebox there was a pack of cigarettes. Trevor had forgotten Mitchell saying he used to smoke and that he still did on occasion. He looked at the strewn papers across the small square table in the corner and found mostly things like bank statements, credit card information. It was the only sign of sloppiness as far as Trevor could see, though he hadn't seen the bedroom yet.

He was *not* going to look in the bedroom without Mitchell's permission.

He went back to the sitting room and plopped himself down on the sofa. Mitchell had mentioned he had a laptop; did he have a cord to plug it into the TV so they could watch Netflix on a larger screen? Trevor had brought his contact case and solution in case he did end up staying the night, which he hoped he did. He wondered how Naomi knew to write that message in the front of the poetry book.

It was nearing eight o' clock when Trevor heard a door open. He turned to look and saw Mitchell walk to the corner he'd disappeared behind, still dripping and wearing just a red towel around his waist.

He loved the look of Mitchell's hair completely wet. It appeared black instead of its usual amber and dark brown, and seemed longer. Dry, it was above Mitchell's shoulders, but only just. Wet, the tips brushed skin. It brought out the shape of his head as the straight strands lay pressed flat to his skull, made his face look more angular yet more young and vulnerable. His fringe made droplets of water slide down the side of his face and drip off his chin.

It was like from the neck up he was almost a girl, while from the neck down he was decidedly not. Trevor wanted to kiss below his navel, push his nose into his skin, taste and smell him.

"Hey. Just lemme get dressed, alright?" Mitchell said.

"If you feel that's entirely necessary."

Mitchell laughed. "I *would* like to eat something first."

"Fair enough."

"You can come watch though, if you like," he said, shooting Trevor a grin.

Trevor was up in a second, following Mitchell to the bedroom.

After putting on jeans and a t-shirt, Mitchell had ruffled his towel-dried hair and combed fingers through it. Trevor, unable to filter himself as quickly as he would've liked to, had asked if he could brush it.

Mitchell didn't often blush, so it was worth the embarrassment of asking to see him do it then. He shook his head, laughing and saying, "What? No. It's fine. My hair is so thin it hardly ever tangles."

Trevor, who was sitting on the edge of the bed, leaning back on his hands, asked, "Why do you keep it so long? Do you like the style?"

Mitchell shrugged and brushed away a few strands of his fringe out of his eyes. "Yeah, I guess I do. I like being able to do different things with it. I wanted it about this long when I was younger too, but didn't really feel I could, y'know? Because I was already, like, being, um, handled? Treated. Like a girl. With guys."

"It's okay, I get it."

Mitchell exhaled, rocked back and forth on his feet with his hands in his pockets. "Yeah. So I didn't need to add long hair to the mix, make things worse. I was too pretty already. But I have the freedom to wear it the way I want now, so..." He trailed off, finishing with another shrug.

"I'd still like to brush it, even if it doesn't get knotted and tangled as easily as mine."

"I don't even have a brush. All I have is a comb."

"Comb, then. Come on, it's not like there's anyone around to see. It's just us." Trevor rolled his eyes.

"Fine."

Trevor smiled in victory and got up to follow Mitchell to the bathroom. Mitchell opened the cabinet above the sink and took out a black comb before handing it to Trevor handle-first. Then he turned to face the mirror and squared his shoulders, taking a deep breath.

"You act like I'm about to cut you," Trevor said, chuckling behind Mitchell as he raised the comb.

"Just not used to other people doing things like this."

"It's okay, you'll get there." Trevor's heart jumped into his throat at the slip, but Mitchell only took a couple seconds to reply.

"Yeah."

Trevor dragged the teeth through the damp strands of Mitchell's hair, from the root all the way down. He started on the left side and worked his way right. Interested in how Mitchell would look, he brushed Mitchell's fringe back over his head, exposing his entire forehead and dark eyebrows.

"No thanks," Mitchell said, ruffling his hair in the front to right it.

Trevor smiled and tried something else. He parted it down the middle, separated the hair that usually swept across so that it fell equally on both sides.

"You're having too much fun, I think."

"Just a little," Trevor said, laughing again. Mitchell turned to take the comb, but Trevor held it behind his back. "I'll put it right, okay?" Mitchell sighed and turned back around. Trevor could see the twitch in his lips that gave away his efforts to keep from smiling.

Trevor was still combing Mitchell's hair—a little lost to the pleasure of such a domestic act—when Mitchell asked, "Would you ever ride in a stolen car?"

Trevor didn't stop combing, but did purse his lips and furrow his brow. "But not steal it myself?"

"Yeah."

"I dunno. Probably not."

"What if it was just borrowed? Like…from a repair shop."

Trevor caught his eye in the mirror before looking back to his hair. "Like from Advanced, you mean."

Mitchell did smile then. "Maybe."

Certainly would be exciting, Trevor mused.

"God help me, but I suppose yes, I would," he said.

Mitchell's smile broadened. "There's a Porsche scheduled for repairs in a couple weeks or so. Collision fucked up the front."

"People often schedule things that far ahead when it comes to collisions?"

"Only when they need some time to get money sorted."

"What kind of Porsche owner needs time to get money sorted?"

"The kind that spent all their money buying the Porsche, I guess. I don't usually care enough to ask those sorts of things."

"Hmm."

"There was, er, something else I wanted to talk to you about."

The tone of Mitchell's voice put Trevor on edge. He nearly froze mid-stroke, but finished, put the comb down by Mitchell's hand, and tried to keep his heart from beating too quickly.

"Okay."

Mitchell turned around, didn't look Trevor in the eyes but did seem to be looking at his face. "You know how when you get really worked up, you put your hand around my neck?"

Trevor's stomach plummeted. He felt a little sick.

"Mitchell, I'm sorry, I never meant—"

"I'm not asking you to apologise." He quickly looked Trevor up and down, and must've seen how nervous he was, because he grabbed hold of Trevor's arms and finally did look him right in the eye. "I don't care that you do it. Do it as much you fucking want if that's what gets you off. But if you hurt me, I'm gonna have to ask you to stop. Especially if you start leaving bruises."

"You've had bruises?!"

"No! Not bad ones anyway. You could barely tell."

Trevor put a hand to his head. "Oh my God."

"For fuck's sake," Mitchell said, sighing in exasperation. "You think you're the first person who's choked me? Look, I wasn't gonna go into details because you're sensitive, but the kind of men who like to fuck underage boys? Not always gentle, la. I couldn't tell them to

147

let up a little, fuck, I couldn't do more than squeak most times. And I doubt they'd listen if I did. But I can tell you. We can find a way to work with it."

Trevor groaned. He wanted to disappear. He wanted to turn back time so he could tell himself to pay more attention like Kay had told him.

At least Mitchell wasn't reacting like Peter, calling him mental. It sort of felt like he was indirectly calling him a pervert, but not one he wanted to break things off with, which was something.

Trevor sat on top of the toilet. "The thing is, I can't really control it. There must be something wrong with me. Most of the time — pretty much every time — I don't even know I'm doing it. Sometimes I realise halfway through and manage to stop myself, but..."

"Let's go to the bedroom," Mitchell said.

Trevor followed. He didn't know what else to do or say. He felt so off-balance. He sat next to Mitchell on the bed.

"You like to see people struggle, right?" Mitchell asked. "In this case, you like to see *me* struggle. Try to catch my breath while you're in control of how much I have? Hear the sounds I make while you're choking me?"

"Stop, stop! You're making me sound like, like — "

"Calm down. I'm not judging you and I never will judge you. It's not a fucking crime to get off on something like this. Jesus. There are far worse things. I just want to know how you feel when you're doing it, what sorts of things about it make you like it."

Trevor took a deep breath and nodded, looking down at his hands in his lap. "Yeah. It's all those things you said. I like the feeling of holding someone's throat. I can feel it when they swallow, try to breathe. It's like I'm holding their life in my hands and... I sound like a fucking psychopath." Trevor groaned again and put his face in his hands.

"No, you don't."

Trevor looked up, searching Mitchell's face. "You don't think it's strange, or weird, or fucked up, that I could do that to someone I like so much? I care a whole fucking lot about you, Mitchell, and nearly killing you shouldn't turn me on."

He could see Mitchell swallow. He flinched a little when Mitchell put a hand on his shoulder.

"I want you to fucking listen to me, 'cause I don't think you are," Mitchell said. It wasn't a tone of voice Trevor had heard him use before, and it was frankly a little scary. "I don't care *why* you do it. I don't care *when* you do it. All I care about is *how* you do it, because as far as I'm concerned, that's the only part that's relevant." He took his hand away and moved toward the centre of the bed. "Lie down on your back."

Trevor warily slid back and lay flat, his head on the mattress. He looked down his body as Mitchell crawled over him, straddling his hips. Mitchell leaned forward, placing his hands on either side of Trevor.

Suddenly Trevor felt his neck held in a tight grip. Instinctively, his mouth opened to suck in air, but it was like breathing through a narrow tube, a straw. He clutched at Mitchell's arms, helpless croaking noises coming from him for once.

Mitchell's eyes were blank, emotionless. He only tightened his hold around Trevor's neck, adding his other hand, until Trevor couldn't breathe at all.

"This," Mitchell said, his voice no higher than its usual soft volume, "this is too tight."

He let up a little, and Trevor pulled in what precious air he could. His heart was pounding and he was starting to feel light-headed.

"This is still too tight."

Mitchell loosened a little more.

"Still too tight. Do you understand?"

Trevor nodded. Mitchell's hands eased up just enough that it hurt, and that he still had to fight for air, but not extremely so.

"This, here, is as far as I want you to ever go."

"Okay," Trevor managed.

"You're not a psychopath, Trevor. A psychopath would choke you to death while they fucked you, and keep fucking your dead body. *That's* what they would get off on. You just like to dance along the line. And you know what? I think that's romantic. It takes a lot of trust to let someone do that to you. To *willingly give* someone your life to play with. That's all you want, right? Someone you can push close to the edge then bring back. It's rather intimate. Poetic, even. But you need to learn control. Have you learned?"

Trevor nodded.

He finally let go and Trevor inhaled as much as he could. It hurt, it hurt so fucking much, and he didn't think he'd be able to talk for a few minutes.

He wasn't expecting the gentle kiss Mitchell planted on his lips a moment later.

"It's alright," Mitchell whispered. "I lose control sometimes too."

Mitchell wished they had time to fuck, but they hadn't woken up early enough. It was either breakfast or sex; there was no time for both before he had to leave for the Overground station.

They'd had a brilliant time last night, though. Mitchell had decided to cook, feeling a bit guilty about not being able to see Trevor sooner, and wanting to make it up to him. Trevor had watched the TV Mitchell hardly ever turned on for maybe fifteen minutes before joining him in the kitchen to help.

They'd talked more about what Trevor had been like as a kid, and eventually, when talk turned to things their parents had always said, took photos of each other. Mitchell knew his mam would cuff him if he showed up without a photo and Trevor's dad had apparently asked what Mitchell looked like as well.

After dinner they'd gone straight to having sex in the living room. It'd started on the sofa, but Trevor eventually lay Mitchell across the table, and from there it moved to the floor when Mitchell wanted to ride the cock he'd been two weeks without. He'd felt high when he came, and had clung to Trevor, elated as Trevor finished inside him. He didn't say as much, but he ranked it their best sex yet, mostly attributing it to the fact that he'd really fucking missed it.

They'd finished the first season of *Hemlock Grove* too, and Mitchell had been surprised to find he wanted more. Trevor said they'd watch *Game of Thrones* in the meantime, of which there was plenty to get through. Then he'd showed Mitchell the website he mentioned so much, Reddit. It wasn't just gore and mutations as Mitchell had thought it was, though that was just about all they looked at. It was certainly interesting to see Trevor's reactions to the gruesome photos and videos. He was pleased to discover that Trevor handled dead bodies much better than the average person, and that they could spend a whole hour looking at them.

Mitchell rolled over and looked at Trevor lying in his bed, brown curls on one of his pillows. Trevor looked back at him, lips pouty with sleep.

Ay really wish we 'ad time ter fuck, Mitchell mourned.

He sighed and pushed his face into Trevor's shoulder, groaning at the prospect of getting out of bed. Trevor stroked his hair.

"If you want, I can drive you to the station," Trevor said after a few minutes. "Save you some time."

Mitchell sighed. What he really wanted was to take Trevor with him, but like fuck was that going to happen.

"Thanks."

Chapter 18

Eye

Two weeks passed, and they'd been on two more dates. On the eleventh of April, they went to see *Oculus*, the horror film that Trevor wanted to see so badly, then gone back to Mitchell's. On the sixteenth, they'd had lunch together, then stayed in at Trevor's later that night.

It was on the seventeenth that Adam came back to Advanced and told Mitchell what the next order was for Kane. Nothing fancy this time, just an escape car, one they'd probably be destroying after two or three jobs. Mitchell started ordering the parts the next day.

Now it was the day after, the nineteenth, and Mitchell was nervous about the night ahead. He and Trevor were going on another date, only this time Mitchell was picking him up in the recently repaired Porsche and surprising him with where they were going. And that wasn't all he had planned.

He'd talked to his mam about a lot of things during his two-day visit—the Gilman job and how things stood with regards to his business with Kane first, and Trevor second. He'd showed her Trevor's photo, suffered through her sexual innuendos, then told her all about him. She was pleased by his being a Libra, said he would do just fine with her Scorpio son.

Then Mitchell had said, all joking aside, that he thought things were getting really serious with Trevor. He was trying to remember her advice and not fall for him too quickly, especially since Trevor was his first real boyfriend, but he felt he was at the point now where he should tell him about his ferrokinesis. He'd already told him about the things they'd done together to get by when he was a teenager (admittedly, he'd left out stealing, drug dealing, and going to prison).

He wanted to be able to show more of himself, and wanted to know what she thought.

She'd held his face for a long time, looking deep into his eyes. Then she'd looked an equally long time at Trevor's photo on Mitchell's mobile. Finally, she'd said okay. Mitchell had felt a weight lift off his shoulders and hugged her.

During the day-long journey back, the weight had returned. He had no idea how he was going to tell Trevor. Then, a couple days after their movie date, he'd thought of a plan. It was something over-the-top romantic, and not his usual style, but also something that would let Trevor know the depth of his feelings without getting too close to "love" territory.

The last time he'd been this nervous was on their first date. This wasn't even his worst secret.

Trevor was slipping his feet into a pair of socks when he heard someone knocking on his door. He finished putting the second one on before getting up to open it.

Mitchell looked every bit the gorgeous creature he did every time. Besides the black leather jacket he nearly always wore, there was also a crimson shirt beneath it, the collar brushing Mitchell's throat. As Trevor's eyes travelled up, he saw Mitchell's lips, rosy and sensuous, smiling in greeting.

"Hey," Mitchell said, stepping in. Trevor leaned forward and met him for a quick kiss. "Ready? I've got the Porsche on the kerb outside."

"Yeah, just a second." Trevor picked up his own coat and shrugged into it. "Alright, let's go."

As soon as he left the building his eyes fell on the silver Porsche. Mitchell unlocked it with the fob and Trevor got in, slammed the door shut.

"Is this going to be a ride like last time?" he asked.

Mitchell pulled from the kerb smoothly into traffic and chuckled. "Maybe. How's it feel to be riding in a borrowed car?"

"I thought it might be a little too adventurous for me, but so far

153

it feels good."

Mitchell grinned. "Good. I don't take out punters' cars often, but it's a fun perk, like." His smile turned filthy and his hand on the gearstick tightened. "Now for some real fun."

Trevor heard Mitchell slam the clutch, saw his hand jerk the gearstick almost violently, and the car accelerated with a loud hum. Mitchell easily cut someone off at a turn, nearly causing an accident, and Trevor's stomach did somersaults as the tyres squealed against the road. He heard more than one horn blaring at Mitchell's stunt.

Mitchell's loud, manic laughter filled the small space, and even though Trevor's pulse was racing from what he was sure was a near-death experience, he found himself laughing with him.

"Shouldn't you be more careful? Especially if the car is stolen. Reckless driving is a good way to get the attention of the police."

"Nah, I'm not really worried about the police."

Trevor quirked a brow. "Do you know how that sounds?"

"It'll be fine, trust me." When Trevor continued to stare at him, he finally sighed and added, "I have friends in the police. Look, don't worry about it."

Trevor didn't believe it at first, but then he remembered the conversation he'd had with his father about Mitchell. Not just the fact that he'd apparently been at an event with people his father knew, meaning they were most likely affluent, but the fact that a man with a presence like Mitchell's leaves a lasting impression. If Mitchell had connections like that, was it so out of the question for him to know people in the police?

It slightly unsettled him again. He was certain he knew Mitchell well, but it was impossible to get away from the fact that he was still keeping things hidden. He hoped wherever Mitchell was taking him tonight it would reveal at least one of the many puzzle pieces that seemed to make up who he was under the surface.

"Friends in the police. Right. Well, you continue to be full of surprises. Which, speaking of, are you still keeping our destination a secret?" Trevor asked.

"Yes. Just be patient, you'll see."

They didn't talk for a while, but it was a pleasant silence between them. When Mitchell turned the volume up on the radio, Trevor didn't feel like it was to discourage more conversation. He revelled in the feeling of things being so easy with Mitchell despite the selective honesty, loved how far they'd come in only a little under two months.

Mitchell parked near Trafalgar Square, and as they exited the car the mystery continued. Trevor kept himself from asking any more questions, which wasn't difficult when Mitchell took hold of his hand without warning, walking as though the action was of no significance at all. Trevor focused less on their secret destination and more on the sweat gathering in his palm. It was the first time they'd held hands in public.

After they'd walked across the Jubilee Bridges, it became obvious where they were headed, and Trevor decided he had to say *something*, even if it would disappoint Mitchell.

"I am, actually, a resident of London and have been to the Eye before," he remarked.

"I haven't."

"Are you serious?" Trevor asked incredulously. "And you've lived here how many years?"

"Yes, I'm serious. If you're such an experienced visitor, tell me what you thought of the Cupid's capsule."

"Never been in a Cupid's capsule. Never had someone fancy me enough to take me." Trevor turned to Mitchell, gaping. "Wait a minute, Mitchell, did you...?"

Mitchell was keeping his head held high, but Trevor thought he saw the faintest sign of a blush. "I did." He glanced at Trevor, his confidence apparently wavering. "It's not... too much too soon, is it?"

Trevor swallowed and tried to calm the quick beating of his heart. After just six weeks of dating, Mitchell had got them a capsule for couples that cost over three hundred pounds, a capsule with champagne and truffles.

He hadn't realised Mitchell felt so strongly about him. It was that, or the money just wasn't all that much to him. Either way, the gesture was above and beyond what Trevor had expected, and he was glad he'd been so persistent in flirting with Mitchell in the beginning. Otherwise, he wouldn't have *this* now.

He squeezed Mitchell's hand. "No. It's amazing."

The inside was like all the other capsules, but with the guide pouring champagne and offering chocolate, the atmosphere was embarrassingly romantic, even a bit sappy. Mitchell, however, was paying less attention to their interior surroundings and more attention to the city below, not even once giving their chaperone a second glance. He stood near the glass with wide eyes, speechless, while Trevor stood a little ways behind him, sipping his drink and unsure what to do with himself.

"Do you think I believe in aliens?" Mitchell asked out of nowhere.

Trevor furrowed his brow, not sure if he'd heard correctly. Mitchell turned around, spared a glance at their audience, then looked back to Trevor.

"What kind of question is that?"

"I want to see how much you know me by now. Like a game."

Put like that, it did pique Trevor's interest. "Alright then, yes, I do think you believe in aliens. Do you think I do?"

Mitchell smiled, letting Trevor know he was right. "I think you haven't ruled out the possibility."

Trevor took a few steps forward, closing the distance between them. The fact that Mitchell had answered so spot on made him feel a step past happy, something that went much deeper.

"Do you think I like rap music?" Mitchell asked.

"No. Do you think—"

"You don't let yourself be restricted by genres. You like songs based on how they make you feel."

Trevor was a little stunned. "Wow."

Mitchell smirked at him. "Come on, you're the artsy type. Of course you'd be open-minded about stuff like that." He took Trevor's glass from his hand and drank from it. "Do you think I'd like going to the theatre?"

Trevor pursed his lips, tried to imagine Mitchell going to see a play. The trouble was, he both could and couldn't.

"No," he finally said.

Mitchell nodded. "I think it would depend on what play it is and who's in it for you."

"Right again."

They were nearing the full height of the wheel now. Facing the river, there was Westminster Bridge, Big Ben, and the Houses of Parliament on their left, beautifully illuminated and casting a golden reflection onto the murky water below. It seemed to outshine everything surrounding it, even Westminster Abbey just to the right. Just ahead was where they'd come from, Trafalgar Square, and down below, impossibly small now, were the bridges they'd crossed to get here. Further to the right, way over beyond Covent Garden, lay the lively Soho where they'd gone for their second date. Even further right of that was St. Paul's Cathedral, lit up as majestically as everything else. Trevor's eyes followed Waterloo Bridge, crossing the Thames again, then, after turning nearly in a full circle, there was the forest of skyscrapers in the distance, the newly built Gherkin, Cheesegrater, and Walkie Talkie. Finally, directly behind him, was Waterloo Station, a bit unimpressive after the magnificent sights surrounding it.

Trevor had to admit, the view at night was quite different than it was during the day, the only view he'd seen. The swaying reflection of lights on the river below was beautiful, even if the river itself wasn't, and Trevor began to think about maybe sketching the scene.

His attention was drawn back to Mitchell when an arm wrapped around his waist, bringing their bodies close in a half embrace. Trevor slid a hand into Mitchell's back pocket as Mitchell let his head rest on Trevor's shoulder.

Both Imogen and the person who'd written the messages in the poetry book were right; Mitchell kept a lot to himself, that much was obvious from the fact that Trevor hadn't known he felt strongly enough to get them a whole private capsule. However, he thought he was starting to get a clearer picture. Mitchell was apathetic, certainly, but he could also be playful, loving, funny, sarcastic, thoughtful. He could be unintentionally cute when he tucked his hair behind his ear, or tilted his head when he was confused. He could be sheepish when he did something embarrassing and tried to subtly hide his face by scratching his forehead.

But the mystery message writer — Naomi? — had also said something about equal parts good and evil. Trevor found it hard to imagine Mitchell doing something considered evil, but not entirely impossible. He had felt terrified when Mitchell had choked him, and he'd seen Mitchell get a certain look in his eyes more than a few times, a look that sent shivers down his spine. The Mitchell he saw moaning and keening in bed was not an easy image to put next to a Mitchell doing something "evil."

What was also hard to process was how someone could be so nice, *and* have the potential to be bad—especially while the person in question had his head on his shoulder. It would be different if Mitchell wasn't also kind and brilliant, toward him, at least.

"So, you know me," Mitchell said. "The important little things. The things that make me *me*, yeah? What makes me laugh and all that."

Trevor turned his head as much as he could to look down at him. "I suppose so, yeah."

"There's something I have to tell you."

Mitchell looked up at him and Trevor could see in his eyes what he wasn't saying. *You know me, and I hope what I'm about to say doesn't change the way you think of me.* Trevor looked back at him, squeezing him and nodding earnestly.

"Guess that means it's been long enough for you to feel comfortable revealing another piece of the Mitchell puzzle, eh?"

Mitchell dropped his eyes. "Something like that."

"Is it about Essex?"

Mitchell's head snapped back up and he pulled away a bit. Trevor took his hand out of Mitchell's pocket and let there be a little more distance between them. The look in Mitchell's eyes was suddenly guarded.

"It's just, when I was talking to my father about you, and how our second date was interrupted, he found it interesting because he had friends who were also called to attend something there the same night," Trevor explained. "I've been wondering about it ever since, but considering how upset it made you, I didn't want to bring it up. And I figured if you felt it needed any more explanation, you'd tell me. Either way, the fact that you're somehow connected to my father was a little weird."

Mitchell's face pinched in thought and after a few seconds he sighed, rubbed his forehead. He walked back over to the champagne and truffles and had their chaperon refill the glass he'd borrowed from Trevor.

"Who's your father?" he asked after draining half of it in one gulp.

"He's just a solicitor, I told you. David Lewis."

Mitchell shook his head. "Nah, the name doesn't ring a bell. But I never give a shit enough to remember names if I don't think I'll meet the person again."

"He didn't know your name either." Mitchell chuckled at that. "So I don't think you've ever met him. When I described you to him though, he said he'd might've seen you in passing. Said a man like you is hard to forget or something."

"Christ," Mitchell murmured. "He didn't say anything else about... me?"

"No. He did tell me to be careful. He told me to be sure that my goals were the same as yours or something?" Trevor walked over to him, glancing at their silent observer. "Look, what is this about, Mitchell?"

Mitchell emptied his glass and held it out to be refilled. "The Essex thing was just, just a social event, like. I had to go entertain well-off cunts and didn't really want to. It's part of a whole different thing that I want to tell you later. If you take this first thing well."

"Alright. What's part two of three, then?"

Mitchell took another long drink. Trevor hoped it wasn't enough to make him too drunk to drive.

"We have to go back to my garage," he said, licking his lips as he looked down into the glass. "I'd rather show you."

Chapter 19

Revelations

Mitchell suggested they get something to eat first, and they stopped to have a quick curry. Trevor could tell that what he'd said about his father knowing him was weighing on his mind, and that he was doing his best not to think about it.

He wished Mitchell would stop being so tight-lipped, because there were no secrets on *his* side of the relationship. He had to trust that Mitchell was doing it for good reason, though; while it was obvious that Mitchell was hiding things, it was also obvious that he cared about him. It was because Mitchell cared so much that he worried his secrets would push him away. It was frustratingly understandable.

When they got to Advanced, Mitchell parked the Porsche in a space near the front. It was as if they hadn't taken it on an illegal joyride. Trevor followed Mitchell inside.

After putting the Porsche key on the rack, Mitchell led Trevor through the staff only door behind the counter. Trevor's pulse raced at being allowed back there, and he continued to follow Mitchell down a tiled corridor. It was dark with all the lights off, but he could make out four doors — two on the right, one on the left, and one at the far end, with a window looking into the empty garage. One of the doors on the right read STORAGE, the one further down, M. MORGAN. They passed both and went into the garage.

Mitchell flicked on one of the overhead lights and the first bay lit up. It was relatively clean, with a few tools here and there hastily pushed to the side to give the appearance of orderliness. Safety glasses and goggles were stored in a large yellow bin next to a bin full of dirty rags and another full of rusted car parts. Mitchell walked over to the bin containing the rusted metal.

"I asked you on our second date if you believed people have the potential to be psychic," he said. "You said you would if there was proof."

Trevor quirked an eyebrow, the only move he made for a moment, but then he nodded. Mitchell picked up the bin and carried it over to him, setting it down. There were old coils, bolts, gears, some pieces that Trevor didn't know the names of but that looked important. All of them were old and seemed like nothing more than junk metal, useless. He supposed they *could* be saved, but he wasn't learned enough in rust removal to know how.

"What if there's no solid proof because it's the psychics who are burying it? If those who could tell the future were always taking the required steps to keep discovery from happening?" He looked up at Trevor as though to gauge his reaction before going on. "Imagine what would happen if it was common knowledge, like, what some of them can do."

It wasn't too hard. "For one, the government would turn them into weapons."

"Exactly," Mitchell said. He picked up one of the rusted components, a medium-sized pipe. "So in actuality, it benefits them that people don't think they exist."

Trevor stared at Mitchell, saw his hands gripping the pipe as though to keep not just it steady, but himself. After a few seconds of no sound but that of their breathing, Mitchell put down the pipe and pulled off his jacket. It wasn't that warm. Was Mitchell sweating?

"You keep saying 'they,' but something tells me you mean 'we.' Am I right?" Trevor asked.

Mitchell clutched the pipe again. "I'm not mad," he pre-emptively insisted, finally looking Trevor in the eye. "I brought you here to give you proof."

He held out the pipe. The outside was worse than the inside, red-orange rust built up around the curved edge. Trevor didn't know what he was supposed to be seeing until slowly, from the left end of the pipe to the right, the rust began to disappear. He rubbed his eyes and squinted to make sure he wasn't imagining things.

It had to be real when Mitchell held it up, sparkling and shiny like it was new. He set it aside and picked up a small bolt, did the same thing. Then an old coil, repeated it with that. He went through half the bin, removing the rust one by one.

Eventually he upended the whole thing, scattering parts everywhere. Trevor jumped back, his heart stuttering at the abruptness and volume. Mitchell stood in front of the mess and held a hand out over it. From Trevor's right to left, the rust across everything on the floor disappeared, like an invisible, magic wave washing it away.

He didn't have any words.

"That's not all I can do," Mitchell said. Trevor raised his eyes from the newly shined metal to meet his. Mitchell held his gaze for a moment, then bent down to right the overturned bin.

Trevor gaped. As he watched, the metal pieces began levitating, bringing themselves back together in a neat group. They slowly lowered into the bin and settled.

Mitchell stood with his hands at his sides. Trevor replayed what he'd seen over and over again in his head, trying to make himself come to terms with it. He'd asked for proof—here was proof.

He swallowed and searched for words. "You can... control metal?"

Mitchell opened his mouth to speak, then just nodded.

"The slogan on the business card, 'the magic touch.' It's actually magic."

Mitchell tightened his mouth and rubbed the back of his neck. "Magic is more like fantasy, this is more, y'know, like, supernatural. I just needed something that would let people know I can do a little more than those other repair shops."

"Are there others? No, wait, you said there are. Oh my God, the support group!" Trevor slapped a hand to his forehead.

Mitchell cracked a smile. "Yeah. My mentor could see the future. She found me and taught me a lot. I was the only one in the group with ferrokinesis, but a lot of the mental techniques are the same as other things. Like pyrokinesis, for example."

"Wow."

It was a lot to take in, not just because he had to acknowledge the existence of psychics. Mitchell had been hiding this from him all the time, had so much more power and capability than Trevor could've possibly imagined. A poor kid from Liverpool with the ability to psychically manipulate metal.

"I know this changes things," Mitchell said, "but hopefully not too much?"

Trevor blinked, coming out of his reverie. "What? No. Of course it doesn't. You're still you, Mitchell. You're just even more amazing than I thought."

Mitchell's body visibly sagged with relief.

Trevor walked around the bin to Mitchell's side, slipping an arm around his waist and smiling. "No wonder Imogen said you were special."

Mitchell raised his hand to Trevor's face, staring into his eyes. "It's not too weird?"

"Nope. Weird, certainly. Too weird? It'll take a bit more than that to freak me out and make me run for the hills."

Mitchell smiled and kissed him. It was in the language of kissing that Trevor heard "thank you."

It would be a little while before Trevor got used to Mitchell's being psychic completely. Truthfully, he would probably always be a bit in awe. Like a rare gem or crystal, it was something one could get used to, but that didn't mean one ever lost the ability to admire its unique beauty.

With the Porsche left at Advanced, they'd taken the tube back to Mitchell's, where Mitchell showed him more of what he could do. He explained—or tried to explain—what it felt like for him, saying that like any of the normal five senses, his sixth sense was always on, he was always "feeling" the metal around him. He used what he felt to manipulate.

Trevor had never seen him so excited. A few times Mitchell had actually nervously apologised, explaining that he'd never really had anyone besides his mother and Imogen to talk about it with. He'd gotten flustered, kept running a hand through his hair, and talked almost nonstop to answer Trevor's questions as thoroughly as he could. Trevor had also never heard him talk so much, so freely.

What was probably the most interesting of all was that, the whole time, Mitchell had been playing with one of the metal trinkets that'd been sitting on his bookshelf, bending it and reshaping it like it was putty. When it got too hot to hold in his hand, slowly beginning to turn fiery red, he'd simply made it hover beside him and continued, making his hand dance like it was controlling a marionette.

It'd been a brilliant night, eventually ending with them sucking each other off in Mitchell's bed in a spectacularly coordinated sixty-nine. Trevor had woken up the next morning to the feeling of his dick being sucked *again*, and tasted come when Mitchell kissed him. Now he was back home, alternating between doing research for work and research on psychics.

As Mitchell had said, there wasn't much on people with psychic abilities, buried by the psychics themselves. Much of what Trevor came across were forums where people claimed to have powers, but as far as he could tell there was no substance to those claims. He did find a synonym for what Mitchell could do, metallokinesis. The term made more sense to him considering he'd seen Mitchell manipulate more than just iron, but further searching proved ferrokinesis to be more widely-used and commonly accepted.

After switching back to work research for ten minutes, he found a series of books by a Dr Vera Hunt, written throughout the 60's and 70's, called *Understanding Parapsychology*. Each book touched on a different topic, from telepathy to levitation, and even, as Trevor had thought, ferrokinesis. There were no written reviews on Amazon; zero, not a single one for any of the books in the series. Nor was there much of a biography about the author—besides a couple sentences—and not a word on the original publisher. It did, however, have a decent number of purchases and five-star ratings, which made Trevor wonder if it was legitimate. Handbooks for the inexperienced psychic.

He managed to find some excerpts from the volume in the series relevant to him, *Metal Manipulation and Ferrokinesis*. Mostly it reiterated what Mitchell had told him the night before, but it was good to see it in writing. Mitchell wasn't the most eloquent of speakers, through no fault of his own, and there'd been many times when he'd simply given up, saying he couldn't explain to someone who didn't have an extra sense. There weren't words. Dr Hunt was good at setting up elaborate metaphors that average people like Trevor could understand, while also referring to things that only a psychic would be able to comprehend or practise.

For example, Trevor knew what it was like to meditate, to close his eyes and shift his awareness to his toes. He knew how to identify things by touch alone, or by sound and smell. He also knew what it was like to have his senses overloaded, to be blinded by sudden light or have a taste on his tongue that was too spicy. Perhaps he couldn't feel exactly what she was describing, but he figured he could get damn close.

Like straining to hear a high-pitched ringing, narrow your focus to a single metal object, Hunt wrote. *This is most easily done when in direct contact with the metal in question. Try holding a small, insignificant piece of jewellery in your palm. Tap into its potential energy and feel it. You possess the power to take control – follow your intuition and take it. Make it bend to your will. Metal's energy is not sentient, does not have feelings. Use all the force you need, keeping in mind your end goal. In your hand is a sculpture, and you are the artist.*

"Hello?"

"Mr Lewis?"

"Speaking."

"My name is Mitchell Morgan. I'm dating your son, Trevor. We need to talk."

There was a beat of silence on the other end of the phone before David spoke again. "Trevor showed me a photo of you. You were smiling, so you looked a bit different, but I did recognise you. Kane's driver."

"You didn't tell Trevor."

"No."

"Why not?"

A sigh. "He's very taken with you. From what he's said, you're not all bad. I don't get the feeling you mean him any harm. Figured I'd stay out of it until then."

"You're not worried about what it means, him being with me?"

Mitchell asked.

"You mean him being with a cold-hearted killer as well as an underground street racer?"

"I'm not cold-hearted all the time. And that's not what I meant. You know how Kane operates. If someone's not entirely compliant, he doesn't always go after them."

"I know. Sometimes he goes after the ones we love. But Trevor's already been in that position for a while."

"You are a solicitor for Kane, then."

"I am. Have been for nearly ten years. I remember when he... acquired you."

Mitchell winced. "So we're both cooperative. That means Trevor should be fine."

"Seems that way. Do you plan on telling him?"

Mitchell frowned, chewing his lip. He wasn't often open with people he'd only just started speaking to, but he figured he owed it to this man, considering it was Trevor's father.

"He means quite a lot to me," he admitted. "I want to tell him everything, even if you haven't."

"Would you like me to give you a bit of insight?" David offered.

"Sure."

"Trevor is a man of principle when it comes to these sorts of things. With regards to morality, he thinks the way he feels he's supposed to. I'm guessing you know about his horror enthusiasm?"

"Yes."

"And his so-called artwork?"

"Yes."

"He's been that way since he was a kid. Fascinated with gore, loved to scare himself shitless just for fun. But if you ask him if he'd ever do it to someone else? He'd say, 'No, that's wrong.' Would be disgusted with himself if he ever did end up doing it. All his fantasies, his darkest desires — it's like they're buried in his subconscious, and he channels them into things deemed safe, like movies and art. On the surface: 'No, that's wrong.' He listens to his moral code because he knows that's what he's supposed to do."

"But you don't think he actually cares? If he killed someone, once he got past being disgusted with himself — "

"He might not. He has a tendency to shy away from things that upset him and doesn't like to think about them too hard. He'd probably try to put it behind him and not address it again. He'd shove it to the back of his mind where the rest of the darkness is."

Like with what Mitchell had told Trevor the previous night, this was certainly better than he'd ever thought to hope for. He'd seen Trevor as almost fragile before, was positive he wouldn't be able to handle Mitchell being a killer. With the horror films, and artwork, and of course the choking, his hopes had risen, albeit very little.

This new information from his father was promising. What if it was possible to have it all, to keep working for Kane *and* be with Trevor?

"Then there's two different outcomes," Mitchell said. "He shies away, leaving me altogether. Or he tries to forget it and pretends that part of my life doesn't exist."

"There is a third outcome... If he cares about you enough that his built-in moral code allows this to pass, and he comes to terms with it."

"Which is?"

"He'll want to watch."

Chapter 20
First Time for Everything

It wasn't like Mitchell wasn't acquainted with Trevor's arse. They'd been together for two and a half months now, so it was impossible not to be. He'd fingerfucked Trevor multiple times, Trevor's cock halfway down his throat. He'd stuck his tongue deep into his hole, eating him out while Trevor sat on his face and moaned. He knew all about Trevor's perfectly firm and perky backside.

He didn't know nearly as much about putting his dick into it.

He'd wanted to celebrate somehow, though. It was always good to have finished a job for Kane, and Adam had picked up the finished escape car the day before. Besides that, he'd felt it was time. He'd texted Trevor on the tube ride over and said he wanted to try something different in bed tonight. Trevor had texted back, saying, *About bloody time!*

Mitchell took a deep breath. They were in Trevor's bed and Trevor was on his knees, arse in the air, head pillowed on crossed arms. His hole was all lubed up, ready to take Mitchell in after it'd already taken two of his fingers. Mitchell had a feeling Trevor had stretched himself a little before he'd got there, because the rim had been unnaturally pliant.

"It'll be *fine*, Mitchell," Trevor said, pushing his arse back impatiently. "I want you to fuck me, even if it's only for thirty seconds."

"It's not that," Mitchell muttered. He shuffled forward on his knees, holding the base of his cock, and lined up with Trevor's hole. It was such a pretty thing, begging Mitchell to fill it, the same way Trevor was begging him to.

He knew there'd be a little resistance, that he'd have to apply a little force to get past the ring of muscle. But when he went even deeper, his jaw went slack.

Jesus *Christ*, that was good.

"Oh God, finally," Trevor moaned just as Mitchell bottomed out. He pushed himself up onto his hands and arched his spine, sighing in pleasure.

Mitchell placed his hands on Trevor's hips and started easing his way into a rhythm, every exhalation forcibly slowed and a bit unsteady as a result. It was more than good—it was perfect. Mitchell had never seen a sight more beautiful than his cock sliding back and forth into Trevor's arse, had never felt anything similar to pushing into such brilliance and being given the opportunity to do it again and again and *again*. Trevor seemed to feel the same way, because his hand reached back and gripped Mitchell's thigh hard, hard enough that Mitchell was sure to have crescents in his skin. He grunted every time Mitchell buried himself to the root.

This was the easy part. This, making himself feel good, Mitchell knew how to do. He pushed Trevor's knees a little further apart with his own and spread Trevor's arse with his thumbs, picking up speed. They found a pace that worked and Trevor pushed back, meeting him halfway on each thrust. He took Mitchell's cock like it was the greatest thing in the world and let go of Mitchell's thigh to lean on his elbows, moaning shamelessly as Mitchell started fucking him faster.

"Mitchell," Trevor said between gasps of breath.

A knot formed in Mitchell's stomach. Was it not as good for him? Did Mitchell just *think* those were sounds of pleasure Trevor was making? "Yeah?"

"H-Harder."

Mitchell laughed in relief. "No problem."

They shifted so that Trevor could lie flat, so that Mitchell could have more control over his thrusts and fuck Trevor into the mattress. He started snapping his hips forward as hard as he could, hard enough for the smack to pierce through the sound of their heavy breathing.

"Yeah, that's—oh, oh *fuck*—yeah, that's good, faster, fucking faster."

Mitchell picked up speed. He thrust his hips in hard, quick motions, breathlessly fucking Trevor as hard and fast as he was able. He couldn't stop, couldn't hold himself back now even if he wanted to because it just felt so damn *good*. He didn't realise he'd put a heavy palm to the centre of Trevor's back, pinning him down, until the palm of his hand got sweaty.

Out of breath, he slowed down. He put his elbows on either side of Trevor's shoulders and dropped his head to the back of Trevor's neck, huffing between his shoulder blades. He was still sliding his cock into Trevor, the feeling too good to stop, but it was lazy. He rolled his hips forward at the end of each easy thrust, a jolt of pleasure making his thighs tense when Trevor clenched.

"God, Mitchell, we should've done this earlier," Trevor said, his voice a little higher than usual. "Let me flip over, yeah?"

Mitchell let his cock slip out and moved back to give Trevor space to turn over. He'd never seen Trevor on his back, legs spread and arse open like he was now. He knee-walked into the space between Trevor's thighs and pushed the head of his dick back inside, exhaling unsteadily again when Trevor lifted his hips to better take him in.

Mitchell shuffled forward a little more, bent his knees to accommodate his thighs under Trevor's. It was a different angle, and when he started fucking again, Trevor's body rocked back and forth on the bed.

Trevor, propped up on his elbows and looking more like a porn star than Mitchell had ever seen him, let his head fall back as he moaned. Mitchell thought he was starting to get the hang of things. He snapped his hips forward, slamming in, and made Trevor cry out.

He did it again, forced his cock in as hard and abrupt as he could, and adrenaline pulsed through his veins. Soon enough he was pumping in and out of Trevor's tight arse, hands gripping Trevor's thighs.

He loved the dazed, almost blissed-out look on Trevor face. Trevor had taken the weight off his elbows to lie flat on his back, and now seemed to be simply enjoying the constant pleasure of Mitchell fucking him. Every so often he'd tilt his hips down a bit and Mitchell would hit his prostate, eliciting a sharp gasp and twist of fingers in the sheets. It was when Trevor moved a hand to his cock and started quickly stroking that he figured him to be close.

Mitchell managed to hold off his own orgasm, walking the line by changing up the speed. As soon as Trevor came, milky white spunk spurting onto his stomach, Mitchell picked up the pace one last time, chasing release.

Trevor had said he could come inside beforehand, when he'd been stretching him with a finger. The thought of filling Trevor with his come was what made him break now.

He panted a few seconds afterwards, catching his breath. "Wow," he said. He carefully pulled his cock out, felt it twitch and pulse one last time at the sight of Trevor's fucked, come-stained hole.

He'd done that. The wrecked, sated state of Trevor's body was *his* cock's doing.

"Yeah," Trevor said wistfully. "My thoughts exactly. Fancy doing it again?"

Mitchell smiled, sat back on his heels and caressed Trevor's calves. "I definitely don't mind it, and I admit I like seeing you this way. But I'm still very much a bottom, that hasn't changed. Just let me know when you're craving a cock up your arse and we'll set an appointment, yeah?"

Trevor guffawed. "Sure thing."

It was almost laughable, which was why Mitchell didn't say anything aloud, but he felt he'd gotten closer to Trevor after fucking him. He'd taken a big step, not just for their relationship, but for himself. Being on the giving end of things was a different dynamic, and he was beyond glad that it clearly worked well for them just as much as any other.

Not telling Trevor the truth about his business with Kane had stopped being a nagging worry in the back of his mind. He didn't feel so bad about keeping that part hidden these days, not when he had a sort-of ally in Trevor's father. They were happy, had a good thing together, and bringing up his third and final secret would just put a major damper on things. Surely it wouldn't be so bad to simply enjoy the way things were now.

It'd been a fucking brilliant two and a half months. Trevor's friend Kay, who apparently worked as a barman at a club Kane owned called Felicity, had been interesting to meet. Mitchell had had to explain the reason why he'd been let in free of charge, casually brushing it off by saying he had friends there too, to which Trevor had raised an eyebrow but said no more. Then he'd led Mitchell to where Kay was serving neon-coloured drinks. Mitchell hadn't said much, mostly because nobody would be able to hear him in such a loud place anyway, but Kay was talkative enough for all three of them.

Trevor had met Lydia when Mitchell nervously suggested a double date to Imogen. They'd picked a relatively warm Saturday and walked the streets with no real destination in mind, ended up at a Starbucks because it was warm but still too fucking cold for strolling. Trevor and Lydia had got on right from the start.

Besides working on the escape car, Mitchell's life had taken on a sort of normalcy during the past four weeks. He should've known it couldn't last for long. He didn't have that kind of luck.

It was a phone ringing that woke Trevor in the middle of the night. He was jerked out of sleep, and groaned into his pillow. It wasn't a ringtone his mobile made, so it could only be Mitchell's. "Mitchell."

Mitchell was a deep sleeper, but after a few seconds of grumbling and shifting, he abruptly sat upright and jumped out of bed. Trevor was too glad for the sound to stop.

"Hello?" Mitchell whispered.

Trevor sighed and turned over. Now that he was awake, he found he wasn't comfortable, had to find a better position. Great.

There was the quiet buzz of a voice speaking on the other end of Mitchell's call, and the rustling of clothes on the other side of the bed. Trevor frowned in his half-waking state. Was Mitchell getting dressed and leaving?

He lifted his eyes enough to see, and caught Mitchell walking out of the room with his things in his arms, his mobile pressed to his ear.

"No, I'm not at home. What the fuck, this is way too soon..." His voice trailed off as he walked out of earshot.

It was too interesting for Trevor not to eavesdrop. He'd waited for weeks for Mitchell to tell him his last secret, and nothing. Here was finally a chance to get an idea of what it could be.

He sighed, mourning the loss of sleep, but made himself get up.

He tiptoed out of the bedroom and walked just far enough to hear what Mitchell was saying. He didn't see him getting dressed, but he could hear the slide of fabric over skin, the teeth of a zip.

"This wasn't the fucking agreement, Nathan."

Nathan? Who the fuck was Nathan?

"No, I know that." Trevor heard the sofa cushions depress under Mitchell's weight, then a sigh. "What kind of job is it?... The one Adam picked up yesterday?... And I'll just be driving?... Have I worked with this woman before?"

Trevor swallowed. He was starting to sweat, and couldn't help thinking of what Kay had said months ago.

Once a criminal, always a criminal.

What the fuck was Mitchell doing?

"Who's the mission?" Mitchell asked. "You've gotta be fucking kidding me... No, it doesn't matter, but fuck, isn't that a bit ambitious, even for Kane?"

Nathan, Adam, Kane. Trevor wished he had a pen and paper so he could write them down. He'd have to wait until Mitchell left and hope his tired brain could remember it in the meantime.

"Guess that explains why it has to be me... No, I'll, I'll text you a location in ten minutes and he can pick me up there. As long as you're sure the police won't be a problem, even with something like this... Okay."

Trevor squeezed his eyes shut. He couldn't believe what he was hearing. He wanted to rush out into the living room and pull Mitchell back into bed, tell him not to go. Trevor's first thought was that it was an assassination, and a high-profile one at that. It was making his stomach turn.

"Wait. Just between us, I was wondering if there was any way to make another deal. I don't wanna go straight to him, he might not take it well. But you know him... Not that kind of deal. I mean I want out, for real this time. Once he gets this man of his in Parliament, he'll be really set, yeah? He won't need me."

Parliament? Trevor's head was reeling. Mitchell was *not* about to help someone assassinate a Member of Parliament, was he? Was he actually insane?

He had to figure out who Kane was, since he seemed to be the man in charge. Someone who could organise murders and have multiple people on his payroll. The police? Apparently so, which would explain Mitchell's laughing it off when they rode in the borrowed Porsche. Who else? Trevor would have to do some snooping around, but carefully.

"I understand that. No deal then. But listen. Kane's working to make everything legitimate. If I can see that, I know you can see it. Once he has Parliament in his pocket, he'll be so busy with his legitimate business, *you'll* be the one left to run things behind the scenes, stuck with the rubbish. The dirty drug dealers, the naive street racers. You'll be just as fucked over as the rest of us. But if we, if someone kills him, like, we can all be set up for life."

Trevor's jaw dropped.

"No! Nathan, no, it was just a suggestion. Not even a suggestion. I was sleeping just now so I'm still not thinking clearly. I was just throwing ideas out there, but I wouldn't ever, y'know, like, plot against him. That's just, just mad. Don't say anything, yeah? Nathan. Nathan, come on."

Trevor knew what Mitchell's fear sounded like. He knew what it sounded like when Mitchell was trying to play it off, too. He didn't want to think about what would happen if whoever Kane was got wind of Mitchell planning to kill him. He hadn't known about the man for five minutes and he knew it would be more than just bad. A man who could have an MP assassinated could do anything.

"Yeah. Ten minutes. Bye."

Trevor darted as silently as he could back to the bedroom, sliding into bed and closing his eyes. He didn't know if Mitchell would come back in, but he didn't want to be caught standing around the corner when he got up to leave.

His heart was still racing when he heard Mitchell's soft footsteps enter the room. He hoped his breathing came off even and steady.

"Trevor? You awake?" Mitchell whispered.

Trevor said nothing, didn't make a single noise or shift in position. He kept his eyes closed, glad he'd faced himself away from the door.

He nearly flinched when he felt Mitchell's hand touch his hair, sinking deep into his curls, but managed to stay still. Mitchell sighed, the drawn out exhalation sounding more like a tortured, weary soul than Trevor had ever heard it before. It stabbed at his heart and he wished more than ever that Mitchell would get back in the bed so he could put his arms around him and keep him from going out.

After ten whole seconds of Mitchell petting him, Trevor couldn't take it anymore. He feigned a sleepy groan and rolled over just enough to furrow his brow up at him.

Mitchell gave him a sad smile and knelt beside the bed. "Sorry, didn't mean to wake you. I have to go."

Trevor yawned, a genuine one that'd sneaked up on him. "Where? What time is it?"

"Almost one in the morning. Go back to sleep."

"Is everything okay?"

Mitchell's hand returned, stroking his hair again. He leaned forward and kissed him. Trevor tried not to feel the goodbye in it.

"If I tell you something, will you promise not to freak out?" Mitchell asked.

Trevor's stomach twisted. "Okay."

"I think I..." Mitchell shook his head and looked down, laughing. "I think I love you."

Trevor stared at him, eyes wide. He certainly hadn't been expecting that.

"You don't have to say it back or anything," Mitchell said quickly. "I'm just a divvy who falls in love easily. But I wanted you to know, in case... Because I'm feeling particularly brave at the moment, I guess."

That's not what you were going to say.

Trevor grabbed Mitchell's hand when he stood up to leave. "Wait. Come back tomorrow, okay?"

Mitchell bit his lip, but finally nodded. "Okay."

Trevor dropped his hand. He didn't say goodbye.

Chapter 21

The Driver

Mitchell had based the body of the latest escape car on the 2013 BMW M3, not too flashy but obviously elite. Like most orders, Kane had given him about a month's notice before he needed it, and therefore a month to get it done. Being a busy man himself, it was at least thoughtful of him to take into account Mitchell's other clients.

It was only an M3 in exterior design—the rest was all Mitchell. Bullet-proof glass. Carbon-fibre body, chassis, and interior. V8 engine, reaching sixty miles per hour in two point seven seconds, with a max speed of two-eleven. Brake disks optimised for better braking. Dual mufflers, LED lights, a sleek black paint job.

Every car Mitchell built had a piece of him in it, but he'd learnt not to get too attached early on. If it wasn't customised for certain purposes—like the torture ride job—it got destroyed. Transported from Kane's garage to a junkyard where it was crushed into a heap of metal that even Mitchell wouldn't be able to salvage.

When Adam had picked up the black escape car the day before, Mitchell had no idea he'd be driving it. The details of the order had been like that of any other escape job: fast, discreet colour, quiet, and in this case, only two seats necessary.

Kane had to have known at the time of his order what it would be used for. The assassination of an MP was something one generally took a while to plan. He had to have known he would need his best driver for the job, that there could be absolutely no chance of fucking up.

In Mitchell's opinion, it was too fucking soon. He was only supposed to be called five or fewer times a year. This was the third, and it was only the twenty-third of May. He hoped Kane wouldn't try to pull something later in the year.

He also hoped that there would *be* a later in the year for him. What had he been thinking, suggesting to Nathan that someone kill Kane?

Right. After hearing how Kane was going to have someone in the government, a sort of sleeper agent he'd apparently been prepping for years, he'd been thinking that this was his chance, his opportunity to get out. How long did the man plan on keeping him as a show pony and on-call mechanic anyway?

But he'd acted too hastily, didn't stop to think things through because the idea had come to him suddenly and at the prospect of a way out, he'd been desperate. Trevor was fucking with him, making him lose his edge and composure.

He really fucking hoped Nathan didn't say anything to Kane. He knew it was a long shot, which was why, sitting in the escape car two blocks from the MP's hotel and waiting for his unnamed partner to finish the job, he couldn't stop sweating. Nathan was Kane's closest man, his personal assistant, practically his best friend. The last time Mitchell had fucked up this badly was when he'd tried to get out the first time.

"Fuck, fuck, fuck," he muttered, hitting his head against the window.

He forced his thoughts back to the job at hand. With something like this, he couldn't afford not to be alert. There'd be men guarding their target, Daniel Williams, for sure, but the unnamed assassin had said it wouldn't be a problem. "You just handle the driving, sweetheart," she'd said, which was just fine with Mitchell considering where his head was.

She'd been one of the fiercer women Mitchell had encountered in his time working under Kane. With shoulder-length light brown hair and hazel eyes, she struck Mitchell as someone who could be your best friend or worst enemy, with no in between. Even without the inclination to find her attractive, Mitchell had thought she'd looked sexy. A long, grey leather jacket with the sleeves rolled up, a white Oxford shirt unbuttoned enough to hint at a lacy black bra. Black shorts that looked more like knickers and thigh-high stockings to show off gorgeous, slender legs. Dressed like that, Mitchell didn't have to wonder how she planned to get past any security she ran into. Provided they weren't as gay as him.

It was close to two in the morning, almost fifteen minutes since the woman had left for the hotel. Mitchell tried to take into account the time it took to walk two blocks, take the lift up to the room, and charm her way in. No sane man would turn down a surprise like that, no matter what time of night it was. Then it was simply a matter of taking him out quietly, probably slitting his throat. She could walk out looking a bit ruffled, and it'd be a few minutes, maybe even hours until the body was discovered. If they were lucky, there wouldn't be a police chase at all.

Just as Mitchell checked the time again, the passenger door opened and the woman got in, all lean limbs and graceful movements. It'd been exactly half an hour since she'd left.

"Drive."

Mitchell's pulse quickened as he released the brake and pulled off, shifting gears as he picked up speed. There were no sirens so far, but he didn't want to stick around for them.

Two o'clock on a Friday night meant plenty of opportunities to blend in if used correctly. Driving through the less crowded back streets of the suburbs, houses on each side, Mitchell felt out the area with his senses before turning anywhere. He kept off the more major roads—and their cameras—as much as possible.

Beside him, the woman reached up to pull down the passenger vanity mirror and took off her wig. She went from medium length light brown to long, black, and curly. She wiped off deep red lipstick and put on deep purple, as easily as if Mitchell wasn't weaving through traffic. Using an eyeliner pencil, she gave herself a beauty mark on her left cheekbone.

Once Mitchell got deeper into the city, closer to the Thames, it wasn't five minutes before trouble came. Mitchell was nearing Westminster Bridge, the one difficulty he'd expected from the job, when he heard the sirens. To make matters worse, he was certain he heard the chop of helicopter blades in the distance.

Mitchell tightened his hold on the wheel. Cars he could deal with; they were on the ground, easy to spot, easy to lose. Helicopters were a whole different story. The only way he'd be able to lose it would be to slip into some dark alley or quiet suburban area, or mentally control it himself.

He slowed and turned down a narrow street. Shadowy figures were standing around in a group not too far ahead, but jumped quickly to the side at Mitchell's approach. Considering the area, Mitchell thought maybe he'd interrupted a drug deal of some sort. Either way, they scattered like pigeons after Mitchell passed.

There was no way the police knew which car they were after, not when Mitchell had been waiting two blocks away. The body must've been found, and they knew the woman was the murderer, but as far as anyone knew, she'd simply disappeared. Not nearly enough time had passed for the police to go over camera footage and follow her to him, especially if Kane's men had any say in it, slowing the process.

It was a first response team, not a chase, and wouldn't be if Mitchell could help it. He just had to blend in for the rest of the drive, drop her off at the assigned destination, then drive the car back to Kane's office where it'd be transported to the junkyard the next day. MI5 would most certainly be involved soon, but Nathan had assured Mitchell that Kane had one or two contacts even there. It'd be a hurricane of activity for a few days, probably a few weeks, but eventually it'd be taken care of as quietly as possible.

Everyone had a price, or something they held dear. It was practically Kane's specialty, backing people into a corner to get what he wanted.

Mitchell killed the interior and exterior lights, got off Waterloo Road, then took a winding route to Westminster Bridge, flickering views of the London Eye on his right until finally it was in his rearview mirror. Up until then, the helicopter had been just a noise, nothing but a nuisance and a reminder, like the ticking of a clock. As he came to the bridge, he saw it there in the sky, and it set his heart racing, his blood pumping.

Blend in, blend fuckin' in. He turned the lights back on and adjusted his speed to go with the flow of traffic. There wasn't much.

The woman put up the vanity mirror and leaned over to look out the window up at the aircraft hovering above. "That won't be a problem, will it?" she asked.

"It shouldn't be. They don't know what the car looks like. Probably standing by for when they do. We're just another car crossing the bridge at the moment."

Victoria Embankment was just about dead at this hour, with only the one camera at the corner of Northumberland Avenue. With the Thames and the London Eye on his right again, it was a straight shot to the next bridge—the same set of bridges he'd walked across with Trevor, he recalled with a thump of his heart—a squealing turn down Northumberland Avenue, and into the thick of the city, the tricky bit that he'd been dreading.

Piccadilly Circus had been the decided drop-off point, as it was crowded enough even this time of night. Mitchell pulled up to the kerb and unlocked the doors.

"Thanks for the ride, luv." The woman left as smoothly as she'd got in, slamming the door behind her and disappearing into the mass of drunken patrons spilling out onto the street. There was another car waiting a few streets away to take her a secure location, but that had nothing to do with Mitchell. His part of the job was almost done.

He turned toward Coventry Street and drove as innocently as he could. He was wary of people crossing, but for the most part, traffic was moving quickly enough that it was a steady flow. He felt his pulse returning to normal, but didn't fool himself into thinking he was in the clear yet.

He was relieved when he finally saw Kane's building come into view. He checked all his mirrors, checked the sky, but all the activity was still south of the bridge from where he'd come. He turned into the underground garage entrance beneath Kane's offices and slowed to a stop in front of the security window.

The guard didn't even ask for his ID. He took one look at Mitchell's face, at the car he was driving, and raised the gate with a nod. Mitchell drove in.

The furthest row of spaces was reserved for escape cars like this one. There was a back entrance where they could be loaded into a lorry for transport. Mitchell parked there and left the key on top of the front right tyre.

He was so fucking exhausted. He trudged to the lift, pressing the button for the ground floor when he got in. It was too late, he was too tired, and he wanted his fucking bed. He wanted *Trevor's* fucking bed.

Mostly he wanted this night to end.

He walked out into the lobby and was about to pull out his mobile and let Nathan know the job was done when he saw Nathan leaning against the receptionist counter, his arms crossed. Mitchell felt all the worries he'd pushed to the back of his mind come rushing back full force. Nathan greeted him with a toothy smile, his ebony skin gleaming under the lights.

"You look like shit," Nathan said.

"Fuck off."

"Chipper as ever, I see. Kane wants to talk to you."

Mitchell's heart stopped. He leaned in, lowered his voice. "Did you tell him? Nathan, I told you, I was just—"

"He wants to talk to you. Follow me."

Mitchell tried to stay calm, outwardly at least. Following Nathan back to the lift, all his instincts were telling him to run. The ding signalling the lift's arrival sounded like a death knell, and stepping on was like stepping past the point of no return.

He was glad he'd told Trevor he loved him before he left.

Chapter 22

Briefing Room

It was some fucking building that Kane had set up for himself. Not as tall as the skyscrapers that had just gone up in the City, but not a squat, poor sort of structure either. He'd been here since before Mitchell had got involved with him, but if Mitchell had his way, the bastard wouldn't be here much longer.

Unfortunately, that was probably why Mitchell was still here now.

The doors were made of glass, the floors were a sparkling white marble, and it had all the cutting edge technology that came with having loads of money to blow on such things. It was all a front, though. Behind the cheery, ever-present receptionist, there were men in suits walking around even this late at night. Despite the elegant music in the lift, there were pistols in hidden pockets, cameras watching the comings and goings, and locked doors that led to rooms Mitchell didn't ever want to be in again.

In the lift, Nathan dialled a number into his mobile and said, "We're on our way up."

Mitchell could hear the voice on the other end, raspy as it travelled through the sound waves of the phone. "Bring him to Briefing Room Three."

Mitchell's pulse skyrocketed and he was filled with dread. *Not the briefing room, not the fuckin' briefing room, for fuck's sake, Trevor Trevor Trevor Trevor –*

"Come on."

Mitchell was pulled from the lift, the long corridor ahead seeming to look narrower with each step forward. He could get out of this.

182

He could feel with his metal senses that Nathan had a gun; he could destroy it, force open the lift doors, and make a run for it.

Then where would he be? With a dead mother, probably, a dead boyfriend, too. Not to mention a wasted car shop, running the rest of his life, and sleeping with one eye open. He could forget about being happy again, that was for fucking sure.

There was no way to undo this fuck-up.

From the outside, the Briefing Rooms were just ordinary locked doors, doors that could've led to supply closets for all the general public knew. Mitchell knew better. He'd never been in one himself, but he'd seen what had happened to someone who had. Or rather, he'd seen what was left. Seven of these rooms, seven glorified torture chambers, and now Mitchell was being led down the hall to one of them.

Might not evun be that bad, Mitchell told himself. *You've takun a beating from these lads before, loadsa times as a kid, a few times in prison. It's jost a few punches, maybe a kick in the ribs. You'll be sore as 'ell, but you'll survive.*

Mitchell swallowed as they passed the first two rooms. It was worse that the corridor was carpeted, that the place even had the audacity to have Monet paintings on the walls, potted plants in the fucking corners. Here he was about to have his face bashed in, and it couldn't even be in a fucking rank place like some dark alley.

He nearly bolted when the heavy grey door swung open and Nathan walked calmly in. The inside was grey too, like a regular interrogation room, with a hanging light throwing shadows across the walls. With the fluorescents shining directly down onto his skin, Nathan looked like an actual demon, his dark skin as smooth as black marble, his eyes gleaming hungrily. Mitchell tried not to think of how the deep red of his leather jacket would easily disguise any bloodstains.

The door slammed shut behind him, and just like that he was alone with the beast, trapped in the soundproof, concrete walls of a cell.

"So where is he?" Mitchell asked.

A heavy fist to the side of his face knocked the wind out of him. Everything went black, his head spun, and he heard nothing but the sound of blood pulsing in his throbbing head. He blinked a few times to clear his vision, and after a few seconds it was just blurry enough that he could see the meaty fist coming at him again.

It hurt more the second time, and he was pretty sure he heard something crack. The pain in his teeth meant it was probably his jaw, and when he tried stupidly to move it, he figured that was it.

The third blow hit him in the stomach, so hard that he thought he would pass out or throw up or both. He groaned and tried not to fall to his knees, knowing from experience that would just leave him open for a knee to the face. It seemed not to matter, as the next hit was a punch square in his left eye.

The blows stopped just long enough for his body to start throbbing proper, and he finally got a look at his attacker.

"Keep it comin' then, Harry, you fat fuck," he spat at the thick bastard. It was then that he realised his nose was bleeding.

"No broken limbs," Nathan's throaty voice intoned. Mitchell was glad at least for that, though just because none of his bones were broken didn't mean he wouldn't be aching for weeks.

He didn't even try to dodge — there was no way out of it anyway. That wasn't to say he didn't try to soften the blows a bit by turning away, clenching his stomach, and stiffening his muscles. Harry was huge, a sledgehammer pounding him again and again, but to keep the people he loved safe, to keep his garage? It was no contest what Mitchell would rather go through. He could recover from physical pain.

Better me than Trevor. Than Mam.

The hate and rage kept him standing a good while, too. It wasn't until clammy fingers grabbed a hold of his hair and slammed his head against the wall that Mitchell was dizzy enough to finally collapse. He couldn't tell which way was up, and when he stretched his arms out to get his bearings, it only gave Harry an opportunity to push him down to the floor.

There was so much blood, Mitchell thought he was going to choke and die. He couldn't breathe, couldn't open his eyes past slits. He felt a swirling concoction of sensations, boiling inside with anger, making him feel heavy and explosive, but light-headed and far-away, blind and aching with pain, making him feel like he could float right off his back.

"Get the fuck up, you worthless piece of shit."

Mitchell hadn't heard Kane come in, too dazed from the beating to be fully aware, but that was Kane's voice. He rolled over onto his stomach and weakly pushed himself up.

"HURRY THE FUCK UP!"

The volume made Mitchell's head pound. He groaned, though that didn't much help. When he was finally on his feet, his head was yanked back by the roots of his hair, forcing his eyes up. He could only barely make out Kane's form through the slits of his eyes.

There was only one time when Mitchell had hated Kane as much as he did now, and that was the last time he'd been beaten, in this very same office building. That time hadn't been in a Briefing Room, but it'd been just as bad.

He wanted to split Kane's fucking head open. He wanted to stomp on his smug face until the bones of his skull crunched beneath his foot. He wanted the man on his knees crying in pain and agony, wanted to burn him alive, drown him in the Thames, drop him from a skyscraper. He wanted to do anything but fucking stand here having to look at him with blood on his face.

One of Kane's clawed hands reached out and grabbed the front of his shirt, yanking him closer. Mitchell was too tired to be scared by this point, too beat for his heart to even palpitate nervously. He stumbled forward and only just managed not to fall into the man.

"You think you're fucking indispensable, is that it?" Kane growled. His breath reeked, and Mitchell was close enough to make out what looked like every individual strand of coarse hair in the man's black moustache. "You think some kid from the Liverpool slums with a knack for driving can't be fucking replaced?"

The light-headed dizziness from before was gone. It was all heaviness now, all lead limbs and pent up rage. Everything went to Mitchell's head, fuelling his anger — the smell of Kane's breath, the throbbing of his head, his own pathetic wheezing. He was trembling with the effort not to bring the entire fucking building down around them all, to bend the steel frame inward and collapse the whole fucking structure. Kane didn't have a fucking clue who he was, what he could do. All he saw was some low-life just like everybody else, some "kid with a knack for driving."

'E'll get 'is one dee, 'e'll fuckin' get 'is.

"You don't tell me when you're fucking done," Kane said.

He was almost yelling now, the veins in his neck bulging, and for a moment Mitchell did feel a trace of fear. He'd known blokes like Kane growing up, blokes who were just downright mental for no fucking reason, liked taking the piss out of old geezers and mugging defenceless women. When Kane started yelling, it was fucking serious.

Kane let him go and Mitchell nearly fell again, forced to hold up his own weight. He wasn't upright for long either way. Kane pushed him down, the table suddenly rushing up to meet his face. He squeezed his eyes shut as his head banged the surface, and his ears started ringing as colours danced behind his eyelids.

If there was ever a reason ter cut me fuckin' herr, this is it, Mitchell thought bitterly. It was too easy for people to grab hold and jerk him around.

He snapped his eyes open when he felt hands roughly undoing his jeans. *No, no, no.* He started to raise back up but Nathan sprang into action, pinning his shoulders down. His jeans fell to his ankles a second later, followed by his pants.

This wasn't happening. It couldn't be happening.

"How stupid can you be?" Kane sneered, pushing up Mitchell's shirt and jacket. Mitchell tried to get free again, only to feel a blade on the back of his neck. He froze. "Nathan? You talk to *Nathan* about trying to kill me?" There was the sound of a zip, then Kane dropping his trousers.

Mitchell's breath was coming faster, not at all helped by the pain in his ribs. He'd never had a problem with being naked in front of others, or at least never thought he did. Now he felt more exposed than he ever had in his life, stripped and vulnerable with his arse bared.

"Kane, listen, I, I didn't mean it. Please, I—"

"Look at that. He's begging," Kane said. "Bet I can make you cry, too. I missed it the first time."

Mitchell closed his eyes again, willing tears away. He could feel the head of Kane's dick nudging into the cleft of his arse, searching out his hole.

No, not searching. Playing. Teasing. Enjoying.

"You belong to me, understand?" A callused hand turned into a claw and spread his cheeks further apart. "You don't stop being mine until I get bored of you and feel like giving you up. I was lenient when you acted out before. Now I see someone like you needs a firmer hand." He slapped Mitchell's arse so hard it stung, the sound ringing out in the room.

"Get on the floor, and don't even think about fucking resisting. Keep in mind you're outnumbered, son."

Nathan eased up enough to let Mitchell slide off the table, slowly lowering his knees to the floor. He was roughly pulled backward, slid through a spattering of his own blood and got his knees scraped in the process. Still, he didn't cry out. He refused.

"That's better. Now turn toward good old Harry. There you go."

Kane got behind him, and Mitchell kept his head down, tried to take his mind out of the situation, out of his aching body. A black hole had formed in his chest, sucking all the good out of his life. He felt more than hopeless, more than alone. He wouldn't even call it despair. Even the hate and rage was sapped out of him. Now he just wanted to die.

"I'll show you who you belong to, and this time you won't forget," Kane said, slapping his dick on Mitchell's arse. "I'm gonna fuck you so hard you won't ever be able get the feeling of my cock out of you."

Mitchell closed his eyes again, hunched his shoulders. He would not cry, he would not cry —

"AHH!"

"Ah, fuck, yes, that's nice. There we go."

Searing pain made him feel like he was being fucked with a knife. How big was Kane's cock? He hadn't seen. It pushed relentlessly in, and struggling to get away only made him clutch Mitchell's hips and force it in faster. Mitchell whimpered, unable to hold it back.

It was a different sort of pain. The throbbing of his head, his jaw, the aching in his ribs — those were an entirely different nature. This was more extreme, more invasive and internal. Worst of all, it was a place where Kane wasn't supposed to be. It was a place meant only for Trevor.

Kane sped up, his grunts punctuated with the slap of flesh. His coarse thighs against Mitchell's. Eventually the constant pain became a bit bearable.

Tears started falling from Mitchell's eyes, though. He felt like a fourteen-year-old boy again, weak, useless, defeated. He tried to tell himself again that it was better him than someone he loved.

"Ah—ah—ah."

Kane slowed, traded speed for force. He snapped his hips and fucked Mitchell hard, slamming in deep. His hands pulled Mitchell back into it, made Mitchell feel dirty, more like a whore than he'd felt in years.

It got worse.

"I'll—*mmm*—show you who you fucking belong to," Kane repeated. "Show you I can do whatever the fuck I like with you. You don't fucking try to turn my best mate on me. You see, we do everything together." Mitchell's head was yanked back by the roots of his hair again. "Now open wide."

In front of him, Nathan was looming, taking a large cock out of his pants. Mitchell's jaw ached just as the prospect of opening that wide.

"I'm not getting down on that filthy floor," Nathan said. "Raise the fuck up." He pushed Mitchell's shoulders back, forcing him upright.

Kane's dick slammed into him from behind again, making him cry out and pitching him sharply forward. For lack of anything else to grab onto to regain his balance, he ended up with his hands on Nathan's hips.

There was no pause between then and Nathan shoving his cock into Mitchell's mouth. The pain was just as bad as Mitchell had expected, forcing fat droplets of tears to roll down his cheeks.

"I like you better with your mouth full of my cock."

The taste of Nathan's dick was tangy and bitter on his tongue, both precome and girth making him gag. As Kane picked up speed again, fucking him like he was trying to finish a race, drool dripped from his lips, running down his chin and mixing with his tears on the floor.

He forced his eyes shut again, tried not to feel the way his body was being used, tried not to hear the moans as both his holes were mercilessly fucked. Gripping Nathan's thrusting hips as Kane's hands possessively ran up his chest and back, he thought his life was a cruel joke, thought it was almost like this was what he was made for. Raised a whore, by a whore—there was no getting away from who he was meant to be, no matter how much money he made. Was Harry going to get off beside them, come on him while these two had their fun? Or was he going to get a turn after Nathan was done?

Nathan came first, holding Mitchell's head in place to empty his load down his throat. It was thick, stuck to the roof of his mouth. As soon as Nathan pulled out and stepped away, Mitchell fell forward onto his hands and spat, wiping come from his lips. The taste was still there, wouldn't go away for a while.

Kane finished a few seconds after Mitchell bent over, digging his fingernails into Mitchell's skin. Pulling out abruptly and making Mitchell gasp in pain, he slapped Mitchell's arse again. Come dripped down Mitchell's balls and the inside of his thighs—Kane's come, hot and claiming him from the inside out, impossible to get away from.

He was too weak to do more than collapse. More than that, trembling on the bloody floor, he didn't *want* to move. He felt small and violated, out of his body, out of his mind. When he started to smell urine, felt the warm, wet sensation of someone pissing on him, he hardly registered it.

"Well, I think we've made progress tonight, boys. Definitely an educational experience," Kane said after a minute. A shoe prodded Mitchell's aching side, making the pain in his ribs flare up and eliciting a pitiful whimper. "Give the cunt his money and get him out of my sight."

Chapter 23

Results

There was no way Trevor was getting back to sleep. His body was tired, his eyes were tired, but too many thoughts were running through his head, keeping him from settling down. How could he rest when Mitchell was out being an accomplice to a fucking government assassination? The whole thing was bloody mental!

Before he started asking himself the most obvious question of all — Was it even worth it, dating someone who brought with him so many problems? — he had to have more information. Whoever this powerful, almighty Kane was, it was clear Mitchell didn't want to be associated with him anymore. It was clear he was he trapped and scared.

Trevor *could* end the whole thing now, get himself out of whatever mess he'd blindly run into, but how could he do that to Mitchell? The man had just professed his love! He didn't know much, but he knew Mitchell didn't deserve that. He had to at least see if there was something he could do before he gave up.

A simple name wasn't much to go on, but he put it into the search engine anyway, hoping the uniqueness would help narrow things down. He didn't even know if it was a first or last name. He also wasn't sure how it was spelt. He typed in "Cain" at first, which pulled up predictably biblical results. Then "Kane," which loaded a few more promising things, but nothing relevant. "Kane England" seemed to be a winner.

Alfred Kane, white, fifty-six years old. Most well-known for owning the cyber security company Kanine, which was how he made a name for himself in the business world. More recently he was the owner of two nightclubs and two fine dining restaurants. Trevor was shocked and, soon after, terrified to see that one of those nightclubs was Felicity. Overall, it seemed Kane was just a very rich man.

Trevor looked at the image results. The man *looked* seedy, and grudgingly good for his age. Black hair with a widow's peak, not a single trace of grey, even in his beard. Bushy eyebrows, a hooked nose. Trevor didn't look at him too long. Just photos of him and his piercing eyes made him uncomfortable.

There was nothing on him about anything illegal. Trevor sighed. Of course. Cyber security? Sounded like hacking. It shouldn't have been a surprise his internet presence was sparkling clean.

Trevor closed the web browser and shut his laptop. Kane was a dead end. He couldn't do anything with random first names like Nathan and Adam, which were far more common. What next?

He turned on the television, hoping there'd be breaking news about an assassination or something. Police investigation, MI5 mobilisation, anything. It hadn't been a full hour since Mitchell had left, but it was better than being alone with his thoughts.

He had to have fallen asleep there, because one minute he was watching TV, and the next the sun was shining into the room. He rubbed his eyes and blinked against the light. He had a crick in his neck and tried to massage it out, stretch a bit.

It was Saturday, and he was caught up enough on work that he didn't have to put in any extra hours. There were a few emails he should probably respond to, other people who worked remotely in different time zones. That could wait for now, though.

Before he dared let himself think too hard about anything, he made tea and toast. He distracted himself with good thoughts, thoughts that were okay.

Mitchell caressing him. Mitchell joking with him, the sound of his laugh and the way his smile stretched his face. The way Mitchell's cock had felt, filling a void after months of longing.

Trevor had never really taken into account the noises Mitchell might make when on the other side, and had been surprised at how much it did for him. An out of breath and grunting Mitchell was definitely his new favourite sound.

It was a sound he'd like to hear again, he thought as he sipped his tea on the sofa. He wouldn't be able to if he broke things off.

"Member of Parliament Daniel Williams was found dead in a London hotel room last night. Williams, a Conservative Member of the House of Commons since the early 90's – "

Trevor nearly choked on his tea, his blood running cold. He picked up his glasses from the table and read the scrolling ticker across the bottom of the screen.

MP DANIEL WILLIAMS ASSASSINATED

They were showing footage of police in front of the hotel, a place in south London. Trevor listened for the details, of which there were frustratingly few. Nothing about how he was murdered, who the suspects were, how the assassin got in. Just the time frame, which matched up with when Mitchell had left.

Trevor's heart had started hammering and he realised it was because he had stopped breathing. He exhaled heavily and leaned forward, elbows on his knees, but they'd moved onto the next story already: *Is the internet addictive? New studies show why parents might want to monitor their teen's computer usage.*

Trevor set his tea on the table hard enough for it to slosh over the side and ran for his mobile. His hands trembled as he pulled up Mitchell's number, but he wasn't sure if he was ready to call just yet. He was probably sleeping, and there was someone else Trevor felt like he needed to call first.

"Hello?"

"Dad? I need your help."

His father sighed. "Never calling just to ask how I'm doing. What is it?"

"It's Mitchell again."

"What about him?"

"I think he's in trouble. Big trouble. Catastrophically colossal trouble. I, I don't know what to do. You're the only person I could think of to phone because, I guess, you're a solicitor and I know you sometimes help bad people. Not that I think Mitchell is bad, but – "

"Calm down, Trevor. Take a deep breath."

Trevor took a deep breath. He kept taking deep, even breaths all the way to the living room, where he retrieved his tea.

"Have you seen the news?" he asked. "Someone killed a Member of Parliament."

His dad was quiet for a few seconds, then, "I'd not seen that yet, no. Do they have any suspects? Why is it that you think Mitchell has anything to do with it? You know you can tell me anything, Trevor. I've heard a lot in my time."

Trevor sat down and placed his free hand over his knee. It was bouncing. "He was here last night. We were sleeping and his mobile rang, it woke us up. I nearly went back to sleep but the way he was speaking to the person on the other end sounded weird so I, I followed him out of the bedroom and eavesdropped. Dad, he was part of this, I know he was. He said something about driving and working with some woman and how it was ambitious, even for Kane. Nathan, that's who he was talking to, some bloke named Nathan. I think Nathan works for Kane too. I tried to search the internet for more information about him, but—"

"Trevor, I don't want you sticking your nose into this, d'you understand me? Stay right fucking clear of it. It's too dangerous."

"But Mitchell—"

"Can take care of himself. Trust me on this, Trevor."

"Dad."

"No. Listen to me. I know Alfred Kane, and he's not someone you—"

"You know him?!"

His father sighed again, and Trevor could hear him rubbing his face. "Yes, Trevor. He's one of my clients. He has been for a while."

"That's how you knew Mitchell," Trevor said in realisation. He was glad he was sitting down, because he felt more than a little taken aback. This was too much.

"Yes. I'm sorry, Trevor, but Mitchell's not who you think he is. Or maybe he's just half of who you think he is."

"Equal parts good and evil," Trevor murmured.

Naomi. It all makes sense now.

"Why not," his father said. "I won't tell you everything. That's for him to do. But he can be dangerous, and he can be heartless. I've had to help clean up some of the things Kane's asked him to do. You said he had a bad childhood? Keep that in mind. I told you things like that leave scars you can't see."

"Dad, I don't know what to do. I feel like I'm in over my head, but I don't want to leave him."

On top of that, what else could Mitchell have been lying about? What else had this Kane asked him to do? This had to be his last secret, but it seemed to be a lot more complicated than the first two, even the ferrokinesis. It was a complex chain of lies, a whole side of his personality kept hidden.

"I told you to think about his goals. You should know him even better by now, liar or not. What do you think he wants?"

Trevor thought about the Mitchell he knew. The one who'd nervously topped for the first time last night. The one who'd blushed when Imogen told stories about him on their double date, poking fun at how his accent had been thicker when he'd worked for her father and how he'd been thin as a twig. He thought about Naomi's message, what she'd said about him being Mitchell's crossroads and how there was a boy who longed to be loved.

"When he was talking to that Nathan bloke, he said he wants to get out. He doesn't want to do whatever he's doing forever."

"Kane doesn't let people leave, Trevor. *He* tells them when they're done working for him. Trust me, I know."

Trevor didn't even want to know how long his father had been working for the man. He only cared about how much longer the people close to him would have to endure it.

"Trevor, we're all in over our heads. Kane is the type of man who'll go after someone's family if they don't cooperate. I hate to tell you this, but you've already been in danger for years through me. Whether you're with Mitchell or not, that won't change."

Trevor was furious, but not at his father. His father was trapped just as much as Mitchell. No, it wasn't either of their faults. They should've been able to have normal lives without worrying about putting the people they love in danger, about putting innocent bystanders like him in danger.

He was furious with Kane.

"Why hasn't someone fucking killed this pillock already?!" he screamed. "He needs to be stopped and he needs to suffer as much as the rest of us!"

"Calm down, Trevor."

Trevor was shaking, his hand gripping his knee. He felt hot all over, felt like he needed to tear something to shreds with his bare hands. "I, I want to rip his fucking intestines out! I want to cut off his fingers and watch him choke on them! I want him dead in the worst fucking way possible, I don't bloody care how —"

"Trevor."

"He doesn't get to do this and get away with it. Nobody fucking does. IT'S WRONG!"

"Get yourself under control, Trevor. Think about who you're dealing with, how much power this man has. Before you do *anything*, talk to Mitchell."

Mitchell. Trevor snapped back to the present, fantasies of mutilating Kane dissolving. He had to talk to Mitchell.

Call me when you're awake.

Trevor had sent the text two hours ago, right after he'd gotten off the phone with his father around 11AM. He'd already called twice, and got no answer. He was starting to worry.

Trying to take his mind off it didn't work. He busied himself with tidying up, paying bills, responding to those work emails. Though his usual day for exercise was Sunday, he felt he needed to get rid of some excess energy and worked out.

Another hour passed. He called again, his heart in his throat as he waited for Mitchell to pick up.

There was no answer, but he got a text.

Can't make it. Took ill suddenly. Sorry.

Trevor knew it was a lie, and he hated it. He angrily typed a reply.

I'm coming over. You better open the door when I get there.

The response was immediate.

Please don't.

Trevor put on his shoes, grabbed his jacket and keys, and left.

Chapter 24
Glitch

He'd come bearing gifts. On the off chance that Mitchell really wasn't feeling well, he'd stopped and bought soup on the way, still hot in the paper bag. If Mitchell didn't eat it, he would.

Raising his hand to knock, Trevor paused. This wasn't a situation for rapping his knuckles on the door. This called for banging. He turned his fist sideways and pounded three heavy times, shaking the door in its frame.

"Mitchell!" he shouted. "Mitchell, open the fucking door!"

Trevor heard the lock click. He turned the knob and pushed the door open.

It was dim inside and reeked of cigarettes. The smell went up Trevor's nose as he closed the door and his face immediately pinched by itself. It took a few seconds for his eyes to adjust and find Mitchell standing behind the wall across the room, peering out from the kitchen. He wasn't sure if the human-shaped figure was just his imagination at first.

"I brought you soup. We need to talk," he said. He started walking over, his vision finally managing to see Mitchell more clearly. "You've been smoking."

"Thank you for the soup. Please go."

There was something off about Mitchell's voice, something besides its usual quietness. There was something off about the whole thing.

He walked closer, tried to get a better look at Mitchell. He was wearing loose black clothes, a large t-shirt that hung off his shoulders and sagging joggers, the overall effect making it seem as though he were wearing his father's clothes. His fringe, usually pushed back somewhat out of his eyes, fell over half his face. When Trevor raised a hand to brush it back, Mitchell shrank away, making himself small behind the wall.

"Thank you for the soup, please go."

Trevor turned, put the paper bag down on the coffee table. He stormed over to the window and yanked the curtain open, letting in harsh light.

Turning back, he saw what Mitchell was trying to hide before he could slip completely out of view.

"What the hell happened to you?" he demanded, lunging forward. The single eye he could see was purple, swollen nearly completely shut. There was a cut across the bridge of his nose, a nasty split in his lip, and discolouration took care of the rest of his face, varying shades of red, yellow, and black.

"Trevor—"

Trevor grabbed his forearm before he could get away. "Who did this to you? Was it Kane?"

Mitchell froze, his eyes opening as wide as they could. "What? How do you—"

"I heard you on the phone last night. Mitchell, sit down and eat this soup, I told you we need to talk."

He slowly released his hold on Mitchell's arm and stepped back. Mitchell hesitantly came out from behind the wall, into the light of the sitting room.

Trevor swallowed and tried not to reveal his shock. He backed away and sat down on the sofa, waiting for Mitchell to sit beside him.

"You smell terrible," he said as Mitchell took the soup out of the bag and peeled the lid off. "Have you showered?"

Mitchell shook his head.

"Alright. Just listen to me while you eat, okay? After you left, I couldn't get back to sleep. Who would after hearing their boyfriend was going out to take part in a murder, right? I'd heard you mention some names, and Kane seemed like he was the man in charge."

Mitchell had tensed up at the man's name, flinching a little. Having eaten two spoonfuls of soup, he looked down at it then as though he'd lost his appetite and was having second thoughts. After a moment, he stirred it, frowning at it like he was thinking he *should* eat it even if he didn't want to.

Trevor went on after Mitchell brought another bite to his mouth, satisfied. "I didn't find anything on him on the internet other than that he's rich. I rang my father this morning and he was able to tell me a lot more."

Mitchell looked up. "You spoke to David?"

"You do know him then."

"I phoned him after you mentioned he might know me. We only spoke a few minutes."

"I told him what I heard you say, how you don't want to work for Kane anymore. You don't, do you?"

Mitchell's hands were shaking and he set the cup of soup down. He didn't say anything.

"Mitchell, I *heard* you. My dad told me you've had to do some rather terrible things. He called you heartless and dangerous. But you're not that way with me."

Mitchell was still silent.

"Keep eating," Trevor said. He picked up the soup and carefully put it back in Mitchell's hands. "The news is talking about David Williams' murder. You said you have friends in the police, I guess that meant through Kane. Are you worried?"

Mitchell shook his head. "I'm more worried about you," he finally murmured.

"Mitchell, I'm not leaving you. Did it cross my mind? Of course it fucking did. But you're just as trapped as my father, and that's not your fault. Apparently that means I'm in danger too, one way or the other."

"I didn't kill Williams last night—"

"I know that—"

"—but I have killed before." His eyes met Trevor's, holding his gaze steadily. "Many times before."

Trevor swallowed again, nodded. "I'd figured something like that."

"I race for him too, in street races. That was what Essex was. Think I told you how I was part of the entertainment," he said bitterly. "I build him customised cars at Advanced. That's how I got it so young, because he paid off people to take care of my certifications as a mechanic. Sometimes he uses them once and destroys them, sometimes he saves them for special purposes. I'm his getaway driver, his executioner, his undefeated racer, his torturer. He does whatever the fuck he wants with me," Mitchell finished with a choked off sob.

Trevor gently wiped the tears from his eyes.

"I've always been violent, always had problems with my temper, like. And I've never really cared about people I'm not close with, to the point that when I have to hurt them for Kane it's like I just... don't feel anything. Even though I know I should."

Trevor slowly retracted his hand and stared at Mitchell.

"That sounds fucking sociopathic, I know it does, but you know I'm not like that. Trevor, you know me." He clutched Trevor's hand, eyes desperate and a little wild. "It's just, like, a glitch in my brain. The same way you can look at all those photos online and not be horrified like most people would."

"This is a bit of a step further, Mitchell." Trevor glanced down to make sure the soup didn't spill, but Mitchell's other hand seemed to have it.

"I know, but it's not like I enjoy having to do it. It's a job. David was right, I can be heartless and dangerous, but only when I need to be. It's not who I really am."

Trevor rubbed his forehead and took a deep breath, but truly Mitchell's explanation made sense, and made him feel a bit better. What did it say about himself that he was taking something like this so well? He didn't really want to think about it.

He touched the back of Mitchell's hand reassuringly, urging him to loosen his grip. "I understand."

Mitchell relaxed, wiped a stray tear, and went on. "I've got better with my temper, but, like, I'm not perfect. I still lose control. And Kane fucking knows that, because one time I lost control in front of him. He *uses* it. He uses the fact that I *can* hurt people to his advantage."

Mitchell's breath was audibly quickening, his nostrils flaring. Then it was like a switch flicked and he was suddenly extremely tense, his teary eyes murderous. Trevor watched the steady shift with equal parts wonder and trepidation.

"I never wanted any of this. I never wanted to have to let myself be fucked for money. I never wanted to sell drugs or go to prison. I didn't want to be some arsehole's fucking errand boy. I just wanted to get out of that fucking neighbourhood, use my powers to fix cars, and live a simple fuckin' life!"

Trevor took the soup from his trembling hands and set it down. Mitchell's entire body seemed to be shaking, rocked by its own earthquake.

"AY WANTED TO BE FUCKIN' NORMAL! AY JOST WANTED TO BE FUCKIN' NORMAL! Me mam never let me fuckin' 'ave that, she never let me *fuckin'* 'ave it! And now Kane took tha' away from me too! Ay never 'ave control over me own goddamn life and now ay've brought yous fuckin' inti it."

Knowing exactly what Mitchell needed to calm down, Trevor slid closer and put his arm around his shoulder. Mitchell instantly leaned into him, putting his head on Trevor's shoulder and breaking down at last.

The anger apparently past, he seemed hopeless and lost again, was weeping when he said, "I meant what I told you last night. I know I'm fucked up, but I really do think I love you. I just wanted you to know the truth."

Trevor stroked his hair, let him get the tears out of his system. Eventually Mitchell calmed, curled up on his side, and draped an arm across Trevor's chest, letting it hang from Trevor's opposite shoulder. Trevor sat a bit numbly, his body focused on comforting while his mind was otherwise occupied with trying to process everything.

He hadn't known Mitchell's anger issues ran so deep, but then, Mitchell was adept at hiding things. Even so, it wasn't difficult to imagine him suddenly snapping. Trevor still remembered the calm, measured look in Mitchell's eyes when Mitchell had his hands around his throat. He remembered the abruptly violent way Mitchell had punched the dashboard of his Fiesta on their second date, and how he'd stood there with his hands in fists a moment after ending the call that had interrupted them.

Trevor also hadn't known Mitchell's carelessness extended into sociopathic tendencies, yet here he was, holding onto Mitchell like he was a child as he cried in his arms. He wasn't afraid, not of Mitchell at least. He trusted Mitchell not to hurt him if they ever got into an argument that resulted in his temper spectacularly flaring.

It was just that he had the ability to get lost in the moment sometimes, to become something he really wasn't. He didn't feel anything when he hurt people, but they could work *with* that before they worked *on* it.

He was weak, had been bruised and beaten for a reason Trevor could guess, remembering the tail end of the phone conversation the previous night. He'd been broken. One of them had to be strong and put things back together.

Trevor caressed Mitchell's arm before softly pulling it away and leaning forward to retrieve the soup again. "Eat, Mitchell."

Mitchell sniffled and wiped his eyes, took the soup again with unsteady hands. Trevor watched him bring a bite to his mouth and swallow before he said anything.

"There's no use regretting things now," he began. "You need to stop thinking about the past and start focusing on what the fuck you're gonna do to get the normal life you want. We could have that. We could have a normal life *together*, and so could a lot of other people if you killed Kane."

Mitchell looked up at him.

"You have the power, Mitchell. You just have to use it as a weapon."

Mitchell's face twisted. "Am not a fuckin' superhero, la."

"Mitchell, look at what he fucking did to you!" Mitchell dropped his eyes. "I understand you'll have to keep working for him in the meantime, and I understand all that entails. We can try to make a plan, though. There has to be something we can do to get out of this."

Mitchell sighed. "No, Trevor. There's nothing. He controls everything. He even has people in MI5, and soon he'll have someone in the House of Commons. You can't win against someone who has half the UK on his payroll."

"And I'm telling you that doesn't matter if you put a bullet in his head."

Mitchell stared at him.

"Look, just finish eating, then I'll help you get cleaned up. You look like you should be in hospital with a brace on your nose or something."

Mitchell's face looked horrified as he brought a hand to feel his nose. "Oh my God, is it fuckin' broken?"

Trevor leaned in, eyeing him closer and trying to keep his face straight. "No. I mean, I don't think so. It could've always been that way?"

"No, really," Mitchell said, much more distressed.

Trevor looked at him sceptically a moment. Then he smiled. "I'm kidding. It looks fine."

Chapter 25
Beaten, Bruised, Broken

Mitchell looked worse directly under the bathroom lights. He stood with his back to the sink and mirror while Trevor brushed the hair out of his eyes and studied his face.

It'd grown longer during their time together, and now reached his shoulders even when it wasn't wet. Trevor tucked it behind his ears and smiled at how young and innocent it made him look.

Trevor reached behind him and wet a flannel. Mitchell closed his eyes as Trevor wiped his face down.

There wasn't much in the way of first aid supplies, so a thorough, gentle cleansing had to do. When Trevor was done with the face, he told Mitchell to raise his arms and took his shirt off.

Mitchell's body was just as bad, his entire torso and back covered in fresh red bruises. The worst was a large region on his upper right side, extending down to his stomach.

"Are you sure nothing's broken?" Trevor asked after Mitchell winced at his feeling around.

"I've been putting ice on my ribs the past few hours in case they're bruised, but I think they just really fuckin' hurt and it'll be fine in a few days," Mitchell said. "At least I hope. My jaw, too. I took pain relievers. I don't need a hospital, really. They'd just tell me to get rest, which I can do here."

Trevor frowned, but supposed Mitchell was right. He started to pull down Mitchell's joggers.

"I can take a shower myself," Mitchell said, stopping him. "If you really want to help, you can go to Boots and get antiseptic cream, healing cream. Was also hoping you wouldn't mind buying a pack of

Marlboros?"

"I'm not buying you fags, Mitchell. Especially if your ribs end up being bruised."

"Was worth a try. I don't wanna go anywhere until my face is less swollen."

"I told you I don't like smoking."

"I know, I'm sorry. Sorry. But the cream?"

Trevor stepped back. He didn't want to leave Mitchell alone, but part of him thought he did need some space. Small doses of comfort and touching seemed best for him in his current fragile state.

"Alright. I'm a bit hungry myself so I'm going to get something while I'm out. Call me if you think of anything else you need." He kissed Mitchell's cheek and left.

Mitchell sat under the hot spray of the shower, the hole in his chest slowly returning now that Trevor was gone. He'd lied to him, had, in fact taken a shower already to get the stench of urine off him, but nightmares had made him sweat profusely in his sleep, and he wanted another. He'd scrubbed himself down again and again, but couldn't seem to feel clean, especially between his legs.

Might as well let the whole fuckin' world bend me over!

He wanted to scream it aloud, but it'd made his chest hurt when he'd yelled earlier.

The inside of his arse still felt torn and ravaged, but he hoped the healing cream would help. It throbbed, burned like he could still feel Kane's phantom cock fucking him. Just as Kane had said it would, he couldn't stop feeling it, couldn't get away from the feeling of come leaking out of him. No matter how hard he closed his eyes and willed the images away, they flashed through his mind, etched into his brain.

The bitter taste of Nathan's semen flooding his mouth, the way Kane's hands had clawed at his skin, under his shirt, the piercing pain of his jaw being forced open. Where he'd been numb immediately following it, he only relived the sensations now.

Harry and another one of Kane's men had dropped him off at

home, leaving him in front of his door with a briefcase full of money. Used, fucked, and paid, just like old times.

He'd wanted to be alone, to not be seen by anybody. He'd been hesitant to let Trevor touch him when he came in, hadn't wanted to let *anyone* touch him, but after feeling Trevor's hand on his arm, it wasn't so bad. In the end, he'd wanted Trevor to hold him and never let go, wanted to be wrapped up in him so he could cover all the places Kane had invaded and wash it away.

There'd been no way he could tell Trevor about it though, at least not then. When he got back, perhaps, but it hadn't been the time. He needed a while longer before he brought it up. He needed to feel clean again, close up the hole in his chest. He needed to feel less broken and more like himself.

He also felt like he was feeling *too* much. His emotions seemed to be set to some extreme setting, and it was overwhelming. Extreme sadness, extreme anger, extreme hopelessness. One minute he was so furious he could explode, the next he didn't want to move, just wanted to lie still in the dark. He hated feeling so weak, but at the same time he couldn't bring himself to care. What was the point of anything? He couldn't do anything anyway.

Trevor was optimistic. As someone on the outside, he hadn't seen what Mitchell—or even David—had seen. He had a vague understanding of the facts, and knew enough to want Kane dead but not enough to know it was impossible. A man like Kane had plenty of enemies and knew it. It was why he had so many bodyguards.

Mitchell was relieved Trevor had handled the murdering well, at least. He really didn't deserve a man as perfect and understanding.

He stood up and turned off the shower. Towelling himself dry, he felt like he was just going through the motions. He stared at his bruised body in the mirror then turned off the lights.

After a few seconds of standing in the dark and listening to his own slow breathing, he turned them back on and picked up the bottle of paracetamol next to the tap. He took one then left to get dressed and get more ice, wishing he'd savoured his last ciggy more.

Trevor stayed a few more hours after he got back. He'd bought a few proper ice packs for Mitchell to put in the ice box and pain relieving gel in addition to the antiseptic cream. He'd put plasters over the cuts on his face and told him he'd rub the gel on his body after dinner.

While Mitchell rested in bed with ice, Trevor put away laundry, cleaned the loo, and did the washing up. He opened the windows and tried to clear out the smell of smoke, tossing out ash and cigarette ends. He found vitamin supplements in the kitchen, bought but apparently rarely taken. Later, as they ate the dinner Trevor had made for both of them, he forced Mitchell to swallow a couple.

He massaged the gel into Mitchell's chest, back, and legs, which Mitchell said made him feel a lot better. He even fell asleep near the end, while Trevor was massaging his feet. Trevor pulled the duvet over him and let him rest.

He was reluctant to leave, but he'd done all that he felt he could. If Mitchell needed anything else, he knew all he had to do was ask. Trevor had made that perfectly clear. He went home, responding to a text from Anya on the tube and politely declining her invitation to go out.

Mitchell still felt really shit on Monday, and not just emotionally. He'd been able to get through Sunday on his own, and had even started to feel a bit more whole, like he could stand on his own two feet again. He wanted Trevor to come back that night though, take away the hassle of feeding himself and massage him again. He planned to finally tell him about what else Kane had done.

When he woke up around 9AM, he texted Imogen to let her know he was too ill to go in, that he'd probably be out the entire week. She said she hoped he felt better soon and told him not to feel too bad about taking off. He never gave himself a holiday and he deserved one.

A few hours later she woke Mitchell up from a nap with a phone call.

"Hello?" Mitchell answered groggily.

"Jesus, you do sound like shit," she said. "Sorry, I wouldn't call if it wasn't important."

"What is it?"

"There was a man here just now, asking for you. Dressed like a normal bloke, but he showed me a badge, so I guess he's some sort of officer."

Mitchell's blood ran cold. "What'd he look like?"

"Dark, spiky hair, freckles all over his face. Bluish grey eyes, big pointy nose. You seen him before?"

"No. Who was he?"

"Said his name was Emmett Dyer and that he wanted to talk to you. Something about making a deal? When I told him you weren't here, he left his mobile number." She lowered her voice, her mouth closer to the microphone. "He asked if I knew some guy called Alfred Kane? Is that who buys all those street cars?"

Mitchell ignored her second question. "What'd you tell him?"

"I told the truth! I don't know who the hell that is. Mitchell, what the fuck is going on? Are we in trouble?"

"No. Imogen, don't worry. This has nothing to do with Advanced, it's all about me." Mitchell got up to find a paper and pen. "What's this man's number?"

He phoned right away. Dyer answered after a couple rings.

"Emmett Dyer."

Mitchell's throat clenched. What was he doing? What did he plan to say?

All he knew was that he was desperate, and after what Kane had done to him, he'd gladly grasp at straws. He'd hear whatever deal this man had in mind, and if he didn't like it, he'd turn on him and tell Kane, who'd take care of it.

He could also play the compliant civilian if he needed to. This had to be about the investigation into the Williams murder, and Mitchell had plenty of experience in deception if that was what he needed to fall back on.

"Hello," Mitchell said, putting on his most posh, friendliest tone. "This is Mitchell Morgan, I own Advanced Auto Repairs. I believe you spoke to my shop manager, Imogen, not long ago? She said you wanted to talk to me about something."

"Ah, yes. You're quick," Dyer said. "I'm going to cut to the chase, because I think we're both men of few words, and not keen on beating around the bush. I know about you from my colleague, Sydney Arnold. Does that name ring any bells?"

Mitchell frowned. What the hell was going on? Was he being played? "The woman from New York?"

"Not quite, though she does a convincing accent, doesn't she? I've been watching you for some weeks now, Mr Morgan. I'm well aware of who you are and where you're from, what you've done. Quite a busy man, but still making time for your personal life."

"What the fuck?"

Dyer laughed. "There you are. Listen, after what happened early Saturday morning, my... friends and I think you're a suitable candidate to help us get rid of the man we suspect orchestrated it. We'd like to make a deal."

"What sort of deal?"

"Not the sort to be discussed over the phone. I understand you're home from work today. Why is that, Mr Morgan?"

"I'm not feeling well."

"I should think not after we saw you dragged out of a car and into your flat."

Mitchell hated him already. He wished he was there so he could glare at him.

"I'd like to meet as soon as possible. When do you think you'll be up and about again? I can do Friday at the latest."

"Thursday should be fine," Mitchell said. "I'd feel more comfortable if we met in public."

"I understand completely. We can make that work. Thank you for getting back to me so quickly, Mr Morgan. I think you'll find the deal satisfies both our parties rather well."

"Wait. If Sydney works with you, why isn't she enough?"

"We'll talk on Thursday. Goodbye, Mr Morgan."

Mitchell stared at his mobile. Sydney Arnold, that rich cunt, had been a spy the whole time? Kane had spilled Mitchell's whole story to impress her, and she'd sat there sipping fucking wine!

More importantly, there was no way Dyer was regular police, not if he worked with undercover agents and spoke of "his people" the way he had. Higher up, then.

He sat down on his sofa and wrapped his head around it all. He needed to process it for when he explained it to Trevor later that evening.

He'd apparently been watched for weeks, but how many? Since Sydney met him at the race? It'd been long enough that they knew about Trevor, but did they know about his mam? Did they follow him all the way to Liverpool when he last visited her? Did they know about the ferrokinesis?

No, Mitchell had been careful with that. The bay doors had been closed and they'd been alone when he'd told Trevor. He was *always* careful with that, and it definitely would've come up, even in a discreet phone conversation. They probably knew just about everything else, though.

If they knew about everything, Mitchell didn't see why they still needed him. It seemed like they should have the resources available to know just as much about Kane. Why *him*? Why the street racing mechanic who made the cars?

Dyer had mentioned Saturday morning. Early Saturday morning, when Williams was assassinated. He would've noticed someone following him on the roads, so they hadn't been *there*, but they knew. He'd been part of that, and they fucking knew. He'd been beaten and raped the same night, and they apparently had an idea about that, too.

Of course. He was high enough to be trusted with an assassination job, but low enough to hold a grudge. He was perfect.

Chapter 26

Another Deal

Trevor was exhausted. Between taking care of Mitchell and staying caught up on his own work, he hadn't got much sleep. Since Monday night Trevor had slept at Mitchell's. For two days in a row he'd stayed with him, feeding him, massaging him, switching out ice packs. Putting him back together after Nathan and Kane had shattered his spirit. Mitchell hadn't said the word for it, had hardly managed to get anything about it out, but Trevor had been able to decipher his stuttered confession. He'd stopped him halfway through so he wouldn't have to finish.

They'd raped him, and Trevor still couldn't believe it. It had made him tremble with rage when Mitchell told him and it made him tremble with rage just thinking about it. If he ever got his hands on Nathan or Kane, the things Mitchell had done in the past would pale in comparison to what he would do to them.

He'd taken his laptop, but without his tablet and creative workspace he couldn't get any artistic work truly done, could only make notes and sketches in his sketchbook for later. Even then he could only work while Mitchell slept, either at night or during his periodic naps.

Mitchell had become rather clingy, not wanting Trevor to leave. Trevor didn't mind *too* much, it just would've been easier if Mitchell didn't demand his constant attention whenever he was awake. He was stressed out about the work he wasn't getting done, but didn't want to let it show in front of Mitchell, who needed the comfort more than he needed to feel like he was being a burden.

They spent much of the three nights and two mornings lying in bed, Trevor holding and petting Mitchell with relaxing indie music in the background. During the day they watched ridiculous anime, because Trevor felt something light would be best, and he was glad every time something made Mitchell laugh. He drew things for him, mutated creatures from his imagination that Mitchell then wanted hung above his bed. He cooked easily digestible meals ever since the one time he heard Mitchell whimpering and crying on the loo. They sat in the bath together and Trevor washed Mitchell's hair. He lit candles, hoping pleasing scents would lift his mood.

It was a draining experience, but Mitchell started looking a lot better, and it wasn't just that the bruises began changing colour as they healed, the cuts closing up. The vitamin supplements, the healing cream, the massages, the ice, the things Trevor did for his mental health—it made a world of difference. Trevor didn't think Mitchell had ever been taken care of like that. It was especially obvious whenever Mitchell climbed into Trevor's lap without preamble, settling himself with his head on his shoulder and making himself comfortable like a big, needy cat.

By Thursday morning, Trevor was guiltily glad for the excuse to go home, and glad Mitchell was going to venture out into the world again. It was even better that it was to talk to some government man about a deal to get rid of Kane. It couldn't have happened at a more perfect time.

"Will you be okay?" Trevor asked at the door. "You don't need me to be here when you get back?"

Trevor planned to go straight back to bed when he got home. As soon as he woke up, he planned to start working on the designs that needed to be finished and sent the next day. He hoped Mitchell would be fine on his own.

With his hands in the pockets of his leather jacket, his hair in his eyes, and his legs gorgeous in black skinny jeans, Mitchell looked like his usual self again. He'd claimed his chest felt better, so thankfully his ribs hadn't been bruised after all. Apart from the greenish bruise on his left eye, the healing cuts on his face, and the hesitance to leave the flat, he seemed normal.

He shrugged. "I'll be fine. I know you have work to do."

Trevor tried not to exhale too obviously in relief. "Okay. Remember the vitamins. And I swear to God if you buy more cigarettes—"

"Trevor, I'll be fine." Mitchell smiled and took his hands out of his pockets as he stepped forward to hug him. "You're amazing. I don't know what I would've done without you."

Trevor put his arms around him and held him close. "Depending on how much I get done, I may be able to come back Saturday." Mitchell pulled away and Trevor dropped his arms. "Probably not to stay the night, but I want to know what Dyer says, and I know you'll have to tell me in person, not over the phone. Don't over exert yourself, okay? Get a cab if you have to."

"I know not to push myself, Trevor. I feel a lot better, really. People have done more with worse."

"Yes, but you're not a soldier." Trevor put on his jacket, hoisted his laptop bag on his shoulder, and took one last look around before pressing a quick kiss to Mitchell's lips. "I'll try to see you Saturday. Good luck with Dyer."

The coffee shop where they'd agreed to meet on Chancery Lane wasn't overly crowded, but crowded enough to make Mitchell feel comfortable. Walking in, he ruffled his hair a little, hid most of his bruised, cut face.

Imogen had described Dyer just well enough that Mitchell was able to pick him out immediately. Dark, spiky hair with lots of freckles. He was seated as far as possible from the window.

He was dressed to fit the scene, in jeans and a checked shirt. Combined with the style of his hair, he looked younger than he had to be. He certainly didn't look like he worked for the government.

He stood up and extended his hand with a smile when Mitchell reached the table. "Mitchell, hi."

Mitchell shook his hand but kept his head down, didn't make eye contact. "Dyer," he muttered.

"Please, call me Emmett." He leaned in closer. "Try to look a bit more friendly, yeah?"

He let go of Mitchell's hand and sat down. Mitchell slid into the chair across from him, easing his rear down gently.

"As I said before, Sydney told me all about you," Dyer said, keeping his voice professionally low, private. "The name took a bit of digging, but she was eventually able to trace you back to your place in Hackney. With a name she was able to do a background check. She looked into your records, saw you'd served a little time for drug dealing when you were eighteen and grew up in Liverpool. Toxteth, I think she said?"

"How long have you been watching me?"

"Jesus, you *are* hard to talk to. Go order an espresso or something." Dyer waved a lazy hand toward the counter.

Mitchell looked in his blue-grey eyes for ten long seconds. He sighed and got up.

When he returned with his drink, Dyer continued. "It wasn't so much watching as it was keeping an eye on you. Believe it or not, we have better things to do than keep twenty-four-hour surveillance on someone we may or may not be able to use. There were other candidates, though of course you were our top choice. You're close to him, but not too close."

"And my phone? Were you listening to my calls, monitoring my text messages?"

"Naturally."

Mitchell clenched his fists under the table.

"Please try to get yourself under control," Dyer said. "I'd hate it if your little anger problem prevented you from being of use to me."

Mitchell did try, but Dyer's personality made it a bit difficult. "Could you please get to the point?"

"I've personally suspected bribed agents in MI5 for a while, but couldn't be too certain. After this recent case, when I took it upon myself to look into it, I saw street camera footage 'malfunctioned' or images too blurry to be of use. Witnesses with convenient lapses in memory, the crime scene itself offering absolutely no leads. I finally took my suspicions to my superior. Your *employer,* we'll call him, has been on a watch list for a while. With regards to the bribed agents, we have no idea who, how many, and for how long. You can see why we have to be incredibly careful about this."

"Tell me why Sydney wasn't enough," Mitchell interrupted. "She had to have gotten more than enough information for you to have solid evidence on him."

Dyer sipped his own drink. "Sydney was only able to capture him in the act, and only for things deemed appropriate for a guest to see. Yes, there's evidence of illegal betting on illegally organised street races, and a verbal confession of instances of getaway driving. We want more. He's gotten away with so much, we want to be able to pin down his ties to as many crimes as possible. You can provide us with a bit more insight and information, not just what's in front of the curtain.

"There's also the matter of his other properties. Besides the mansion and racing roads in west Essex, we need to know places that might not be *owned* by him but that are controlled by him. Places like the tucked away marijuana greenhouse previously run by the late John Gilman.

"You can also tell us more about the people who work for him. I said you weren't the only person we were considering extending this offer to—which I'll explain more about in a minute. Who's innocent, who shouldn't we hold responsible, and who's helping pull the strings? What roles have they played? Where's the line between the people on the top and the people on the bottom? We don't want to take down one man. We want to take down the whole system. Do you think you'll be able to tell us that?"

Mitchell nodded, though truthfully sometimes the lines became a bit blurred. Trevor's father, David, was definitely innocent, simply caught up because of his profession. People like Adam were a bit trickier. He was still really just a kid, and Mitchell considered him innocent, even though he didn't particularly like him. He was a drug dealer, yes, but his involvement with Kane was mainly as an errand boy. He benefited from it, but he'd been threatened into a corner just as much as Mitchell had. Just as much as anyone as low as them and lower on the totem pole.

"Good. Here's the deal. We don't know everything you've done for him, but we know a lot. We know what he's done for *you*. We're willing to pardon all of it—let you keep your garage, the money you've earned, all of it—if you cooperate. *And* if you swear to be an upstanding citizen after this is all over. If you're so much as caught taking Ecstasy in a club, the deal is off, and you'll be found guilty for all of it."

Mitchell nodded, but inwardly he mourned the loss of his casual car-stealing days. He just wouldn't be able to risk it.

"There'll be a signed confession of everything you've done while under his employment. You'll want to list all of them, because only the ones listed will be pardoned. If it's later discovered you've been involved in a crime not listed, you'll be charged then as well. No matter how bad it is, list it."

"And all I have to do is tell you everything I know about him? You'll take care of everything?" It sounded too good to be true.

"I'll be honest, it'll be difficult," Dyer admitted. "It's hard to work in an area where you don't know who you can trust. We're trying to get together a task force we can use to raid the Kanine building, but having to be incredibly selective about who we choose. If someone on his payroll even gets a *hint* of what's going on, we're certain he'll disappear into hiding. Government servers may suffer from a conveniently timed cyber security breach, that sort of thing."

"But you can do it, can't you?" Mitchell had to believe he could. "How long will it take? When will it be over?"

"We want to do it right and not rush things, but we also want to do it soon, so you'll not have to work for him too much longer and put yourself in danger. We're looking at about a two-week window, which should give us time to organise the team. That means the thirteenth of June as the absolute last day to act." He took another large gulp of coffee then set it down. "Our work *today* needs to move fast. When we leave, we'll take different routes to a black van parked across from the telephone boxes on Carey Street."

Mitchell knew where it was. It wasn't far. "And once I get in?"

"We'll drive around. You'll talk a lot, tell us everything, and it'll be recorded. A transcript of the conversation will be printed out, you'll go over it, make sure nothing's slipped your mind. That list of offences I mentioned earlier. That'll be your confession, which you'll sign and date. I'll sign it as well, showing I was there and can confirm. Then there's the contract, which states everything about the deal I've just told you, only in print. We'll both sign that, too. After that, we drop you off wherever you like, maybe a few streets from your flat. You'll know when it's over, so I won't need to phone you. It'll be on the news, and your involvement as an informant will be left out of it."

Mitchell thought it over, drank from his cup mostly for appearances. He wanted it over so badly. He was rather disappointed he wouldn't be able to kill Kane himself, but he'd take what he could get and not complain. This was his chance at a normal life. He'd get to keep the benefits from working for Kane *and* get out in one piece.

He set his cup down, licking his lips. "Alright."

Saturday afternoon, Mitchell looked even better. He and Trevor were sitting on the sofa watching *Game of Thrones* after talking about the deal with Dyer, which Trevor had been overjoyed about. Mitchell had said he was done with anime for now and wanted the usual bloody fare.

He seemed to be on better footing since the meeting, visibly more optimistic, but still only a week had passed since he'd been raped and beaten. Trevor still saw a dead, faraway look in his eyes sometimes.

"I think you would've liked some of the stuff I did," Mitchell said as someone died onscreen. Trevor looked at him, kept stroking Mitchell's hair, but Mitchell kept his eyes on the television.

"What the hell makes you say that?"

"Don't look at me that way. I was just thinking, because of all those things you look at online, you would've been just as fascinated with it. Like when you slice someone's throat, it doesn't kill them right away, not always. They make these wet, gurgling sounds while blood pours from their neck and mouth, and if their hands aren't tied they'll put their hands over it, try to keep the blood from gushing out. It kind of looks and sounds like they're choking."

Trevor could see it, just the way Mitchell described. He saw someone lying on the ground, hands desperately raised to their throat as they tried to save themselves, blood pumping out with each beat of their heart. He heard the gurgling, the choked off gasps of breath.

"If they were lying on their back, could they choke on their own blood?" he wondered aloud.

Mitchell nodded. "If bleeding out doesn't kill them, that will."

"Sort of makes me wonder how all that blood would taste. Can you imagine? All that in your mouth, like you're drowning in it."

Trevor thought about it a bit more, saw the blurry-faced, struggling victim in the theatre of his mind. Feet scrabbling against a wood floor, blood pooling around them.

He stopped himself in his tracks, horrified. What the fuck was wrong with him? Looking at it online was one thing, talking about actual murders so lightly and fantasising about it was, was—

Mitchell's fingers entwined with his and pulled him out of his head. "That'd be a pretty cool thing to draw, wouldn't it?" he suggested.

Trevor looked back at the TV. A man was being tortured for information, a rat chewing through his chest.

"Yeah. Yeah, it would be."

Trevor got home a little after eight that night. Over dinner, he and Mitchell had discussed where things went from here. Mitchell currently had no orders from Kane to take care of at Advanced, and no jobs in the near future. He had enough money stashed away in bank accounts and personal hiding places that he'd be set pretty much for life, able to live more than comfortably on what he made at the garage without Kane's continuous contributions.

He didn't bother turning the lights on when he walked in. He toed off his shoes, shrugged out of his jacket and went to his study, plugging his mobile into the computer to charge.

Dyer had said there was no definite set date for the raid and arrest, but with the final day of the two-week window being the thirteenth of June, they were so close to being free. Trevor used "they," but really he personally hadn't been too involved for long. Or rather, he'd been blissfully unaware of his involvement, considering the position his father had put him in ages ago. It was depressing to think about how many others had suffered the same fate, people who'd been killed or tortured just because someone they were close to got caught up in Kane's world.

But soon it would be taken care of, not just for him and those close to him, but for everyone. Within the month. Trevor couldn't wait for the feeling of relief to finally come when he saw Kane brought down on the news.

Expecting a long night of catching up on work ahead, he left the study and went to the kitchen for a drink. Something sweet and fizzy for him to sip on for a while. A large glass of Coke.

He turned the light on in the kitchen and his heart stopped. He saw the eyes first, the whites starkly contrasting dark skin. Then he saw the gun pointed at his head.

"Hello, Trevor."

Chapter 27

Kanine

Mitchell looked at himself in the mirror. He leaned forward, nearly touching his face to the reflective surface. He blinked, watched his eyelashes sweep through the air.

The skin around his left eye was still faintly green, and turning yellow. He ran fingertips softly down the side of his face, past the nearly healed cut on his cheek and over the stubble he hadn't bothered to shave. Avoiding a jolt of pain through his jaw, he was careful not to apply too much pressure.

He touched his lips, fleshy and pink. The cut on the bottom one was taking the longest of all his facial wounds to get better. He ran a finger across the bridge of his nose. The cut there was closing up as well.

He stepped back and looked his body over. Tilting his head from side to side, he rolled his shoulders and heard the joints crack. He lifted his arms straight above his head, stretching enough to touch the ceiling.

He was not weak. He had a strong body, strong, powerful muscles. He could bend metal to his will like it was nothing.

He took in a deep breath, keeping his shoulders square, and watched his chest expand. Pectoral muscles, deltoids, abdominals. The bruises on his chest had changed colour just like his eye, blue-black in the worst areas but mostly yellow. He exhaled.

Carefully, he tried to twist, first to one side then the other. He could go pretty far, but didn't ignore the soreness and make it worse. Trevor would yell at him for sure. He knew his body though, knew how it healed after a beating.

He placed a palm over his stomach, right over his navel, and closed his eyes. This was *his* body, not anybody else's. It had been violated, but that didn't stop making it his. This was his skin, his hair. He was himself and the invader was gone, *would be* gone for good.

He opened his eyes.

So far, he'd been doing good not letting any of the overwhelming emotions take over, which he felt was largely thanks to Trevor. Trevor kept him balanced, afloat when he felt like he could sink to the bottom of the darkest depths. Now, looking at his body in the mirror and remembering what had been done, he felt fury rushing to the surface. He suddenly had to clench his fists and place them on the sink, stop his arms from quivering with pent up anger.

It'd be over soon, it'd all be over soon...

He heard his mobile ringing in the other room and immediately turned on his heel to get it, glad for the distraction. When he picked it up, he saw it was Trevor. It'd only been just over an hour since he'd left.

"Trevor?" Mitchell answered.

"Sorry, he can't talk at the moment."

Mitchell's stomach felt hollow as dread flooded his body. His knees went weak and he sank to the floor, one hand clutching the sofa.

"Nathan."

"I didn't know you had such a handsome boyfriend when I shoved my dick in your mouth a week ago, but I should've guessed," he taunted, amusement in his tone. "You deep-throat too well not to be a regular cocksucker. Bet it was just an ordinary night for you, eh, taking it like a cheap whore."

"*Shut your fucking mouth, I'll fucking kill you –* " The sound of Trevor shouting in the background was cut short by a hard punch. Mitchell gripped the phone and struggled not to lose his control.

"We know who you've been talking to," Nathan said. "In the interest of time I'll just tell you that the bottom line is, you're fucked. We're taking your Trevor up to the office for a meeting and your attendance is mandatory. If you even think about calling that new friend of yours, we'll go after your mother next."

Mitchell used the sofa to pull himself up, trying to remember where he'd put his switchblade and hoping like hell that his phone was still being monitored.

"Don't keep us waiting. If we get bored we might just give Trevor the same treatment we gave you."

As soon as Nathan hung up, Mitchell darted to the bedroom to pull on the first clothes he got his hands on. He searched for his switchblade at the same time, scanning the flat with his senses.

The drawer. Of course it was in the drawer. He unlocked it and rummaged through the mass of notes to find it.

Trevor, they have my fuckin' Trevor, they have him.

He almost ran out without shoes. He growled in angry frustration and stormed back to put them on.

He didn't care what the deal with Dyer had been. He was going to kill everyone in the fucking building if he had to.

The man who Trevor soon found out to be Nathan had forced him out of his building and into some horrifically modified car at gunpoint. The inside had looked like a portable torture chamber, with built-in handcuffs and smooth metal flooring. A man had ridden in the back with him, Nathan sat in the passenger seat and someone else driving. He'd received a punch to the face for his outburst during Nathan's call, and had been gagged with a thick piece of rope immediately afterwards.

It was as he was being hauled out and escorted through an underground parking garage, hands cuffed behind his back, that he thought the whole situation was mental. What the fuck had his life become? He'd just been a remote-working graphic designer who ignored the majority of his friends until it suited him, who stayed at home on Reddit. As he was pushed into a lift and taken to the top floor, he wryly thought that this was probably more than exciting enough for Kay.

They walked him into a large office that overlooked the City. He recognised the man sitting behind the desk instantly as Alfred Kane.

"Put him down over there," Kane said, gesturing just past the corner of his desk.

Trevor was shoved forward again. A hand pushed him down

onto his knees in front of the metal desk, and he grunted at the force of bone meeting the floor. Rough hands turned him around to face the other way.

"Don't fucking move," Nathan said, gripping a handful of his hair. "You move and I'll take great pleasure in slicing something open."

Trevor glared up at him as he let go. His jaw had started hurting almost as soon as the rope gag had been tied around his head, and already his knees ached. He didn't dare readjust to sit in a more comfortable position.

His heart started hammering in his chest when he heard footsteps walk around the desk. He looked up. Kane was dressed in a cream-coloured suit, with a matching tie that contrasted a black shirt underneath. His eyes were bone-chilling in person, his gaze making Trevor's skin prickle. He shrank away when Kane crouched in front of him and reached out to touch his face.

"So this is who my driver calls his boyfriend," he mused aloud, stroking Trevor's cheek with a callused finger. Trevor felt unclean just from that alone; he couldn't imagine the horror of being raped by the man.

He wasn't able to look Kane in the eyes, instead looked at the ceiling and forced himself to hold still. He tried not to panic, but the hopelessness of the situation made his courage waver.

"I knew he was a fairy," Kane said. "He's picked up a man or two in my clubs on occasion, you see. Don't think anyone else knew it, but I did. I'll admit he has good taste."

If Trevor wasn't so frightened — and if he hadn't been gagged — he would've spit on him.

Kane stood up. "I made him who he is, you know. I gave him *everything*. And this is how he repays me."

Trevor looked around when Kane turned. There were bodyguards everywhere — two outside the door, two on each side of the room, and of course Nathan. That made seven, plus Kane made eight. Could Mitchell kill that many people at once? All of the bodyguards had guns, and Nathan had both a gun and a knife. He didn't know what Kane had, but he had to have something. If they all shot at the same time, would Mitchell be able to stop the bullets that fast?

"I wonder if he's told you about what he does," Kane said, sitting leisurely in a plush chair across the room. "Not very talkative, is he? Quiet. Fun to wind him up and watch him go, though. You know he built the car they brought you in? He's talented, I'll give him that. Brilliant driver, brilliant mechanic. This whole thing is such a shame."

Trevor thought back to what he'd read in the *Understanding Parapsychology* book. The power worked like a muscle, like a reflex. Individual pieces of metal had to be sensed before they could be manipulated. How good were Mitchell's reflexes? As far as Trevor knew, he only used his power for mundane things. When would he have practised using it as a weapon, fine tuning his ability to sense quickly?

How fucked were they?

"You don't seem quite as terrified as the others I've brought in, so I take it he has told you," Kane continued, tapping a finger contemplatively over his mouth. "Which means he cares enough about you to consider you worth the truth. And you care enough about him to stay even though you know it put you in danger. I wonder, how did you feel when you found out Nathan and I had a bit of fun with him?"

Trevor was jolted out of his thoughts, felt rage course through him in waves. He shifted his attention back to Kane, wishing he had Mitchell's ability to throw a dagger across the room with nothing but his mind.

Kane clapped once, laughing delightedly. "Oh man, if looks could kill, eh? Good. You were getting a bit boring. He has quite the arse, doesn't he? Tell me, who usually tops between the two of you? It's you, isn't it. I bet it's you. That glare tells me all I need to know. I've invaded your territory."

Trevor uncurled and curled his fingers, cracking his knuckles behind his back as he bit hard on the rope in his mouth. He wanted to skin Kane alive, scalp him and hear him scream in agony. Then he wanted to bash his skull in.

"Really, it was his fault. He brought it on himself by trying to turn my best friend against me. I had to show him who's in charge, you understand. He took it well, all things considered. Harry here pissed on him afterwards. Saw everyone else having fun and just had to join in."

Trevor followed Kane's gesture to the large man on his right, one of the two bodyguards on that side of the room. Harry smirked at him.

Kane got to his feet, pushing himself up out of the chair. "Where *is* he? I'm getting impatient. Didn't you tell him to hurry up?" he asked Nathan.

Before Nathan could reply, one of the guards at the door turned and spoke over his shoulder, a hand on his ear piece. "He's just walked in the building."

Kane grinned, pleased. "Good." He turned and looked at Trevor, making him break out into a sweat. "Don't worry. It'll all be over soon."

Trevor rattled his metal handcuffs.

There were more men than usual when Mitchell walked in through the glass entrance. Nearly half of them were standing around, ready to go for their hidden weapons should the need arise, and the other half were moving, hauling boxes out into waiting lorries outside. The sound of so many busy footsteps were loud on the marble floor.

They were packing up, preparing for Kane's departure. Nothing incriminating could be left behind. Maybe he was even moving somewhere else permanently, getting out of the country because he knew what had been set in motion, and there was no way to stop the flow of things now. He wasn't going to just leave without taking care of the person who'd betrayed him, though.

It was eerily silent as Mitchell walked past the armed guards. All eyes seemed to be on him, even those passing by with a load in their hands. He hoped that there were more down here than there were surrounding Kane. Otherwise he and Trevor didn't have a chance of making it out alive.

He'd stolen a car to get there as fast as he did, mapping out a loose plan on the way. He didn't like the odds, how stacked they were against him, but he had to believe it would work. If it didn't, there was always the slim chance that Dyer had overheard the conversation and was en route.

He walked up to the receptionist at the counter. She was pecking away at her keyboard, eyes darting back and forth to various points on the screen. Apparently even she had been tasked with getting rid of things, most likely deleting archived files. She stopped what she was doing and looked up at him, smiled.

"He's in his office. You know where it is," she said. She returned her attention back to the computer. Mitchell headed for the lift.

There was a camera in the corner, a black half sphere opposite the LED floor display. Mitchell curled his toes in his shoes as the lift rose, extended his arms forward and stretched. His heart was racing, his armpits sweating, and he wasn't sure how this was going to end. He had the element of surprise though, hidden ferrokinesis in his favour. As long as the top floor wasn't crawling with guards as the ground floor had been, his plan would work. Hopefully.

The lift reached the top level with a ding and Mitchell took a deep breath as the doors opened. So far, things looked promising. The corridor wasn't lined with guards, as he'd suspected it might be. As he stepped out and began walking, looking around, it seemed the whole floor had cleared out. The only people left were those in Kane's office.

Kane was underestimating him. He'd been able to handle Mitchell with only two men a week ago, so why would he need much more than that to handle him now? He expected a quick execution. It was working out perfectly.

Mitchell's hands started shaking, and he clenched them into fists. He'd never killed so many people at one time before.

There were two guards outside the door, one on each side. The one on the left opened the glass door for him when he was just a metre or so away. Mitchell reached out with his metal senses as he approached, felt the inner workings of their drawn pistols right down to the smallest components. By the time he entered Kane's office he'd rendered them useless.

The door closed softly behind him and his breath caught in his throat. Trevor was on his knees in front of Kane's desk, hands behind his back and gagged with a rope. Nathan had a gun pointed at his head and Mitchell heard the metallic clank of handcuffs as Trevor shifted his arms.

When he turned his gaze on Kane, there was a gun pointed at his head too.

He started feeling out the room, searching out all the weapons one by one. Kane prattled on while Mitchell narrowed his focus. He didn't do anything to the guns he'd locked onto, not yet.

"You're just full of fuck-ups recently, you know?" Kane said. "If it were up to me, I'd torture you *and* your pretty boyfriend, and take my time with it too, but we're in a bit of a hurry. Thanks to a certain ungrateful mechanic, we have to pack up and move out, set up somewhere else. We have to be quick." He stepped closer, pushed the gun right up against Mitchell's forehead. "Would you like to go first? Or would you rather spare Trevor the sight of your brains being blown out?"

Mitchell swallowed his anger, forced himself to stay calm and channel the pent-up aggression into what came next. He looked straight in Kane's dark eyes, pouring all the hate he could into the glare. He didn't speak loudly, but he so rarely did.

"I don't think that's how this is going to go."

Chapter 28
Not a Superhero, Like

It happened faster than Trevor could see. The guns flew out of Kane and Nathan's hands, hovered out of their reach, and while Kane stood staring up in shock, Mitchell threw a punch, sending him falling back and onto the ground.

The guards saw Kane had been attacked and drew their weapons. Beside Trevor, Nathan grabbed his hair and pulled out a knife, holding it to his throat. Trevor felt his handcuffs unlock but didn't move just yet. He stayed frozen in place, watching Mitchell.

Kane got back on his feet, holding his face, but by then Mitchell had taken the man's gun for himself. He had it aimed right at him, while six guards had their guns aimed back.

Kane looked up at where Nathan's gun still hovered above them, then back at Mitchell. Trevor could feel the tension in the room like it was something tangible.

The gun slowly turned in midair, pointing back at Nathan. Then everything happened fast again.

The guns held by the four guards in the room were flung out of their hands, and floated in front of each of their faces for just a single second before firing simultaneously. The noise finally alerted the guards outside, who quickly spun on their heels with their weapons raised as four dead bodies dropped to the floor. They pushed the glass doors open and hurried inside, but two levitating guns shot them in the head before the doors even closed behind them. They fell on the spot, and Trevor had never been so relieved to see people die.

That left only Kane and Nathan. Mitchell still had the gun pointing at Kane's face, and two others pivoted to point at him as well. The rest pointed at Nathan.

Trevor swallowed as a bead of sweat slid down his back. Despite the fact that a knife was still pressed against his throat, Mitchell appeared to have complete control of the situation. Neither Kane nor Nathan moved as they processed the impossibility of Mitchell's power and no doubt tried to quickly come up with a plan to counter it. He saw Kane's eyes dart back and forth between Mitchell and Nathan a few times.

The knife held to Trevor's throat was wrenched away, dropping to the floor with a thud. Without taking his eyes off Kane, Mitchell ordered Nathan, "Step away from him."

Trevor looked up at Nathan, who was glaring but took two steps away. Trevor shook off the handcuffs and got unsteadily to his feet, his legs wobbly. He untied the rope gag and cast it aside.

"I don't know how you're doing this, but think before you do anything stupid," Kane said at last. "There are cameras in this entire building, and my security—"

"Not in the briefing rooms," Mitchell countered. "And not in here. You wouldn't put a recording device anywhere *near* a place where you take care of real business."

"And how do you plan on getting out exactly? You think you can just come in here, kill me, and leave? When I have people crawling all over this place?"

Trevor wanted to know that as well. What exactly was Mitchell's plan?

"That's not really something you need to worry about," Mitchell said. He waved the barrel of the gun a little. "Go stand by the desk."

Kane laughed. "You think you're calling the shots now just because you have more guns than me? Whatever it is you're doing to them, I bet it takes a lot of concentration to control all of them at once. You're not even facing Nathan but the guns still follow him. Tell me, how do you know where he is without looking at him?"

"The metal in his belt." Mitchell shook his head and took a step forward. "Fuck off. Stop trying to distract me."

Kane grinned, sending a shiver down Trevor's spine. "It's working then." His eyes slid past Mitchell to Nathan, and before Trevor could register the dark blur of movement in his periphery, a forceful blow to the stomach made him curl in on himself, grunting in pain.

Mitchell spun around. "Stop!" He didn't shoot, though. Even Trevor knew Nathan was too close and moving too much for Mitchell to have a clear shot.

Trevor managed to dodge the next one, jumping back just far enough that Nathan's fist passed through empty space. But the man was a beast, growling and lunging mercilessly, and Trevor wasn't nearly as skilled at fighting. He found himself backed against the desk with nothing to do but knee Nathan between his legs.

As Nathan groaned and doubled over, Kane made a run for it, dashing out the glass doors and into the hallway. Mitchell's head whipped back and forth, obviously torn between giving chase and staying to make sure Trevor wasn't killed.

Like hell was Trevor going to let Kane get away just because Mitchell had to save him. He punched Nathan in the face hard enough to hurt his own fist and shouted, "Go!"

"Trevor—"

"Kill him quickly and come right back. Just fucking go before you don't get another chance!"

A punch landed on his jaw, forcing his head left. He felt a cut on the inside of his cheek and blood on his tongue, but swallowed it and strafed out of the way of the next blow. Mitchell hesitated, watching them a second or two longer, then turned and sprinted after Kane.

Nathan was fast. When his hands weren't in fists throwing punches, they were in claws reaching out to pull Trevor in. He was relentless, looking like a monster with his pearly teeth bared.

Still, Trevor managed to duck and dodge a bit, to shuffle backward or to the side. It really was a sort of dance, he saw that now. He just needed to find a way to be less on the defensive side, needed to find his own openings.

Nathan laughed darkly. "Fucking pathetic. But not as pathetic as the way Mitchell cried when I fucked his pretty little mouth."

Trevor snapped. All the anger he'd felt toward the man before boiled to the surface, animal rage flowing through his entire body. He no longer saw Nathan as a monster to dodge, but as a man he wanted to tear apart.

With a growl of his own, he charged forward. Nathan side-stepped out of the way, tilting left to dodge Trevor's punch, but Trevor grabbed a fistful of shirt in front of his stomach with his left hand and started pounding into his side with his right. Nathan grunted but punched Trevor in the side just as hard.

Trevor shoved him back against a wall. Another hit landed on his chin, knocking his teeth in his skull again and this time splitting his lip. He drove a punch right into Nathan's stomach, expelling air from him in a short huff. Trevor just as quickly followed it up with a fist to the side of his head.

Nathan kneed *him* between the legs then, and Trevor literally saw stars for a few seconds. He stumbled back to get away, didn't want to leave himself open for another blow while he was disoriented, and ended up knocking his hip on a corner of Kane's desk. It unsteadied him and he fell to the floor.

Fuck.

Once he was down, he knew it'd be almost impossible to get back up. He started to roll onto his stomach, but was too slow—Nathan's fist met his face hard enough to send his head ricocheting off the floor and back again. His vision blurred and his nose throbbed in time with his thumping heartbeat, waves of pain reaching every part of his head.

Another blow and another. Trevor raised his arms over his face to shield them but that left his middle open. He gasped at the sudden pounding in stomach, and felt dizzy. If he hadn't already been on the ground, pinned under Nathan's legs, he would've dropped.

Come on, come on, think.

He tried to think through the onslaught of pain. He tried to push it into the background and clear everything else but his own mind away. If he didn't get out of this position soon, he'd die in it, face beaten to a bloody pulp.

Kane was getting on the lift by the time Mitchell caught up to him at the end of the corridor. Mitchell sensed the metal box, all its inner workings, and forced the doors to stay open. Kane angrily jabbed the close button to no avail.

As Mitchell closed in, gun raised and ready, Kane went for his pocket and pulled out his mobile. Mitchell tapped into it with his senses and flung it out of his hands, smashing it to pieces against the wall.

"Hey!" he yelled, directing his efforts to the camera in the corner of the lift. He waved his arms frantically to get security's attention. "Get me five — no, ten men up here right — *Ahhh!*"

Close enough to be accurate, Mitchell shot him in the knee. Kane fell against the railing, clutched it to stay upright.

"Just hang on, alright?" he began rambling. "Hang on. You don't have to do this. I'll let you go. I'll let Trevor and your mother go. Just don't do this, Mitchell. I'll disappear and you'll never hear from me again. Your government friend never has to know tonight happened."

The lift started up a continuous loud buzzing, the doors having been held open too long. Finally stepping on and joining Kane inside, Mitchell let the doors close to stop the noise, but kept the lift itself stationary.

It was just the two of them now, nowhere to run in the confined space. Mitchell smashed the camera in the corner with the butt of the gun, rendering them completely and utterly alone.

For a prolonged moment, neither of them spoke. Mitchell stared at Kane, took in the blood stain on the trouser leg of his cream-coloured suit, and Kane stared intently back, panting as he waited for Mitchell's next move.

He dodged the sudden punch Kane threw at him, caught his wrist and pinned it against the wall. He shoved the barrel of the pistol into Kane's stomach, reminding him not to do anything stupid.

"I know I don't have to do this," he said, his face just inches away from Kane's. "I could just wait for Dyer to get here and clean the whole thing up. But the thing is, Kane, you fucked me. You... *raped me*," he said between his teeth, digging the gun in further. "You brought Trevor into this. You've brought me and so many others so much suffering. The thing *is*, I want to do this. I've fucking dreamt about it."

Mitchell's finger on the trigger trembled, and he no longer suppressed the urge to shoot. He kept the gun held right up against Kane's stomach and pulled the trigger, the sound deafening in the enclosed space.

Kane inhaled sharply and the colour drained from his face. Letting go of him, Mitchell dropped the gun and pulled out his switchblade. Kane sank to the floor as he flicked it open, exposing the blade, and his weight shook the lift.

Now, Mitchell thought, the adrenaline of sweet revenge coursing through his veins. *Finally.*

He straddled Kane's slumped body and drove the knife into the hollow of his collar bone, yanked it out and shoved it in again. Kane didn't make a sound beside a grunt that turned into a gargle, and he was far too near death to move, but he wasn't dead yet. His head drooped, fell forward, and Mitchell grabbed hold of his hair to move it to the side before driving the knife deep into his neck.

Gushing blood added to the slippery mess already made of both their clothes and the floor, pumped steadily out of the large artery with each beat of Kane's heart. At the thought of Kane's heart, Mitchell ripped open the black shirt, buttons popping off and scattering across the floor, then brought his knife down right in the centre.

Again and again and again. His arms were locked into the movement and he couldn't stop.

How many times had he been forced to use this same blade on people who didn't deserve it? How many times had he been used as a fucking errand boy, a show pony, a taxi? *Years* of living under his thumb, of living in fear with no hope of ever getting out.

"DO I BELONG TO YOU NOW? DO I FUCKING BELONG TO YOU NOW?"

His arms hurt and he was out of breath, but he threw the knife aside and switched to his fists. It didn't matter if the man was dead; he needed to feel the satisfaction of his hands bashing in that stupid fucking face.

"I'll show you who I fucking belong to."

It was as Trevor was trying to block both his face and stomach that he saw the knife on the floor just within reach. Nathan's knife. It was half hidden under Kane's desk.

Trevor left his stomach open to desperately reach for it. For a terrifying second, he worried his arm wouldn't be long enough, that his fingertips would brush the handle and accidentally push it back. He grabbed it though, curled his fingers around it and gripped tight before thrusting it into Nathan's thigh.

"AHHH! YOU FUCKING—FUCK!"

Blood steadily pulsed from the wound, soaking the fabric of Nathan's trousers and even getting into Trevor's shirt. The blade was lodged deep in the outer part of Nathan's leg, piercing flesh, muscle, and bone.

As Nathan raised a hand to grab the handle himself, Trevor twisted it and brought forth another pained wail. The hand that wrapped around Trevor's own was firm, but still too weak to do more than tug.

Trevor wrenched the knife free and shoved the bleeding blade deep into Nathan's stomach. It disappeared into his body with ease, past the shirt, past skin, and into vital organs if Nathan was too hurt to even scream a third time. Nathan pressed a hand to where blood was quickly staining his shirt, pouring out of him and onto Trevor. It was warm, made Trevor feel almost like Nathan was pissing on him.

Trevor twisted the knife again, rotating his wrist in all directions to do as much damage as he could. Nathan's face had gone pale and bleak, his expression at once pinched in agony then suddenly blank. He started falling to the side, eyes already losing their focus.

Trevor shoved him off with the knife still lodged inside, scrambling from under his legs. Nathan's blood made his shirt stick to his skin, and he felt disgusting, unclean. He was trembling from what he'd just done and weak as hell from the beating, his whole body throbbing in pain. He had to use the desk for support to get to his feet.

He wanted to collapse, wanted to sit in a hot bath and have a nice cup of tea, but first he had to find Mitchell and Kane. Panting, he started dragging his feet toward the door.

There was nothing left of Kane's face to readily identify him as Kane. Mitchell's hands were bloody, some of it probably his own, as he'd felt the occasional tooth cut the skin of his knuckles. Everything from Kane's chest up was a ragged mess of blood and mutilated flesh.

Mitchell sat astride the corpse, panting. He couldn't believe how free he felt, how free he *was*. He'd wanted for so long to get that out of his system, and he finally had.

He giggled a little hysterically.

The lift dinged and Mitchell went silent and tense as he waited for the doors to open. The second seemed to drag on, and he wondered if Kane's reinforcements had arrived after all, much too late.

He exhaled a held breath when the doors parted to reveal Trevor, bruised and beaten, though evidently successful. He didn't have nearly as much blood on his shirt as Mitchell, but the stain was still quite large.

Trevor's eyes stared at Kane's body and he swallowed. "Nathan's dead, too. Fuck, I can't believe I actually killed someone. Does this mean it's over?"

"Yes, Mr Lewis, it seems that way."

Mitchell furrowed his brow at the new voice. Trevor turned around and there was Dyer, a team of armed men behind him.

"This was in self-defence," Mitchell said.

"I'm certain it was. Why don't you get up and come out of there before the buzzing starts up and becomes a nuisance?"

Mitchell got to his feet, grabbing his bloody switchblade on his way out. Dyer motioned for one of his men to retrieve the corpse, and he made efficient work of dragging the body out.

"I assure you, everything will work out fine, Mr Morgan. I did *technically* say the crimes you committed while under Kane's employment would be pardoned, and you were *technically* still working for him when this happened."

"But it's not on the list."

"Nothing that can't be amended." Dyer folded his hands together behind his back. "I don't know how you did it, Mr Morgan, but here's the official story. Kane has numerous enemies — people he's cheated, double-crossed, or blackmailed for too long. People with the kind of money that can buy hired killers, not too unlike the woman you worked with last Friday night. It's entirely feasible that before we could catch the man behind Williams' murder ourselves, one of his enemies got to him first. Which wouldn't be too far from the truth, after all."

Mitchell nodded. "Alright. And what about Trevor killing Nathan?"

Dyer looked at Trevor, then back at Mitchell. "I don't believe we ever saw Mr Lewis here." Mitchell sagged in relief just as Trevor did, and Dyer put a hand on his shoulder. "We'll take care of it from here and get back to you in a day or two with that amended contract. Get cleaned up and go home, Mr Morgan."

Chapter 29

Crossroads

The tenth of August was a Sunday, and a beautiful day for a wedding. At twenty-three degrees, with minimal cloud cover, Lydia's desire for pleasant summer weather was fulfilled.

Both of them looked stunning. Mitchell had seen Lydia dolled up often enough, but nothing like now. Her gown had a heart-shaped bodice with a scoop-necked, beaded applique that extended down the front, an elegant silk bow at the waist. The dress flared out from there, falling to the floor and encircling her as though she were a fairy tale princess. She'd certainly put a bit more effort into her hair than usual as well, curling it into loose ringlets that she let flow freely over her shoulders.

Still, it was Imogen Mitchell couldn't stop staring at. When she'd told Mitchell about shopping for dresses, he'd tried to imagine her in one and hadn't been able to. It was so odd seeing her in the white, silk gown, beaded flower designs across one hip. A surreal, unbelievable sight, but a nice one.

Her common exuberance in addition to her petiteness usually made her childlike, but there was nothing childish about her now. Her long hair had also been curled, and flowed down her back with white flowers clipped in at random places. Her makeup was simple, no eyeshadow or blush, just dark eyeliner and rosy pink lipstick.

The dress clung to her at the top, thin straps stretching over her strong shoulders. At the waist it became looser, and ended halfway down her calves, flaring playfully out the slightest bit. Her shoes were flat, open-toed, and with laces crisscrossing up her legs in a way that made Mitchell think of a ballerina.

All that, but it was still the smile that Mitchell had seen a million times before that made her the prettiest.

They'd gotten closer in the two months following Kane's death. Mitchell had put more effort into his friendship with her and Lydia since he no longer had a whole separate life to hide, secrets to keep. Neither of them knew all of what he'd done, but he felt able to open up more in general. They knew just about everything *except* that he'd been a murderer, even his terrible childhood experiences.

Lydia became privy to his ferrokinesis. Imogen was no longer just a work friend, but a life friend, his best friend right after his mam and Trevor. He didn't think he'd be filled with such sappy emotions at the sight of her getting married otherwise.

He had his own hair brushed back in a ponytail, and was wearing a suit that cost more than he thought any piece of attire had any right to cost. A dark grey, pinstripe three-piece, fitted to his form in the places where it should fit and loose in the places it mattered so as to still be comfortable. Trevor had fucked him before they'd gotten dressed, bent him over the bathroom sink, but the way he'd looked at him when he put on the suit—it was like he was fucking him a second time with his eyes.

His mother was there too, and Mitchell might've teared up at how beautiful *she* looked. He'd expressed his worries about her coming to Trevor, about how she might dress, might act, and Trevor had said to leave it to him. Mitchell didn't know how he did it—maybe he had fashion-savvy friends for that sort of thing, or maybe he'd just conspired with Lydia, who he'd become good friends with—but his mam looked amazing. With her brown hair in curls atop her head, dangling diamond earrings, and a white cotton dress with lace overlay, she looked proper elegant for the first time since Mitchell could remember.

She still came off as too sultry than was appropriate for a wedding, considering half the men present kept looking at her, the other half probably gay. It was like she couldn't turn it off, couldn't help but look inviting even in a modest dress. Mitchell hoped that was all in his head though, prayed that he wouldn't catch her in some back room later with Lydia's father's hand up her dress while she jerked him off. Just the thought made him regret letting her come and he glared at anyone who stared too long.

There were less than a hundred people there, a small wedding as Imogen had said it would be, but still wonderful. Mitchell broke out into his widest grin when she and Lydia kissed. Part of him had still been unable to believe it, that they were married, *could* be married under the law. But it had happened. He'd just watched it happen and it could even happen to him. He really could have it, the option was there.

Glancing at Trevor beside him, he saw he was smiling just as wide, probably thinking the same thing. Trevor laced their fingers together when he caught Mitchell looking.

"Have you ever seen either of them look so happy?" he asked, leaning in to speak in Mitchell's ear.

"No, never."

The reception was at a small, private venue, a hall with a lovely garden that Mitchell hadn't picked, but had insisted on paying for. He'd taken to being a bit sentimental lately, largely in part to Trevor, he suspected. Imogen worked so hard as shop manager, coming in even on Saturdays when she didn't have to, and Mitchell never had properly repaid her father John for all he'd done for him before he died. The least he could do was let her and her wife have the reception of their dreams.

He tried to make his mother stay by him the whole time, didn't want her sneaking off, but he couldn't tell her not to dance and keep her from having a good time. In the end, it was Imogen who put a hand on his shoulder and told him not to worry about it, knowing him well enough to read his thoughts.

"It wouldn't be a wedding without a bit of drama," she added with a devilish grin.

"If it does happen, she knows how to be discreet, I promise," Mitchell said hurriedly.

She slapped him on the back, made him get up. "It'll be fine, Mitch. Dance, drink, be merry. Stop glaring at people, you're coming off as antisocial."

He couldn't decline Trevor's request to dance, even though he didn't know how. The occasion was a bit different than a nightclub, but he made himself give it a shot anyway. Mostly he followed Trevor's lead and pretended he knew what he was doing. After three songs he felt uncomfortable and wanted to get away from the crowd.

He and Trevor went out into the garden. Fairy lights lit up the night and a group of people were by the door drinking and having a lively conversation. They passed them and sat at a bench not far away.

"Sorry, I just needed a bit of space," he told Trevor. "It's not like in a club. They're strangers, but they're important strangers, like. It was too much."

"I get it. I've done the same with Kay loads of times. You know how extroverted they are, and I'm, well, not so much."

"Yeah, but you're not as introverted as me."

"No. I'm a bit in the middle, I suppose." He looked away from the flowers and rising moon in front of them and turned to Mitchell. "You really do look good."

"So do you."

Mitchell thought Trevor was the best-dressed man there. Like his father, Trevor knew how to wear a suit, how to hold himself in it. Where a black suit on Mitchell would make him look much too dark for the occasion, it was perfect on Trevor, whose playful curls and deeper complexion made him look a bit like a celebrity, so attractive he shouldn't be allowed to exist.

He'd been different since killing Nathan, less of the innocent graphic designer Mitchell had started dating back in March. The times when Mitchell had gone out with Trevor's friends, they'd given Trevor odd looks, looks that said there was something off about him. Mitchell didn't know if Trevor noticed, and he didn't have any past behaviour to compare to, so he let it lie.

But there were things Trevor said, outbursts that revealed his inclinations toward darker things. Things that normal people didn't talk about, and certainly not so casually. Mitchell saw — while Trevor didn't — that his friends were finding him more and more weird each time they met up, and that they correctly blamed it on his being with Mitchell, who was quiet and even weirder.

Mitchell didn't particularly care, thought the entire group of people was too artsy and oversensitive. He'd realised that even though Trevor talked about his friends a lot, he really had no feelings for them past the surface, except for Kay. Friends come, friends go. Eventually, these would go.

Trevor put his arm behind Mitchell on the back of the bench and leaned closer, placing a hand on Mitchell's thigh as he kissed first his cheek then his lips when Mitchell turned his head to reciprocate. For a minute or two it was just the easy opening and closing of mouths, until Mitchell felt Trevor's tongue sliding into his mouth to find his own.

The temperature was dropping as the night went on, the breeze carrying a chill with it. Mitchell shivered and decided they'd go inside after they finished kissing. Or, better yet, they could leave and continue at Trevor's flat, take things further than appropriate in public. They'd already stayed long enough that it wouldn't be considered leaving too early.

Trevor evidently had the same thoughts as him. He pulled away and stood up, held out his hand for Mitchell to take. "Come on, let's tell Imogen and Lydia we're leaving."

Mitchell took his hand and stood. "My mam?"

"Probably already found someone kind enough to take her back to her hotel," Trevor quipped as they started walking.

Mitchell elbowed him hard in the side.

"Finally," Trevor exhaled as he shoved Mitchell against the wall in his bedroom and forced their mouths together.

Mitchell put his hands on Trevor's hips and pulled him close, felt his half hard cock brush against his thigh. Trevor jerked his hips forward as his tongue plunged deeper, hungry and insistent.

Mitchell understood completely. Seeing Trevor done up had made him feel exactly the same way, though almost certainly for a different reason. Trevor dressed well even on his worst days, but formal events, fuck, it was almost too much. He was all class, all sophisticated and gentlemanly. Mitchell's arse clenched just at the thought of how hard he knew Trevor would fuck him.

The last couple months had been rough. Up until recently, Mitchell hadn't been able to bring himself to have sex, but Trevor had been understanding and patient. Some nights Trevor would simply run fingers over his skin as they lay in bed, caressing him. A few times he'd sucked Mitchell off, never finishing himself but making it about Mitchell's pleasure. Most of the time they just stayed up talking all night, and they'd gotten to know each other even better as a result.

Mitchell raised a leg and let it slide up and down against Trevor's, the sinuous movement of their bodies together intoxicating. That morning had been the fifth time they'd fucked since the night of the Williams job, and Mitchell was slowly but surely regaining his old confidence and sex drive. It helped that every time so far Trevor had had enough control to keep from grabbing his throat, or grabbing any part of him too roughly really. In fact, Trevor had been fucking him lovingly and passionately, had been gentle yet still firm enough that he hadn't been treating Mitchell like glass.

He was a little more pushy now, but he was probably just following Mitchell's lead, being more rough and forceful because that's what Mitchell was doing. Mitchell moaned and did absolutely everything he could to encourage it. Trevor pulled away, and strong fingers yanked the band out of Mitchell's hair to make it fall to his shoulders.

Trevor grabbed hold of Mitchell's leg, brought it up to his waist, and Mitchell hooked it around as he rutted desperately into him. Mitchell began undoing Trevor's shirt as Trevor licked into his mouth, traced his lips with the tip of his tongue. It wasn't the best thing for Mitchell's concentration, and made his hands fumble.

He got Trevor's shirt open though, and immediately pressed his palms to the exposed skin, sliding his hands around Trevor's back and loving the fact that it was all his. He tilted his head back and moaned when he felt Trevor's hand trailing down his chest to squeeze his cock through his trousers.

As much as Mitchell wanted Trevor inside him, he didn't want to rush through this either. How often would he get to see Trevor in an expensive suit with kiss-swollen lips and lust in his eyes?

He did want to move to the bed though, and pushed against Trevor's chest until they were there.

Trevor fell on his back with a short, expelled breath, arms out to catch himself. Without missing a beat, Mitchell climbed on top, shrugging out of the suit jacket and undoing the buttons of his own shirt. He rolled his hips against Trevor's, Trevor's hands planting themselves firmly on his arse to aid the motion.

Mitchell undid his belt, pulled it through and dropped it behind him on the floor. Trevor's hands ran up his bared chest as he undid his trousers. Finally feeling a little less restricted, Mitchell leaned forward, hands on either side of Trevor's head, and lowered himself down to capture his mouth again.

He found Trevor's cock with his and absolutely fucking abused the discovery, chasing the friction relentlessly. Trevor grabbed his arse again, lifted his hips to press harder as he moaned. They briefly parted for air and Mitchell panted against his mouth.

Clothes came off in stages. A shirt here, a tie there, then back to rocking against each other, enjoying the simple dance of tangled limbs and rising desires before pulling away to remove something else.

It was the little things that drove Mitchell wild these days; the feeling of fingertips brushing along the knobs of his spine as Trevor sucked his neck, the flexing of Trevor's thighs as they accommodated his weight. When Trevor rolled Mitchell on his back and kissed his way down his chest, purposefully, lovingly, that drove Mitchell wild too.

After Mitchell's navel, Trevor went a little lower, then a little lower, until he kissed the swelled head of his cock, tongue first with lips slowly closing. It made Mitchell shudder and have to grip the sheets. Then a little lower, a little lower, until Trevor had sucked kisses all the way down to his balls. Mitchell lifted his body, already knowing what came next.

He moaned gratefully at the wet warmth surrounding him, and let his body sink. The smacking sound of Trevor sucking his balls was loud, obscene, and felt so much better because of it. He hitched his legs up and rocked forward, pushing against Trevor's face.

His cock was next, but only for a minute or so, because he could feel Trevor's need escalating along with his own. It was in the way Trevor's hands gripped his hips, holding him down as he bobbed on his dick, the way it was almost sloppy, more enthusiasm than finesse. Trevor hollowed his cheeks, wrapping his lips around the shaft, and took him down his throat again and again, looking too fucking hungry for it.

It was a sight Mitchell could've watched all day, had he the stamina. Trevor pulled off with a pop, Mitchell's cock slapping his belly with its fall. His lips were chapped, his face flushed, and he smiled up at Mitchell as he crawled up his body, not looking like he was about to fuck Mitchell into the mattress, but like he was having a good time and he knew Mitchell was too.

It was moments like that that Mitchell was finding he loved the most. There was Trevor during sex and there was Trevor outside of sex, just like with anyone. Different mindsets, different actions — people weren't the same in the heat of the moment as they were outside of it. But sometimes they mixed, the Trevor that did things like rolling his eyes surfacing out of nowhere.

Mitchell hadn't been able to pin down why he liked it so much at first, but then he realised: after having sex with someone enough, someone he'd spent a lot of time with, it just became another activity that was done together. They could probably hold an entire conversation while Mitchell rode Trevor's cock.

It was something Mitchell had never had before, such an intimate closeness and familiarity. It'd come to be his favourite thing, the simple fact that people could even *be* that close. Tagging along like small print on a contract was the heart-wrenching thought of ever losing the person he'd become so close to, how much it might literally kill him if he did.

His mind drifted back to earlier that day while another part of his mind was dimly aware of Trevor momentarily disappearing for lube. He thought of the wedding, how happy Imogen and Lydia had looked. They felt the same way about each other as he did about Trevor, had to if they wanted to spend the rest of their lives together. He'd known for a while that he never wanted to leave Trevor, but it hadn't been until seeing his friends get married that he thought about the future stretching out ahead of him, what it meant. It meant growing old with him, seeing him every day, feeling the closeness he loved so much constantly.

"Mitchell?" Trevor's voice called him back to the present. "Hey. You spaced out a bit. My cock finally boring you after five months?"

Mitchell sat up. "Christ, has it really only been five months?"

"More or less. Our first date was the eighth of March."

"You remember the date?"

Trevor shrugged, smiling sheepishly even as he stroked his cock with a lubed hand.

"Feels so much longer, like," he said, unable to believe it. "Feels like I've known you for, for a *year* at least."

Trevor sat back on his heels, lowered his hand to the cleft of Mitchell's arse and searched out his hole with slippery fingers. "We did go through a bit of an ordeal," he said, half concentrated on his task. Mitchell lay back down and spread his legs wider to make things easier. "I mean, something like that tends to bring people closer, yeah?"

"Yeah." Mitchell laughed, interrupted by a gasp halfway through when Trevor curled his finger inside and brushed his prostate. "Don't worry, I don't think I'll ever get tired of your cock. In fact, if I don't have it right this second I'm going to hold you down and take it myself."

Trevor's finger slipped out as he grinned. "God, it's so hot when you talk dirty."

Mitchell's reply was delayed by a grunt, Trevor's cock pushing in having forced it out of him. He panted as Trevor went steadily deeper, moaned when he angled his body and took in the final glorious bit of length.

"Is that really what's considered dirty talk?" he finally managed, more than a little breathless. "Telling you how much I want your cock? You know that already, no matter how many times I say it. I always thought dirty talk was a bit more graphic. I would know, I was in the business."

Trevor rolled his eyes and leaned forward over him, started fucking him with shallow jerks of his hips. "Not all of it's the same. Either way, still sexy to hear."

Mitchell licked his lips and raised his legs, shifted his weight onto his back so Trevor could grab hold of his knees and pick up speed. "Then I—ah-h-h—I want your cock. I want, I want, *oh God.*"

Trevor was pounding into him so fast that he had to clench around the rock hard cock, all his muscles taut as he breathed through the onslaught. He closed his eyes and reached both arms over his head to clutch a pillow, Trevor determinedly pumping in and out of him.

"This is why I don't talk because I, I start sounding like I'm in a fucking porno. *Fuck*!"

Trevor snapped his hips hard, slamming in deep enough that Mitchell felt it in his stomach for a second. He chased it when Trevor pulled halfway out again, using his arms to push and take it back in.

"Whatever you're comfortable with," Trevor panted. He was sweating when Mitchell opened his eyes, damp curls plastered to his forehead. "Not gonna force you, but I love whatever comes out of your mouth."

His hands lowered to Mitchell's thighs, holding them from underneath to pull him up into his lap as he leaned back on his heels. Mitchell went with him and planted his feet on the bed. They settled into a new rhythm, Mitchell dropping his weight to meet Trevor's thrusts halfway. The angle was fucking perfect, had Trevor fucking into his prostate and making him keen.

"In fact Mitchell, I, I love everything about you. Even the things I don't like, if that, if that makes sense," Trevor said, slowing to push deep, swivel his hips, and moan before repeating the movement.

Mitchell looked up at him, furrowing his brow. He was sweating too, was breathless and close to coming. He gripped his cock and started stroking, thumbing at the head.

"Stop talking and keep fucking me," he said. "So close."

Trevor nodded and picked up the pace again, until Mitchell was bouncing and riding a wave of pleasure. The hand on his cock blurred as he brought himself closer, the tension in his groin rising. Then everything else blurred as well, his eyelashes fluttering as his eyes rolled back in his head and he came. He felt Trevor throbbing and spilling inside him too, the closest they'd ever gotten to coming at the same time.

Panting beside Trevor a couple minutes later, he'd hardly got his breath back when Trevor propped himself up on his elbow and nudged him. Mitchell turned to look at him.

"I was trying to say I love you, Mitchell. I think I could even marry you."

Mitchell stopped breathing. He had to force himself to inhale and start again.

"I'd like to see how living with you goes first though, if that's alright?"

Mitchell didn't blink. "Yes."

Trevor's eyebrows shot up and he smiled. "Yes?"

Later, Mitchell would feel embarrassed about how he practically tackled Trevor, pinning him down to bury his face in Trevor's chest and hold him tight. At the moment, he didn't care.

"Yes. God yes."

If you enjoyed this story, you can sign up for a free membership
at ForbiddenFiction and discuss it with other readers
and the author at the *Driven* story page
at http://forbiddenfiction.com/story/NK1-1.000216.

We do our best to proof all our work, but if you spot a text error we missed,
please let us know via our website Contact Form
at http://forbiddenfiction.com/contact.

Author's Notes

I have a lot of feelings about this book. I have a lot of feelings about Trevor and Mitchell. My poor broken Mitchell and my poor repressed Trevor. (And then there's Kay, who's a mixture of two awesome people I know, one of them Kay's namesake.)

I've had fun with the way this story has changed and evolved to become what it is now. I learned a lot, and not just about mechanics. One thing I learnt early on was that, sadly, you are not allowed to be shirtless while working in a garage. Foiled! There went my original scene of Trevor catching sight of shirtless Mitchell, muscles flexing as he twisted a spanner. I did, however, also learn that oil, grease, transmission fluid, etc. is nigh impossible to get out of clothes and skin, so although I couldn't have Mitchell shirtless I could still have him work the whole dirty/sexy thing. Zoom in on the details, the black/grey embedded in the whorls of his fingers, or the smear across his collarbone, and ta-da! Knowledge successfully applied.

Finally, special thanks to two wonderful people who I'm fortunate enough to call friends, Lily Benham and Babs. This quite literally wouldn't have been possible without them.

Babs tolerated my endless questions about London, and took me on a lovely guided tour via email with the standard level of British humour included. Lily, having worked a bit as a mechanic herself, was my go-to source for this when internet searches failed. Her help with machinery and mechanics was invaluable, as were the many car-related puns we both had a giggle over.

Hope you enjoyed the ride. I know I did.

—Nicholas Kinsley

247

About the Author

Nicholas Kinsley has been writing since a very young age. After going through school focused on computer science, he discovered that he would rather be a professional author. He grew up with few friends and a love of books, and hopes to create worlds in which others can find enjoyment. Kinsley currently lives in Maryland.

ForbiddenFiction Works by Nicholas Kinsley:

Behind Locked Doors

Driven

Albion Rising 1: Love Is for the Living

About the Publisher

FANTASTIC FICTION PUBLISHING

FORBIDDENFICTION INTELLIGENT EROTICA

ForbiddenFiction.com is a publisher devoted to writing that breaks the boundaries of original erotic fiction. Our stories combine intense sexuality with quality writing. Stories at Forbidden Fiction.com not only arouse readers through sensations, but also engage them emotionally and mentally through storytelling as well-crafted as the sex is hot.

ForbiddenFiction.com is also designed to be a social reading environment. You'll have fun even if just reading the latest post each day, yet you will have the chance for so much more. Readers and authors can be part of ongoing discussions of specific works and individual authors as well as more general topics.

Sign up for a FREE Membership today at ForbiddenFiction.com